TRIPLE THREAT

KATY WARNER

Hardie Grant

BOOKS

Triple Threat
first published in 2022 by
Hardie Grant Children's Publishing
Wurundjeri Country
Ground Floor, Building 1, 658 Church Street
Richmond, Victoria 3121, Australia
www.hardiegrantchildrens.com

A catalogue record for this
book is available from the
National Library of Australia

Text copyright © 2022 Katy Warner
Cover design © 2022 Hardie Grant Children's Publishing
Cover design by Holly Ovenden
Typeset by Eggplant Communications

Hardie Grant acknowledges the Traditional Owners of the country on
which we work, the Wurundjeri people of the Kulin nation and the
Gadigal people of the Eora nation, and recognises their continuing
connection to the land, waters and culture. We pay our respects to
their Elders past and present.

Printed and bound in Australia by Griffin Press, an Accredited ISO AS/
NZS 14001 Environmental Management System printer.

1 3 5 7 9 10 8 6 4 2

The paper this book is printed on is certified against the
Forest Stewardship Council® Standards. Griffin Press
holds FSC® chain of custody certification SGSHK-
COC-005088. FSC® promotes environmentally
responsible, socially beneficial and economically viable
management of the world's forests.

For Dad

ONE

The house is live.

The audience is taking their seats.

I love this moment. The butterflies that tornado around my stomach and flutter down my legs and up my body and through my skin, fluttering, glittering. In the darkness of the stage wings, I bounce up and down on my toes and try to get into Charity mode. Charity Hope Valentine. That's who I am tonight. As in *Sweet Charity*. As in the musical. As in the role originated by Gwen Verdon, as in Shirley MacLaine in the 1969 movie, as in Nancye Hayes and Debbie Allen and Christina Applegate and Sutton Foster and all these amazing musical theatre performers from across the globe and generations. As in 'Hey, Big Spender' and 'If My Friends Could See Me Now'; as in I'm-freaking-out-again-I-can't-do-this.

But I can.

And I will.

The rest of the cast is crowded together in the blue light of the backstage area, stretching and whispering *chookas* and *break a leg*. Warm breath on necks, tight cuddles around waists, sloppy kisses on blushed cheeks, and laughter. So much laughter. There's a lot of love back here, especially on closing night. Everyone is a little hyperactive, a heap of adrenaline and energy and nervousness swishing around us.

I stand apart from them, trying to focus. I'm not a diva. I just want to do a good job. I have to. It's the only way I know how to survive in a school like Arcadia Grammar. A school which is very serious about the performing arts. It's what they do, what they're known for, and it's why I've been coming here since Year Seven. Musicals, stage plays, concerts, dance recitals – Arcadia Grammar does it all. And it does them well.

Someone like me, from where I'm from, isn't supposed to be at Arcadia. I don't come from the right background, don't have the money or any connections. Not like my classmates. They have a right to be here. Me? I'm *lucky* to be here. And every day I am terrified my luck will run out and they'll see me for the fraud I am …

'Um, Edie?' Jay, one of the juniors from the ensemble, approaches me. There were four Year Sevens in the junior ensemble until the broken toe incident. Now the remaining three stand in front of me, all shy and giggly. Jay, the spokesperson for their little gang, clutches my arm and looks at me through fake thick eyelashes and too much blue eyeshadow. 'Thanks for the gift. We love it. You're so sweet!'

I've given everyone a chocolate heart with a handwritten card attached that says: THANKS FOR A GREAT SEASON. LOVE, CHARITY (Edie) xxx. It's not much but it's all I can afford and it's kind of a tradition, so I do it. Always have. And I make sure I remember everyone: cast and crew and front of house. In a musical like this, that's a lot of people. Forty-nine, to be precise. I spent all last night writing the cards and making sure I spelled everyone's names correctly. Most people seem to appreciate it. I mean, Phoebe and Holly both explained the concept of empty calories (*Thanks but no thanks*, they said, but neither of them actually returned the chocolate) and Cody called me a *goodie-goodie suck-up* (um, is this Grade Five?), and Diego thought, out loud, so everyone could hear him, that what I'd done was a waste of time. But people like Jay and their friends make it worthwhile. Not that I do it for praise or whatever. Or maybe I do? Maybe I like being liked. Who doesn't?

'OK, OK, leave the star alone. She needs to focus.' Aubrey, wearing the all-black uniform of the crew, headset on, clipboard in hand, shoos Jay's group away. 'How you feeling?' she whispers as she checks her watch.

'I'm freaking out,' I tell her, because I can't lie to Aubrey. My best friend and stage manager extraordinaire.

'So, is she actually here? Like for real?'

'I think so,' I say, not wanting to get my hopes up. My mum is in the audience. Or she should be. This will be the first time she will see me in an Arcadia show, in a lead role, in a real musical. I have invited her to every show since Year Seven and finally, now that I'm in Year Twelve, she is here. I mean, I *think* she is here. She hasn't cancelled on me.

3

Usually I get a sad face emoji – no apology or explanation, just an emoji – the day before she's meant to come. But this time? I've been obsessively checking my phone and there's been nothing from her. No emojis. No messages. No cryptic voicemails. I'm taking that as a good sign. She probably thinks she's surprising me. Mum loves surprises.

Aubrey holds her hand to her ear, gets this faraway look on her face. The crew and Mrs B are probably screaming at her through the earpiece – *Where are you? We need you! Help!* If they are, she's not letting on. She always looks so calm. So together. Nothing fazes her. Ever. 'We're about to start.' She kisses my cheek. 'You'll be amazing. As usual.'

I close my eyes as the orchestra starts playing the overture and a hush settles over the audience. I know all my lines, I know all my songs, I know every step of the choreography – and I can do this. I'm good at this. I'm what they call a triple threat. I sing, I dance, I act. It sounds arrogant, I know, but Mum always says there's a difference between arrogance and confidence. She's never explained what the difference is, but according to her there is one.

The overture slides into the opening number.

I can do this.

I *will* do this.

When I'm onstage it's like my brain switches into a different operating mode and nothing outside this moment, this song, this scene, exists. Tonight, I am Charity. And I feel her, what it means to *be* her, surge through me like electricity. When she's feeling desperate, overjoyed, in love, hopeful, sad: I feel it, too. Her words and her songs and her dancing take over. The emotions are easy to hit when you sing, the music surging and my voice melding with the orchestra. Mrs B taught us that, in a musical, a character will sing and dance because their feelings are too big or too much or too complex for words alone. It needs more than words. It needs song and dance. And I get that. Because tonight I *am* Charity.

I take a breath and step into the bright lights of the stage … I love this feeling.

And I don't know who I am without it.

*

Tonight we're having the kind of performance where everything just clicks and feels effortless. But there's a sadness in the edges. Every word is one word closer to it all being over. I feel like part of me is farewelling a part of Charity at the end of every number. I wish there was a way to capture it, to hold onto it a little longer. But then, that's what makes theatre so special: it's fleeting. It can't be bottled up and preserved. I mean, how could you even try to capture that fizz of energy that sparks in a scene, or the thrill that rushes through you when you hit that note just right? I'm not saying I blackout or get completely possessed by the character or anything weird like that, but when a performance is going well it sort of feels that way. I am swept away by it. Edie stops existing the moment I feel the stage lights on my face. It feels good to let myself go like that. To immerse myself in someone else's voice and emotion and story.

It's exhausting and terrifying and exhilarating, and I wouldn't trade it for anything.

In the final scene, Charity is pushed into a lake, which is actually the orchestra pit. Aubrey waits for me down there, with a drenched version of my costume to change into and a bucket of water to wet my hair. I love seeing her right at the end of the show like that. As always, she gives me a quick hug before helping me out of the dress, and whispers, 'You are the bravest.' She means the song I am about to reprise – 'I'm the bravest individual' – right at the end of the show, a slower and sadder version than the first time I sang it.

There's not a lot of room in the pit for us. Early on, Aubrey lectured the brass section about the need for privacy and now all of them keep their eyes on their music stands as if their lives depended on it.

'Have you seen your mum out there?' Aubrey whispers as she zips me into the wet version of my dress.

It's a real jolt – bam – and I'm out of my myself, or out of my Charity-self, just for a second.

Why did Aubrey have to mention Mum? Why now?

I shake my head, because I haven't snuck a look at the audience. I don't do that. Others can tell you exactly who is sitting where and what they're thinking about the show at any given moment. I'll hear them rush off stage and talk about *that guy in the third row who was totally cracking up when you said that funny line* or *the girl in the fifth row who's so bored she's using her mobile phone.* That kind of thing. I don't look. No, that's a lie; I do *look* but I don't *see*, because I'd rather not know. I want to focus on the show. I don't need this in my head now. The final moment is tricky enough as it is.

I dunk my head in the bucket of water.

Should I have snuck a look at the audience? Is she actually here? Of course she is. She has to be. She never said she wasn't coming. She has to be here. It's my final musical for Arcadia Grammar. There's the school play later on in the year, but no more musicals. So this is it, this is the last chance she gets to see me sing and dance on this stage. Of course she wouldn't miss it.

My music cue begins and I, a soaking wet, jilted, and yet still somehow optimistic Charity, pull myself up from the pit and land, face down, on the stage. I feel the spotlight on me. Water drips in my eyes, and sparkles as I turn my head to the audience. Take a beat.

'Did you ever have one of those days?' I say as Charity.

The audience laughs, right on cue. I wonder if Mum is laughing.

And then my mind goes blank. Shit. What's next ...
What's next?

Time slows down. Seconds become hours. Everything is blurry. I think I can hear someone coughing. Someone whispers. Someone gets up and leaves. Why are they leaving? The show isn't over yet. Maybe it's Mum. Maybe she's so embarrassed by my performance she had to get the hell out of here ...

The music continues. I stumble to my feet, slip on the water and fall on my arse. Hard. My eyes fill with tears.

The audience laughs.

I pretend it was meant to happen.

OK. This is OK. Deep breath. I am Charity Hope Valentine. I know what I need to do. I open my mouth ... but nothing comes out.

The pause is becoming awkward. It's too long. *Shit, shit, shit.* I look to Flick, the conductor and musical director, who is staring at me from the orchestra pit but still keeping the band playing. She gives me a reassuring smile, the band repeats the intro and she silently counts me in to the cue. I open my mouth again and ... somehow, like magic, the song flies out of me.

But the lyrics are wrong. It feels like my brain is catching up to my voice. I'm not singing the reprise, but the lyrics from the Act I version – but it's working, and somehow I keep going, and then, finally, I'm back on track. I'm shaking – with cold, with nerves, with embarrassment – but I'm back on track. And I let it all out. Everything. I lay it all out there on the stage for this final song. For my mum.

I'm the bravest individual I have ever met ...

TWO

At the end of the show, I wait in the wings while the rest of the cast take their bows. I've changed back into the dry version of the dress and three crew members have tried their best to restore my hair to something that looks a little less drowned rat in record time. No-one has mentioned the fall or the mistakes I made with the words to the song. Everyone must think it was a choice, something I added for the final night. I am not about to correct them.

I'm the lead, so I'm the last one out for curtain call. Diego – who plays Oscar, Charity's love interest – stands next to me in the dark, waiting his turn.

'You were great tonight,' he whispers in my ear.

I turn to look at him. His eyes are shining and he's smiling a real smile, not the fake one he usually reserves for me. He's never given me a compliment before. He says I'm the school's charity case – he made some dumb pun about it when I got this role. Plus, he thinks I have a massive ego. I know because he's told me. Even though it is Diego himself who has the biggest, healthiest ego of all.

'But not as good as *moi*,' he laughs as he flounces onstage to take his bow.

And then it is my turn, and as I walk downstage to take my bow I finally let myself look for Mum. I reserved her the best seat in the theatre. Row E. Seat 15. Perfect spot. Mum is really particular about where she sits for a show. Can't be too close but can't be too far away either, and it's got to be in the centre so she can get the full picture. *The mise en scene*, she says, *is vital.*

But Mum isn't in that seat.

Someone else has nabbed it.

I scan the audience. Maybe she had to move? Maybe there was a mix-up at the box office.

I look out.

Or maybe she just didn't bother to show up.

Again.

I keep smiling. Blink away the hotness in my eyes.

The rest of the cast step forward and join me, and we all hold hands to take the final bow. Diego on my left. Lexie on my right. I squeeze her hand, like I always do, and she gives me a little squeeze back. Diego's friends are going crazy, applauding and chanting his name.

Lexie nudges me, shouts in my ear, 'How much d'you think Diego paid those guys?'

Some people from the audience approach the stage with bunches of flowers. My heart flips when I see a small posy of yellow roses: my favourites, because they're Mum's favourites. She must be here after all … But the roses are tossed towards Angela. She had a couple of lines and was really great and is very deserving of flowers, but still, I feel a twinge of hurt in my chest. More bouquets appear and end up in the arms of various cast members, but there are none for me. Which is fine. Totally fine.

We wave goodbye to the audience, who are still clapping and cheering, and start to exit just as someone runs down the aisle towards the stage, carrying flowers. I don't look, just keep moving with the rest of the cast towards the wings, but Lexie pulls me back.

'I think they're for you,' she says.

My heart tumbles and for a split second I think, *Mum! Mum is here!*

I try really hard to keep the smile in place when I see it's not Mum, but Will. He's holding the flowers out to me and looking a bit shy about it, which is weird because Will is anything but shy.

'Sorry,' he shouts from the edge of the stage as he hands them over, 'I was gonna give them to you after and then I saw everyone was making it a thing and so, yeah, here you go, Eds. Absolute superstar.'

Will's my best friend. Along with Aubrey. I'm lucky. I have two – two of the best. I try to say something but I know if I speak now I will burst into tears or laugh hysterically or maybe both, and no-one needs to see that, so I just take the flowers and kiss his cheek and get off the stage as quickly as possible.

It's not until I'm in the wings that I realise he's bought me roses. Yellow roses.

I take a moment before I head into the dressing room. I don't know why I find this so hard. I should be able to walk right in there and laugh with them about my mistake like it's no big deal, and celebrate the final show and what we all achieved together. I've known most of the people in that room for years. But that doesn't make it any easier to make small talk and pretend everything is OK. I know they'll be nice to my face about it – all sympathetic looks and kind words. Everyone is so *nice* at Arcadia. At least on the surface. But I never know quite what to say, and what I do say always comes out wrong. I think it's because I'm so used to working with a script. Learning the lines, repeating the words of characters so different to me; characters who always find the right words to say at the right time. And if they can't find those words, they sing.

If only real life was like that.

One day I'm going to write my own musical where all the dialogue is just *umms* and *ahhhs* and awkward silences interspersed with amazing songs and dances. I reckon people would relate to that.

I would.

Lexie floats down the corridor towards me. She's slipped a silky dressing gown over her costume and twisted her long, curly dark hair into a messy bun. She looks like a glamorous movie star from the 1940s. Lexie is Dance Captain. If you didn't know that, you'd be able to pick it pretty quickly just by looking at her. Everything she does has this effortless elegance to it. She's graceful, and has this perfect posture that always makes me stand up a little straighter. She played one of Charity's best friends in the show. She's my actual friend by default. The default is Aubrey; our shared love of Aubrey has made us sort-of-maybe-friends, or at least something a bit more than just classmates.

'Good show,' she says.

'And you were amazing tonight,' I gush. I always gush. The minute anyone says anything nice to me off I go, and it's always too much. 'I really loved your solo tonight, like I felt it, you know, the pain underneath her façade.' Geez. Who uses the word *façade* in real life? I feel my face get hot. My brain is telling me to stop talking but my mouth doesn't get the message and I keep going on and on and on, and I can see Lexie doesn't think I mean any of it.

'Thanks,' she says and opens the door to the dressing room. I hesitate. 'You coming in or you gonna live in that costume forever?'

'Yeah, no, I mean, of course not,' I stumble, and follow Lexie into the dressing room. It's buzzing with noise, and smells like the cosmetics section at Myer on overdrive. As I walk through the mist of perfume and deodorant and hairspray, everyone shouts out their congratulations. I smile and say, *Thank you,* and, *You were great!* and try to get to my little corner of the dressing room without having to stop and actually engage with anyone.

But then Tara reaches out and grabs my arm. 'Don't worry, I don't think anyone would have noticed all your mistakes tonight,' she smiles sweetly.

'Thanks, Tara.' I try to keep walking, but she is holding on tight.

'Although that fall looked pretty bad. You OK, hun?' she says.

'I'm fine!' I laugh. I don't know why I'm laughing, but Tara joins in, and the whole thing just feels so fake and forced and awkward. Which basically sums up how things are with me and Tara.

At the start of rehearsals, Tara proclaimed herself my understudy. It wasn't an official thing, but she made it clear that if anything happened to me she'd be the one who would step up. Aubrey worried Tara might *make* something happen to me (*Never take the stairs with her*, she said) but I got through it all fine. No sprains or broken bones, no colds or laryngitis. It meant Tara never got the chance to be Charity. I feel a bit bad about that.

'It did look funny. Your face! Oh my gosh, you have such great comedic timing. I would have died of embarrassment on the spot. But you, Edie, well, you're just so … brave.' She pats my arm before returning to look at herself in the mirror.

I finally get to my spot in the far corner of the dressing room. A little oasis of order and calm among the chaos. I gently place the flowers on the table and flop back into my chair.

'Nice flowers,' Phoebe says, munching on the chocolate heart I bought her. So much for those empty calories she'd lectured me about. 'Got any make-up wipes? I'm all out.'

I hand over my packet of wipes, hoping she won't use them all or forget to return them. I don't want to make a big deal out of it, but whenever I lend anyone anything around here it just disappears. Bobby pins, hair elastics, the last spray of the hairspray. It's not like people are stealing stuff.

They just don't think about what those make-up wipes cost because to them, money isn't a big deal. What's eight dollars anyway? But to me … well … it's a bit different.

I slip out of my costume and hang it carefully back on the rack. I love my costumes. Others will throw theirs on the floor and expect Aubrey and her crew to pick up after them. But not me. I'm kind of a neat freak. All the other tables in here are overflowing with make-up and tissues and food and junk, but mine is clean and clear. Except for my make-up case, Will's flowers and a small framed black-and-white photo of Shirley MacLaine as Charity, which Aubrey gave me as an opening night gift. My good luck charm for the season. I'll keep it forever.

I place my character shoes into the soft shoe-bag Nan made for them and put them into my backpack. I still haven't taken off my make-up because Phoebe has passed my wipes down to Holly, who is sharing them with Tara. They're talking about the closing night party at Tara's house; of course Tara has the kind of house where you can throw a party. Or so I assume. I've never been there, and I won't be going tonight. They're replacing their heavy stage make-up with heavy party make-up, changing out of costumes and into cute party-approved outfits.

I've put on my purple daisy-print dress and white sneakers. My hair is still in the Charity curls, although they're not so bouncy now, and my face is still in the Charity make-up, which is way too much for the real world.

'Hey, um, Phoebe?' I say, 'you done with those wipes?'

Phoebe doesn't hear me.

'Phoebe?' I say a little louder, 'my wipes?'

15

Phoebe gives me a death stare. 'Jesus, Edie, calm down, they're just fucking make-up wipes,' and she laughs as she throws the now almost-empty packet at me.

*

In the foyer, I watch my fellow cast members being hugged and congratulated by their parents and family and friends. Everyone is being told how amazing they were. How they shone in this number or that. How they stole the show. I wish Mum was here.

I can't find Will, and Aubrey's probably still backstage, packing up all our mess. I'd like to disappear back there and help her, but Aubrey hates that. She reckons the actors just get in the way. I'm about to message them an SOS when Mrs B appears at my side, glass of wine in hand.

'Stunning work, Edie,' Mrs B says.

'I am so sorry. I totally screwed up tonight,' I say, but before I can start listing all my mistakes, she interrupts.

'Nonsense!' she says and sloshes her wine over the side of the glass for emphasis. Or because she's tipsy. Perhaps both. 'What are we going to do when you graduate? Talent like yours does not come along very often.'

I like Mrs B, but she can be a bit much sometimes. Like now, as she's listing all the great roles I have to look forward to when I'm older. I scan the foyer as discreetly as possible, searching for a way out. It's then I lock eyes with Imogen. Shit. What the hell is she doing here? She never comes to the musicals. I smile at her. She doesn't smile back, just stares with this look I can't quite work out. It's unnerving.

I turn my attention back to Mrs B, but I can still feel Imogen watching. Her eyes are like lasers burning holes through me.

Imogen describes herself as a 'serious actor' which, by her definition, is the opposite of what I am. She is very vocal about never lowering her standards to singing and dancing in musical theatre, as if it is a lesser form of performing. *It's all in the text*, she always says. *If you need a flashy song-and-dance number to convey meaning then, sorry, you're doing something wrong.*

Imogen and I have a deal. I never do a lead role in a play; she doesn't do a lead role in a musical. Theatre and musical theatre don't mix. There are some exceptions, though, like me. And that's only because the terms of my Arcadia Grammar scholarship state that I'll audition for 'every opportunity', which means all the musicals, plays, recitals and concerts Arcadia can jam into their busy calendar. But most of the theatre kids won't do musical theatre, and vice versa. It's a thing.

Back in Year Seven, before the deal had been struck, we'd both auditioned for the lead role in *Annie*. Imogen could act the heart out of that role; the tears came easy, the wobble of the lower lip, the catch in her voice as she cried over her non-existent parents. But then she had to sing and dance. And she couldn't do it. Couldn't hold a note; couldn't dance a step. But she was so good at the other stuff she decided to claim her territory right there as a serious, dramatic actor. The following year, she blew everyone away in her performance as Abigail Williams in *The Crucible*. I

17

played a much smaller role and I remember watching her and thinking, *I can do that*. Because I can. I do. I just sing and dance as well. Anyway, it doesn't matter, because the deal was made for reasons that must have made sense when I was starting a new school and desperate to make friends. Imogen, it turns out, is no friend.

'So.' Mrs B moves in a little closer and gets this funny look on her face. 'I thought your mum was coming tonight? Thought we were finally going to meet the other talented Ms Emerson.'

'She's so busy in LA ... Sometimes her schedule changes and it can be hard for her to get back. You know what the industry is like over there,' I say.

'Oh, yes, of course, very high pressure,' Mrs B murmurs, even though she has no idea what 'the industry' in LA is like. I feel a little bad for lying to Mrs B. But the truth is boring and embarrassing, and Mrs B doesn't want to hear it. Not really.

As if things can't get more awkward, our school principal, Old Man Healy, makes his way towards me. Crap. Like being stuck with the drama teacher doesn't make me look sad enough.

'I think, no, no, I *know* and can confidently say that was our best show yet,' he announces loudly as he joins us, and shakes my hand.

'Thank you, sir,' I say quietly, aware of Imogen's presence and how pissed off she'd be to hear that.

'I've heard on the grapevine the next production is *Romeo and Juliet*,' he says with a wink, as if it is some big secret. It's not. People have already started working on their audition pieces. Not that I know why they're bothering. We all know Imogen will be Juliet.

Old Man Healy's tone suddenly changes and he lifts his hands into the air. 'But, soft, what light through the window breaks yonder? It is the east and Juliet is the sun. Fair sun arise and, and – damn what's the line – fair sun arise, arise fair sun … '

The whole room has stopped, everyone watching Mr Healy as he loudly attempts to recite the famous speech. My cheeks burn in second-hand embarrassment for him and the fact he is getting most of the words wrong. Really, really wrong. Finally, Healy stops and takes a small bow. People nearby applaud politely. It is awful. But Healy seems so impressed with his efforts and so taken with the half-hearted response, it looks like he is about to launch into another. Thankfully, Imogen appears. I have never felt so grateful to see her in my life.

'What a charming impromptu performance,' she says and gives Mr Healy a little round of applause. 'Are you classically trained, sir?'

A short, loud laugh bursts from Mrs B, who tries to cover it with a very fake-sounding sneeze. 'Sorry,' she says, 'allergies.'

'Oh, Mrs B, congratulations. I was so impressed with your seamless direction and I cannot wait for our next collaboration,' Imogen says, modulating her voice to make herself sound like Cate Blanchett. Low pitched, perfect articulation and an accent you can't quite place. It's not Imogen's real voice. It's Imogen's 'serious actor' voice. And it's a pretty good imitation of her favourite actress, developed

19

from years of private vocal tuition and an unhealthy obsession with YouTube clips of old Blanchett interviews.

Imogen is explaining, in her serious voice, how *connected* she feels to the Shakespearian language and how you need to find the very best actors to carry the *demands* of the text. She looks at me pointedly. Mrs B and Old Man Healy both look a little uncomfortable. I wonder if all of us are wondering how we can politely remove ourselves from this conversation. I know I'm thinking about it.

Someone pops a bottle of champagne and there's a heap of whooping and cheering and Old Man Healy is off to investigate. He is very protective of the new carpet in the foyer.

'Margot! Margot!' Old Man Healy says, 'I may need your help here.' And Mrs B looks at me sadly before she follows her boss across the room. She feels sorry for me. Probably thinks I'm hurt I don't have a crowd of adoring family members throwing flowers at my feet or popping champagne in my honour. Or it could be the fact that I'm now stuck with Imogen. Perhaps all of the above. To be honest, it's all pretty depressing stuff.

'Congrats,' Imogen says and pulls me in for weak hug and air kiss. Imogen is all about the air kiss.

'Thanks.' I pull back and wait for her notes. There's always notes from Imogen. And they're always negative.

'It was a surprising response, wasn't it? Such a vapid, silly show but everyone seemed completely enthralled by it. I mean, I hated it – but then, I am not the target audience, obviously. Still, I found the response rather surprising.' Imogen has this way of speaking that tricks you into thinking everything she is saying is a fact. If the acting thing doesn't work out for her, she will make a mean politician someday. 'It's a tad disappointing, a show like that being your final musical. I mean, it wasn't *terrible*, but it simply wasn't memorable.'

I'm not worried about Imogen or her opinions, even though Imogen thinks everyone cares about what she thinks. She likes to act as if she is already the Hollywood A-Lister she so desperately wants to be when, in reality, she's been a featured extra in one lousy TV commercial for a car insurance company. Still, everyone's got to start somewhere, I suppose. And, apart from the school stuff, she's done a lot more than me. I don't even have an agent. Imogen has had representation since she was ten months old. She was a Bonds baby.

'I find it so sad.' Imogen grasps my arm for emphasis. 'This was your last lead role at Arcadia. Your last hurrah.'

'My *last hurrah*?' I smile. Poor Imogen. She's even more awkward than me when it comes to normal conversation.

'Any decisions on what you're going to do next year?'

'Um,' I say, not quite prepared for this line of questioning, 'drama school. I think I'm going to audition for –'

'Sorry,' Imogen interrupts, 'but have you seen how much those schools cost? Do you know how expensive it is to train to become a professional? Those university fees are extreme. Even for someone like me. I assumed you would be going into nursing or something.'

'Um, a nursing degree isn't exactly cheap either.'

'But there's a job at the end of it. Otherwise you'll just be in debt forever, which I imagine isn't ideal considering your … circumstances.'

'I'll just have to make it then, won't I?'

Imogen starts telling me about all her plans and I vague out, letting her voice wash over me. I have been obsessing over university fees and courses and how the hell I can make this work for months now. I know what I want to do, what I think I was born to do, but the reality … I don't want to think about the reality. Not tonight.

'Where's your mum? Didn't you say she was actually coming this time?' Imogen says as she casts her eyes around the foyer. Suddenly it makes sense why she turned up to the show – Imogen would never miss an opportunity to network with someone from 'the industry'. Even if that someone is my mum.

'She couldn't get away,' I lie. It's scary how easily I can do it now.

'God,' Imogen says. 'I don't know how she does it. I mean, if I was her age and *still* trying to break through, I think I'd just top myself.'

It feels like I've been kicked in the stomach. Hard. Did she seriously just say that? I open my mouth to say something but nothing comes out – no words, no air. It's like I've been winded.

'You feeling all right? You look even paler than usual.'

My mind is racing, desperately trying to find the right words to throw back in her face.

'Anyway, mothers are such bores. Ugh. You're lucky you don't have to deal with yours all the time,' she says.

'I love my mum –'

'Yeah, yeah, who doesn't? Anyway, those are pretty.' She motions to the flowers I'm clutching.

'Oh, yeah, just Will being nice,' I stammer, still recovering from Imogen's words.

'*Just* Will? Don't let him hear that.'

'I don't mean it like that –'

As if on cue I feel an arm around me, pulling me into a sideways hug. It's Will. Great timing.

'I think I overheard Mrs B talking about potential costume designs for Juliet,' Will says.

'Where is she?' Imogen says. Will gestures to the other side of the foyer and, just like that, she's gone.

'Thanks, buddy,' I say.

'It looked like she was going full Imogen on you,' Will says.

The foyer is getting even more crowded as people pile in to hear the speeches, which should have started five minutes ago. It's my job to present gifts from the cast to Flick and Mrs B after their speeches, and after that I can finally leave. I hate these things. I love performing, but being in the foyer afterwards? No thanks. I like people watching me be someone else. I don't do too well when I have to be myself. That's a much more difficult role to play.

'You coming to the afterparty?' Will says. I pull a face. 'I can help you through it.'

'I'll go to an afterparty the day you write a musical,' I laugh. It's our inside joke. Will has been telling everyone for years that he is going to write a musical, but he never has. Usually this reference makes him laugh, or smile, or roll his eyes. But tonight? Nothing. He gets this strange look on his face, and I feel like I should apologise even though I don't know what I've said to upset him.

As Old Man Healy takes the podium and the noise subsides, I turn to Will to say, *Finally*, but he's disappeared into the crowd.

As usual the speeches are long and very earnest and a little embarrassing and Mrs B cries, a lot. As soon as it's done a lot of people start making their escape. Probably heading to Tara's for the afterparty. I get out my phone to check what time the next bus home will be, and see Mrs B standing right there in front of me. Again. This is getting ridiculous. Doesn't she have any of her own teacher friends?

'Come with me,' she says. Her mascara has run and her eyes look puffy. She looks like she should be at a funeral. 'You've been summoned.'

Old Man Healy is holding court with a group of people I don't know. There's a woman who looks older than my nan and is vaguely familiar, like I might have seen her face at another closing night, and a tall and elegant woman who is clutching the arm of an equally tall and elegant man. Rich people. Donors, probably. I can tell by their perfect clothes and perfect haircuts and perfect teeth, and the way Old Man Healy is pretty much drooling all over them.

'Sorry about this, my dear,' Mrs B whispers, then shoves me towards them and disappears.

'And this,' Mr Healy says, and I realise by *this* he means *me*, 'is what your generous donation gets us. Gets the *world*. A superstar in the making.'

He is talking about me like I'm not here. I wish I wasn't. Instead, I have to listen to his embarrassing speech, which I pretty much know off by heart: *An underprivileged background shouldn't diminish immense talent. Everyone deserves the right to be an artist.*

It's not the first time I've been through this.

Old Man Healy has a tendency to drag me out for the big donors. And I feature in a lot of glossy newsletters the school sends out asking for more support. *Help a child like Edie Emerson reach her full potential! The Arts changes lives. Arcadia Grammar changes destinies.*

Ugh.

They're all staring at me, waiting for me to say something. It feels like I've missed my cue. Forgotten my lines. I wish Mrs B hadn't gone. There's never an uncomfortable silence while she's around to fill it.

'You're welcome,' the man says pointedly.

'Oh,' I stumble, 'yes, thank you …'

But the man just looks at me as if he's waiting for me to say more.

'Thank you?' I say again.

Old Man Healy coughs, and I can sense his disappointment. He always wants me to put on an extra show for these people, and usually I play along: smile sweetly, say how grateful I am, how I'd never have this opportunity without their support, and then ask what their favourite part of the show was.

But over the years, I've grown more and more tired of this performance; more and more tired of forgiving these sorts of people for their ignorance, their superior attitudes. Why can't they acknowledge that the Arts changed my life well before I came to this school? Why don't they understand that the Arts exists outside of their little bubble, beyond their fancy postcodes? They can't imagine that my home has original Broadway cast recordings of musicals by Sondheim, and Rodgers and Hammerstein, and Lloyd Webber, which we all know word for word; that Pops does a mean Valjean; that Nan recites poetry in a way that makes you really listen and *hear* it; that we may not have a lot of money, but that doesn't mean we don't have the Arts.

These people, these rich people, seem to think the Arts is only for them.

'I assume you feel quite privileged to be attending a school like this,' the man says. 'Must have been quite the step up from your local high school.'

I stare at the floor. The new carpet Mr Healy chose for the foyer has stars all over it. Mrs B thinks it's beautiful and calls it the Midsummer Night's Dream carpet. I think it's tacky. Right now, though, I'm grateful for it because it's giving me something to focus on. I count the stars. I try not to say all the things that are bubbling up inside of me, because I can't put my scholarship at risk. Performing in a musical is tiring, but these endless, grovelling, cringeworthy performances, right here in the foyer for all these strangers, are next-level exhausting. I grit my teeth. *I am lucky to be here at Arcadia Grammar.* They all like to remind me of that.

'This is the only high school I've ever attended,' I say, as politely as possible, 'so I can't really compare it to anything else.'

The man sneers at me like I'm a piece of gum he's scrapped off his shoe. Although he probably has someone to do that sort of thing for him. He shakes his head and mutters something to the woman, who is gripping his arm a little tighter and looking just as embarrassed as I feel.

'Edie,' Mr Healy says, a bit louder than necessary, 'this is Mr and Mrs Winters. They have just made a very generous gift to the school, which we all appreciate so very much.' Mr Healy looks at me. 'Don't we?'

'Yes, yes, we do, very much appreciated, really,' I say and try my best to smile.

'And you remember Mrs Hewitt,' Mr Healy says and gestures to the woman beside him who, up close, is actually much, much older than my nan. She sort of sniffs at me. Maybe I smell. Did I remember to reapply deodorant?

'Of course, hello, again,' I say sweetly. I don't remember Mrs Hewitt but she seems satisfied with my response. Mr Healy looks relieved. I'm a good actor.

Mrs Hewitt starts talking at me about how she feels she has a responsibility to help those who are less fortunate, and I can't help but stare at the diamonds and emeralds that glitter around her neck. The way she keeps stroking the precious stones reminds me of Gollum with the One Ring. 'If I can add just a little hope, a little spark of something more to the lives of children such as yourself, Edie, then I can rest easy at night,' she says, and sniffs again.

I'm meant to say something here. I know the line, but I can't get it out. I need a glass of water. I need fresh air. I need to get out of here.

'Are you feeling all right, Edie?' Mr Healy whispers.

I nod.

Mrs Hewitt sniffs.

'Well, I thought you were just adorable. Your mother must be so proud.' Mrs Winters smiles brightly. 'Where is she? Your mother. I'd love to meet her.'

'She's at work,' I say quickly.

Mrs Winters' smile drops. 'I really don't know how any mother could choose work over their children but, well, call me old-fashioned ...'

'It's not a choice, Mrs Winters,' I say coldly.

Before I can say anything else, Old Man Healy jumps in. 'Edie's mother is in LA,' he says excitedly. 'She is in the industry, you know.'

'What *industry* is that, exactly?' Mr Winters smirks. 'Hospitality? Tourism? Some other industry ... perhaps?' He raises his eyebrows. What the hell is wrong with this guy? I look to Mrs Winters for some support but she is focused on her bracelet, twisting it around and around her wrist.

'What are you implying, sir?' I say. I am not letting him off the hook. I want to hear him say it, to my face.

Old Man Healy jumps in quickly, 'She's an actor! An actor!' He laughs like it was all some big misunderstanding.

'Ah,' Mr Winters nods, 'so she is in the hospitality industry, then. Waiting tables.'

'She is an actor,' I say, trying to sound calm and composed when all I really want to do is slap his smug face.

Old Man Healy starts talking up my grandparents (*They are so committed to Edie,* he says) and my mum (*She has such a strong work ethic,* he says, *and that's been instilled in Edie*). He is talking really fast, animated, trying to keep these rich people invested in me and, by association, his school.

I breathe deeply, trying to calm down, and wonder how Mum would have dealt with this. Would she have played the role I've carefully built for her? I'm sure she would have charmed everyone. She can do that. Make you feel like you're the most important person in the room. People fall in love with her very easily. Staying in love with her can prove a little more difficult.

'We know a lot of people in LA. Perhaps we could do a little networking. Link them in with your mother,' Mrs Winters says.

As I try desperately to come up with a good reason for that not to happen, I hear someone call my name and see Aubrey and Lexie, hand in hand, weaving their way through the foyer towards the exit. Aubrey has changed out of her theatre-blacks and is wearing a red velvet jumpsuit, which looks as glamorous as it sounds. Lexie looks just as glamorous in a little black dress and very high heels. It looks as if they're VIPs heading to some exclusive club, not a high school party at Tara's house. I feel so childish and basic compared to them. It's like I'm Disney Channel and they're HBO.

'Edie! Edie! Come on, let's go.' Aubrey untangles her hand from Lexie's and rushes towards me.

I never go to afterparties. Actually, I never go to parties. But right now it's the perfect excuse to get away from this terrible conversation. I link my arm through Aubrey's. 'Sorry, I have to go,' I say, as if I am super disappointed to be leaving them, and make my escape.

THREE

I sit in the back of Lexie's car – a sporty, red Mercedes her parents bought for her seventeenth birthday with personalised number plates (LEX1E). It causes her a lot of embarrassment. But if someone gave me a car, I don't think I'd care what the licence plate said.

There's a cartoonish-looking bulldog figurine on her dashboard that keeps nodding its head. Giving me the silent encouragement to tell my friends what I should have told them *before* I got into the car: that I do not want to go to this party. At all.

Lexie and Aubrey are singing along to Doja Cat. Listening to them, you'd really have no idea they had any musical talent whatsoever.

'Um, look, I think I need to get home,' I shout over the music.

'What?' Aubrey turns down the volume and swivels around in her seat to look at me.

'I need to go home,' I say again, but what I really mean is *want*. I *want* to go home.

'Oh my god, Edie, you never want to do anything!' Lexie says.

Lexie is correct but she didn't need to say it like that.

'Just come for like half an hour or something, it will be fun,' Aubrey says. 'Little steps. OK?'

Aubrey always does this. Makes me take 'little steps'. Without her little steps I would have missed out on a lot of things: school socials, joining the school debating team, even becoming friends with Will.

'You look so cute, let's go show it off,' Aubrey says.

Cute? I don't want to look cute. And I definitely don't want to 'show it off'. What does that even mean? But it's not my terrible dress stopping me from wanting to go to this party, and every other party. It's something else. Something I can never quite explain. Not even to Aubrey.

'I'm not driving all the way to your house,' Lexie says and turns the music up again.

'Thirty minutes, Edie, that's all. Just try for thirty minutes,' Aubrey says and restarts the duet with her girlfriend.

We arrive at these huge wrought iron gates with BIRDSONG emblazoned across them in gold lettering. OK, so Tara's house not only has gates but an actual name. Lexie buzzes the intercom and the BIRD and the SONG open up to reveal a long, tree-lined driveway lit up in golden fairy lights.

The circular driveway has a fountain in its centre, and looking over it all is the biggest, brightest house I have ever seen. Except it isn't really a house. It is a proper mansion, with four roman-like columns, a sweeping staircase leading to the front porch, a huge balcony on the first floor and then two more floors including a turret right at the very top.

'Holy shit,' I say.

'Yeah,' Lexie says as she pulls in behind another Mercedes, 'Tara's family are next level.'

Next level is an understatement. They're on a whole different planet. An uber wealthy one.

Tara's mother greets us at the entrance. 'Edie Emerson is here!' she announces to no-one in particular. It takes a lot of effort not to turn around and leave. 'I didn't know if the star of the show was going to grace us with her presence this evening but there you are, as I live and breathe. The star is here!'

The way she's acting, anyone would think I was actually famous. Or giving her one of my kidneys. She gives me a hug that I don't really want. It's a little too tight and goes on for a little too long and I start to worry she may be trying to take one of my kidneys after all.

'The party is in the pool house. I'll take you.' Before I know what's happening, Mrs Belsky has taken my hand and is pulling me across the marble floor and through the French doors and into the lush garden. I hear Aubrey and Lexie laughing behind me.

There must be really impressive ways to show up to a party. Like turning up in a helicopter or being chauffeured there in a stretch limousine – any other way than being brought in by the host's mother. Holding your hand. Presenting you to the group. As if it is the first day of kinder or something. But that's how I'm making my entrance to this party. Mrs Belsky leads me up the stairs and onto the deck.

'EDIE IS HERE!' she shouts over the music and raises my arm up like I've just won a boxing match. Thankfully no-one seems to notice, except Tara, who appears from nowhere, somehow managing to look even more embarrassed than I feel.

'Oh my god. Mum! What the hell are you doing?' Tara hisses.

'She is here. Can you believe it?'

'No-one cares,' Tara says before turning to me to say, 'no offence, Edie.'

'You care,' Mrs Belsky continues, 'you said this morning there was no way Edie would come –'

'SHUT UP!' Tara interrupts her mother with a shout-whisper.

I pull my hand from Mrs Belsky's grasp and leave the two of them to their hushed argument.

Aubrey and Lexie have disappeared, which makes sense. If I could have avoided that entrance, I would have. But I feel so awkward, just standing there, alone. I need to find Will. If there's an Xbox here, that's where he'll be. So I head towards the pool house, which looks how I imagine a five-star resort would look. I have to resist the urge to take photos of this place to show Nan, because she isn't going to believe me when I tell her about it.

The pool house is surrounded by a wooden deck, a canopy of fairy lights creating a starry sky under which people are dancing. The pool, lit up and glowing in neon blue, nudges up to one side of the deck, where couples sit, feet dangling in the water, making out. Inside, the house looks like something out of one of those *Grand Designs* episodes Nan is always crying over. I could live in this pool house. There are potted ferns and palms all over the place. The walls are covered in art. Huge ceiling fans spin lazily overhead. Lush, comfy sofas and beanbags are scattered across the floors. There's a pretty impressive bar that's getting a lot of attention in the corner, and a table full of food that is being ignored. It is going to get very messy very quickly. But right now, everyone seems happy. Except Tara, who is still out on the deck, silently screaming at her mother and trying to push her out of the party.

I grab a bottle of water from the bar. Say *no thanks* to a pink-haired girl I have never seen before who offers me vodka. She shrugs and empties the rest of the bottle into her cup.

'I really like your hair,' I say.

She shrugs again.

'It looks amazing, like it totally suits you,' I keep going. Gushing. As always. Why am I like this?

'Thanks?' she says and gets away from me. Fast. I don't blame her.

I have to find Will. Imagine his face when he sees that I am actually here at an actual party. He won't believe it. I still don't believe it. I try to push away the anxious feeling that is starting to chew at the edges just a little … *You're so awkward,* the voice says, *you don't fit in, you don't belong here.*

There are a lot more people at this party than were in the *Sweet Charity* cast and crew. I thought this was supposed to be a party for us, but there's heaps of unfamiliar faces staring at me. They're probably wondering what the hell I'm doing here. Except, I tell myself, they're not. They're not staring at me. I have to remind myself of that. Everyone is so caught up in themselves they don't really notice anyone else unless something really, really embarrassing happens, and so far everything is OK. I got out of the Mrs Belsky situation without anyone noticing and I can get through another twenty-four minutes. Nothing bad will happen. And then I can go home.

'Oh my god, you're actually here?' Diego stands in front of me with a very colourful drink in his hand.

'What are you drinking? It looks weird,' I say.

'It's my own recipe. Want one?'

'No. Thanks. I'll stick with water.' I shake the water bottle at him and he rolls his eyes.

'Boring, whatever, come with me. We're gonna do *Anything Goes*!' he says and starts to head towards the deck.

I don't move. Are we still doing this? 'Do we have to?'

He turns back and gives me one of his famous death-stares. 'It's our last ever musical afterparty. And you're actually here. For once. So, yes, we have to.' His death-stare melts away into a dazzling smile.

'Fine,' I say and follow him out to the deck.

In the year when everything stopped, *Anything Goes* was meant to be our school musical. We'd had the auditions and started rehearsals but then the school closed down, along with everything else. That year we didn't physically go to school all that much and we tried to keep singing, dancing and acting online. Which, we discovered, doesn't work. Not really. No matter how hard Mrs B tried to make it OK, it wasn't. It was tough. We did a really weird

Zoom concert-version of the show which was recorded in our homes and edited together by the media department and just didn't work. I mean, how can you do a group tap routine online? Answer: you can't.

Diego always says his performance as Billy in *Anything Goes* would have been the greatest thing Arcadia had ever seen, had it not been for the global pandemic ruining everything. Only someone like Diego could take a global pandemic as a personal affront. He likes to prove to people just how great he could have been. I was meant to be Reno Sweeney in that show and we had this number together, which he *always* wants to perform at any and every occasion where there's an audience. We've done it at school open days and assemblies and he even dragged me along to his grandfather's seventieth birthday so we could perform it there. Everyone must be so over it. Not that Diego could ever imagine anyone ever being over him.

He is clearing the deck to make a space for us to perform, and shouting for Tara to change the music. I don't know why people are listening to him. Why would anyone want to watch us do this … again? But they are. Diego has a way, I suppose, of getting what he wants.

A crowd has gathered, phones out, ready to forever capture a performance they have all seen way too many times. I wonder if Diego will ever let this go? Will I be forced to belt out a rendition of 'You're the Top' with him when we're at our twenty-year school reunion? Our fortieth? Will he perform it at my funeral? I see the girl with the pink hair smirking at me like this is the dumbest thing she's ever had to endure. And she's probably right. It is dumb. I mean, for musical theatre nerds like us, breaking into song and dance is pretty normal. But not everyone here is like us.

'Do we really have to do this?' I whisper to him.

'Take off your bag,' he replies, and grabs the handbag strap that hangs from my shoulder.

'Geez, all right, calm down,' I say and throw the bag onto a nearby table.

'Professional, Edie, you should always be professional. You never know who is watching.' He moves into position and motions for me to do the same.

Looks like I'm doing this. Again.

Something takes over like I'm on autopilot – the song and dance are so embedded in my brain and body it just kind of happens. But as I'm going through the motions, I keep wondering why the hell I'm doing this. Why didn't I just say no?

Diego is really playing it up for the crowd. He is so obnoxious. Not that people seem to care. They're actually getting into it – cheering him on, whooping and clapping. I notice even the pink-haired girl is less smirk and more smile. I suppose the song is catchy even if it is outdated. Arcadia doesn't really do contemporary. I mean, pretty much all of the musicals we've done at school were written before our grandparents were born.

I'm singing a line about Fred Astaire (during rehearsals, some of the cast asked Mrs B who that was) when I hear it. It's a noise that only groups of entitled guys can make – a kind of chanting. And even though you can't make out *what* they're saying, just the *sound* of it means trouble. Their voices are getting louder and faster, drowning out our song. And then this guy appears. A blur of colour and bravado pushing the crowd and running straight at Diego like a deranged bull. I can see exactly what's going to happen and, instead of just letting it happen – like any normal person would, because Diego is a pain in the ass – I shove Diego out of the way. And before I can stop it, this bull-guy is bowling me over and we're both slipping backwards and splashing into the pool. The water stings as I land, and then I'm sinking, submerged, my hair in my face, and I can't tell up from down and then I'm kicking, struggling, pushing to the surface.

I tread water and try to catch my breath.

I am in the pool. Fully clothed. Shoes on. In. The. Pool.

I swim to the edge of the pool, look up at the silent, shocked crowd gathered on the deck. 'Come on in!' I say, trying to act like this is all a hilarious joke when really all I want to do is cry. 'The water's fine!'

But no-one jumps in. They laugh. Some take photos. Most turn away. Get back to drinking and dancing and enjoying the party, which does not, it seems, involve jumping fully clothed into the pool. Go figure. Every teen movie I have ever watched has lied to me, obviously.

The bull-guy swims up next to me. He isn't wearing a shirt; I don't want to find out what else he's not wearing. 'Oops,' he says, smiling. 'Sorry about that.'

Seriously? He thinks he can just smile and act all cute and everything will be OK?

'Dick,' I mutter. I push off from the wall and start to swim towards the steps on the other side of the pool.

'Hey! I said I was sorry!' he shouts. 'Don't be like that! Come on. I'm sorry!'

I stop, turn back to face him. 'I don't accept your apology,' I say, trying to keep my voice steady. I'm shaking. 'You're a dickhead.'

'It was just a joke,' he says, and smiles at me again. 'I mean, I was meant to tackle Diego, obviously. Not you. It would have been funnier if it was Diego, I suppose –'

'It wasn't funny at all.'

'Depends on your perspective. Comedy is subjective. You might find this hilarious one day!'

I have this urge to hold his head underwater for a really, really long time. See how funny he thinks it is then. But I don't. I ignore him. Swim to the steps. Leave him behind.

Tara is there, holding a fluffy white towel. 'Oh my god, I'm so sorry, Edie,' she says, and I can see she means it. I wipe the tears from my eyes as I carefully get out of the pool. Tara wraps the towel around me. There's something about someone being genuinely nice to me when I'm feeling genuinely awful that always makes me cry. It's like I have permission to let it all out. But I'm at a party, surrounded by people, and I can't let anything out. Not here.

'NOAH!' Tara turns her attention to the guy in the pool. 'I HATE YOU. GO HOME!'

'It was a joke!' Noah says. 'I said I was sorry!' He pulls himself out of the pool and onto the deck, and I see he's wearing jeans. Which will be super uncomfortable now that they're soaking wet. Good. I want him to suffer.

'Get out of here, Noah!' Tara shouts. He does this exaggerated mime like he can't hear her or something and saunters off towards the pool house. Tara chases after him, swearing and demanding he leave RIGHT NOW.

My dress is sticking to me and my shoes are wrecked and I don't even want to know how my make-up and hair look. I try to slip out of the party quietly but I'm making squelching noises with every step, and now that something bad has happened everyone is looking at me. I'm not imagining it. They give me sympathetic looks and whisper behind my back.

I find my bag, pull the towel around me a little tighter and head towards the main house and my escape. I hear Aubrey calling my name, but I don't want to stop. I just want to get out of here.

'Edie!' she shouts, and I can hear her running to catch up. 'Wait up!'

'Sorry' – I stop, wait for her – 'didn't hear you.'

I know she knows I'm lying but she doesn't say anything, just gives me a big hug. 'Are you OK?'

I nod because if I try to speak I'll cry. Which is so dumb. Because I'm fine. Really. I'm just soaking wet. With ruined shoes.

'Do you want me to sort this jerk out?' She would too. Aubrey always sorts things out. 'What a dick. Who does that? It's assault, Edie, and we should report it. Do you want to report it?'

'I just want to go home.'

'No, don't. You can have a shower here. Tara will have a dress or something you can borrow. The party's just kicking off. Please, please, please stay.'

I want to ask, *Why? Why do you want me to stay when you and Lexie ditched me the moment we got here anyway?* But I don't say that. I say, 'I lasted thirty minutes. That was the deal, right?'

'Are you serious? You barely even ...' her voice trails off. 'Fine. OK. Whatever, Edie.'

'What?'

'Nothing,' she sighs. 'Get home safe.'

I go to give her another hug but she is already heading back towards the pool house.

I hate parties.

*

Ubers are pretty expensive but there's no way I can negotiate a bus timetable right now, let alone sit on a bus, in wet clothes, for hours. I try to justify the expense and ignore how sad my savings look. I tell myself it will be worth it – I'll get home much quicker this way. And the sooner I get home, the sooner I can fall apart. I've held it together pretty well so far. Stood there, dripping all over the marble floors while Mrs Belsky screamed at the staff to make me cocoa and fussed about me. I managed to politely excuse myself – *have to run, my Uber is almost here, thank you for having me, Mrs Belsky* – and now I'm under the watchful, blinking eye of the security camera above the Belskys' front gates. I wonder if it's necessary. Nothing bad would ever happen in a suburb like this.

I'm checking the Uber's progress when I hear it ... a slow clap. Clap. Clap. Clap.

I turn.

The slow-clapper stands in front of me, mid-clap, grinning like he's in on some big joke I've missed. Noah.

'Thank you,' he says, 'for getting me kicked out of the party.'

'That wasn't my fault. You did that all by yourself,' I say, and turn my attention back to the app.

He produces two beers from his bag. 'Drink?'

I shake my head.

'It's a peace offering,' he says, 'because I'm truly, sincerely, and utterly sorry.'

'Good for you,' I say.

Noah shrugs and takes a swig of his beer. 'It's good,' he says, 'for cheap beer. Sure I can't tempt you?' He waves the bottle in front of my face.

'No, I don't drink.'

He pulls a face.

'Sorry if that offends you.'

'You're pretty great at offending people, actually.' He takes another mouthful of beer. 'You called me a dick. I heard you.'

'You are a dick.'

'Yeah,' he says softly, 'you're probably right.'

I don't want to talk to him. I want to get home and into my bed and just pretend this night hasn't happened.

'You waiting for an Uber?' he says. I nod. 'Me too. Actually, not an Uber. A car. We have a driver, so ...'

I don't know what to say to that, so I don't say anything at all.

'I'm Noah,' he says.

'Yep. I know.'

'This is the part where you're meant to introduce yourself.'

I stare him down.

'OK, um, so, you're Edie – I know who you are cos I was at the show tonight and, um, yeah, hi, nice to meet you.' He holds out his hand as if I am going to shake it. I don't.

To avoid Noah and his small talk, I write a long message to Aubrey. I tell her I'm fine. That I'll let her know when I'm home safe. That she should stop worrying about me and have fun. Even though I'd prefer her to be hanging out with me. Coming back to my place for a movie marathon and popcorn and a sleepover the way we used to. Before she met Lexie.

'You're waiting for me to say congratulations and tell you how great the show was or something, right?' Noah interrupts.

I roll my eyes at him. Press send on my message to Aubrey and hope she'll magically appear and save me from this.

'I'm not going to say any of that,' he goes on. 'I mean, you were good. Great, actually. But the show? It was kinda crap, to be honest. I've seen way better versions.'

'In case you didn't notice, it was a *high school* production,' I snap. I can't help it.

Here's the thing. Everyone is a damn critic. It doesn't matter if they've never danced or sung or acted in front of anyone before. If they've never even been on the stage, or helped put on a play. It doesn't matter if they can't sing and have no sense of rhythm and are incapable of delivering a line. People love to tell you that the show was awful, your footwork sloppy, your voice off-key when they don't actually know what a key is or how to sing in one. Nope. None of that matters. The fact they *couldn't* do it doesn't stop them criticising how *you* did it. And it's not like constructive feedback isn't needed. But this sort of shit isn't constructive. It's just mean. It makes you feel like crap. And how dare this guy, who has already ruined my night, try to make me feel like crap?

43

'It was *very* high school,' he laughs.

'Screw you,' I say. 'You don't know what you're talking about. I wouldn't critique your – your water polo game, would I? No. I wouldn't. Because I don't play water polo and I don't know anything about it and so I'd keep my pathetic opinions about it to myself.'

'Water polo?'

'Isn't that what rich kids play?'

'Water polo?'

'Shut up,' I say and head away from the gates. Surely the Uber will be here soon.

He rushes up beside me. 'Sorry,' he says, 'I'm an idiot. I was just being provocative and … pathetic. You're right. I am pathetic.'

I'm not talking to him. I am watching the road for headlights. Noah, however, won't shut up.

'To be honest, I'm not really into musicals so, yeah, sorry, again for being a dick,' he says. 'See? I am a dickhead. I said you were right.'

I smile. At least he's got a little self-awareness.

'Made you smile!' he says.

'Oh, let me guess? You're gonna tell me I look so much better when I smile? That I should smile more? Is that it?'

'You do have a nice smile …'

'You're a walking, talking misogynistic cliché,' I say.

'Ouch.' He grabs his chest as if I've just shot an arrow through his heart, and waits for me to laugh, to tell him it's OK because he is cute and oh-so-funny and lives in a world where he always gets what he wants. 'Look, I'm really sorry, Edie, OK?'

44

'I don't want your apology, Noah,' I say with all the force of my voice training. Projecting. Like I'm onstage. Like I'm playing the lead role – a braver, stronger version of myself. He takes a step back. 'What I want is for you to go back in time and make some better decisions. Like, maybe, not being a complete jerk tonight. But that's not gonna happen. So, instead, how about you just leave me alone?'

He nods. 'I really am sorry,' he says, and this time there is no smile, no laugh in the voice. This time he sounds real.

A moment later, headlights appear. My Uber. Finally. I get into the back seat and as the car pulls away I sneak a look back at Noah. He catches me looking, and he waves.

I stop myself from waving back.

FOUR

I know Nan and Pops will be waiting for me when I get home. Sitting in their old, rundown armchairs, dressing gowns on, watching some very violent action film because my grandparents are into that sort of thing. I open the front door as quietly as I can, hoping perhaps they've fallen asleep in front of the TV and I can just get to the shower and bed without having to answer all their questions. Because I know they'll have questions. Hundreds of questions.

The sounds of screaming and explosions come to an abrupt stop as I enter the living room.

'You look like a drowned rat,' Nan says. No *hello, welcome home, nice to see you*. Nope. Not my Nan's style. 'What the hell happened?'

I know if I mention some boy pushed me into a pool they will lose it and turn it into a big thing and I can't deal with a big thing right now, so I say, 'I slipped . Into the pool.'

'Slipped?' Nan raises an eyebrow. She's staring at me like she's trying to read my mind.

'What?'

'I know what teenagers get up to at parties, Edie.'

'How was closing night?' Pops changes the subject. He is good at that. Avoiding conflict. At all costs. 'How was our super-star?'

'Meh,' I say.

'Meh? Bullshit. My granddaughter is never meh.' Nan gives me a quick kiss on the cheek as she makes her way to the kitchen to put the kettle on. No-one asks if anyone wants a cup of tea around here. It is a given.

'Come here, come here,' Pops says, arms outstretched. I give him a hug. 'Sorry I didn't get to see this one, Little Ed.'

'Don't even worry about it, Big Ed,' I say.

Pops will tell anyone who listens that I'm named after him. Edward Emerson. Edie Emerson. Mum always tells me it's not true and that I'm named after a singer she loves, but Pops refuses to believe that. And so we've become Big Ed and Little Ed. Although, these days, he isn't so big. He used to be a giant of a man, tall and strong and always on the go. When I was a kid I read *The BFG* and I always imagined him as the Big Friendly Giant, and me as Sophie. The little girl he plucks from the orphanage. Anyway, now he's a sharp-angled shadow who sits, all day, in his old armchair. But he's still my BFG. And he is my number one fan, which makes him completely biased but very sweet.

'Feels like only yesterday you were the little Christmas Elf and now you've just closed your last Arcadia musical,' he

47

says, wiping tears from his eyes. He can get very sentimental at times. 'I should have been there ...'

'Nah, you didn't miss much, Pops, and tonight I was not great. Really. I was bad. Totally off. I'm kinda glad you missed it ...'

'You were incredible on opening night so I can only imagine that your closing night performance was even better,' Nan says as she brings in the tray of tea. Milky and weak for her, strong and dark for me, in between for Pops. 'Cheryl even raved about it. Did I tell you? She never has a good thing to say about anything. But there you go. She said it was wonderful.'

'Really?' Pops says. 'Cheryl used the word *wonderful*?'

'OK. Adequate. She said it was *adequate* but that's big bloody praise from Cheryl,' Nan laughs.

'Have you heard from Mum?' I say.

Nan's face slips. Just a tiny bit, but enough for me to notice. She puts it back together pretty quick. She's always like this when it comes to Mum. Little cracks appear, frays at her edges, that she tries to cover over so she doesn't upset me. But I can always see it.

'I reserved a seat for her but she didn't show up.'

'I told you not to get your hopes up, sweetheart,' Nan says.

'But she said she'd see this one. She said she'd come. Closing night. She promised.'

'Your mum says a lot of things,' Nan says. Not unkindly. No. My nan isn't like that. When it comes to Mum, she's just sad. And tired. Like the rest of us.

Pops takes hold of my hand, squeezes it tightly, and it takes all I have to stop myself from bursting into tears right then and there. I don't know why I want to cry. I knew Mum wouldn't be there tonight. Deep down, I *knew* she wouldn't show up. I'm used to it. So why am I upset?

'We need some biscuits with this tea,' I say as brightly as possible, and make a quick exit for the kitchen.

*

I can't sleep. I stare at the glow-in-the-dark stars on my ceiling, which I can barely make out because they've lost all their glow-in-the-dark abilities. It feels like a metaphor or something. I check my phone and stare at the notifications. Messages in the group chat with Will and Aubrey. I don't want to look at them. It will just be about the party. All the stuff I'm missing. I put the phone down and go back to staring at the ceiling. I should take all those stars down, or replace them. Maybe I could stick new ones over the top of the old ones.

My phone lights up again. I should probably respond. They'll just be checking in, wanting to make sure I actually made it home. I should tell them I'm fine. I should have done it hours ago.

But it isn't Will or Aubrey messaging me. It's Mum.

A message from Mum. At three in the morning. I shove the phone under my pillow. What's worse than *not* hearing from my mother is actually hearing from her. It makes no sense. I know that. But that's how it is. Especially when a message is coming through at three in the morning. No good messages arrive at that time. This is the time of bad news and ugly scenes and things you don't want to deal with right now. Or ever.

I'd rather not know.

But I can't not know. I reach for the phone, my hands shaking. It's stupid. It's only a text message. Words on a screen. But sometimes words on a screen can hurt. Especially when your mum has written them.

Another phone starts ringing, loud and shrill. I jump. The landline. That phone sits, usually silent and forgotten, on the little table next to Nan's chair. I don't know why she insists on keeping it. We don't need it. We don't use it. And now all it's doing is waking everyone up. I rush from my bed to answer it. No-one wants to be the reason Nan's eight hours of sleep is interrupted. Believe me.

I grab the receiver. 'Hello?' I whisper down the line, my heart thumping loudly in my ears. I can't hear anyone on the other end, but I know who it is. 'Mum …'

Still no-one speaks. I think I can hear her chewing the edge of her fingernail, the way she does when she gets nervous, or maybe I'm just imagining things.

'Hi Edie,' Mum's voice sounds small and unsure and very far away, but it is hers.

I sink into Nan's chair. Hold onto the receiver with two hands. Tight. Like it's going to fly away from me or something.

'You were ignoring my texts,' she says.

'Sorry. I was asleep,' I say.

'Not anymore you're not!' she laughs. A full, throw-your-head-back, eyes watering kind of laugh. It's her stage laugh. She's putting on a show for whoever is watching her make this call. I hear her compose herself. Clear her throat.

'Darling, I am mortified, absolutely mortified I missed your show tonight.'

'You remembered?' I say stupidly.

'Of course! I just remembered a couple of hours too late.' She is probably shrugging now, or pulling a funny face at her adoring audience. I wonder who is there with her. I wonder where she is. 'I feel terrible. Just terrible. Tell me everything!'

I don't want to tell her everything. Actually, I don't want to tell her *anything*. But Mum has this power; she has this way of making you completely forget you're annoyed at her. Just like that. It's like she's put you under hypnosis or something and, instead of being pissed off with her, you desperately need to impress her. It's weird. But it's how it's always been. Which is why I am now sitting here in the dark, when I'd rather be sleeping – or trying to sleep – telling her all about the show.

Before I came along, Mum was a triple threat herself. She performed on cruise ships wearing those awful show-girl costumes of feathers and sequins alongside other identical women with matching toothy grins and tiny waists and impossibly long legs. I used to love looking at those photos. She doesn't have them anymore. On one of her bad days she ripped them all up and that was that. Nan still has some of her theatre programs and pictures, though, and a review cut out of the newspaper in which the critic calls Mum things like *sensational* and *breathtaking*. She was probably going to be famous – until I stuffed it all up for her.

Mum was an actor. Or rather, she is still trying to be one. She isn't famous. She isn't even C-grade celebrity famous. Like, no-one would recognise her from a TV commercial or anything like that. But then, fame and talent don't always go together. *Not all famous people are talented, and not all talented people are famous*, that's what Mum says. There are exceptions. Mum says that, too. And one of those exceptions is her hero, Meryl Streep.

It was because of Meryl that Mum disappeared to New York City. At least, that's where she said she was going. I was only ten, but I remember it like it happened last week. Her stuffing things from her wardrobe into a suitcase. Not folding them. Not even looking at what she was taking. Just shoving armfuls of clothes into it and crying – *I didn't want this, I didn't want this.* And by 'this' I knew she meant me. I'd ruined everything. *I'm an* actor, *not a mother,* she said. *Be both,* I said. But she didn't hear me, or pretended not to. She just kept shoving things in her bag. And the more she put in there the harder it got to breathe, as if all the air were being slowly sucked out of the room. Mum took my face in her hands, told me it would be OK, and because she's such a good actor I believed her. For a moment. What else could I do?

Meryl Streep has children. Four of them. I wish I'd known that back then so I could have told my mum. Maybe that would have changed things. I like to imagine she would have laughed: *Meryl has kids? Meryl is a mother* and *an actor? Well, if Meryl can do it, so can I!* And she would have unpacked all her poorly packed clothes and seven years later I wouldn't be stuck in a weird early-morning phone call with someone who feels more like a long-lost relative than my mother.

Mum yawns loudly.

'Anyway,' I say, feeling bad for talking for too long, 'I'm sorry you missed it. It was my last musical at Arcadia.'

'Really?' Mum says.

'Um, yeah I …' I start to explain that the school's next production is *Romeo and Juliet*, and why I won't get a lead role, but Mum has started talking to someone else. She's covered the phone so it's a little muffled, but I can hear her. Giggling and saying, *Stop it, not now, no, no.* And then more giggling. 'Mum?'

There's a pause. I wait.

'Sorry, darling,' Mum says. 'I'm exhausted. Can we finish this conversation later?'

She doesn't sound exhausted or sorry at all.

'Sure,' I say, because what else can I say?

'Mwah!' she makes a stupid, exaggerated kissing sound. 'Love you. Bye.'

And just like that, she's gone.

FIVE

Will's musical is something of a legend, a myth, a dream he has gone on and on about for the longest time – but we've never seen any evidence of it actually existing. It's why it's become an inside joke. Not just for me and Aubrey and Will himself, but pretty much everyone in our year group. I think I even overheard Mrs B referencing it at one point.

His big idea started in Year Nine. That was when we did *Guys and Dolls*. There we were, a group of kids pretending to be gangsters and gamblers from 1930s New York. The musical was heaps of fun to be in, but not at all relevant to our lives or experiences or anything we cared about. Will was in that production with me. He had a small role but was so funny he stole the show every single night. Which can be disheartening when you're up there, singing your guts out and working super hard, and the guy with a couple of funny one-liners gets all the attention. Anyway, that's

Will. He always nails the comedic roles – his timing is perfect, and he finds details in characters or moments in lines that other people would miss. I don't know why he never went for lead roles; he was always good enough for them. Better than good. And then, this year, he didn't do the musical at all. Even though I begged him to audition for *Sweet Charity*. *What's the point?* he'd said, and when I tried to tell him the point was he was better than Diego and would make a much better Oscar, he just shook his head and wouldn't talk about it.

Anyway, it was during the season of *Guys and Dolls* that it all started. We'd gone to Aubrey's house after opening night. The three of us were devouring pizza and peanut M&Ms and fighting over which movie to watch when Will started playing this YouTube video. It was a StarKid show. A low-budget, hilarious musical based on *Harry Potter* that we all immediately fell in love with. We stayed up all night watching everything they'd ever put up on YouTube, and it changed everything. I never knew musicals could be like that. All the musicals we'd done seemed so far away from stuff we actually knew and liked and understood, and then here was StarKid Productions – a group of friends who'd got together and made something fun and contemporary. And Will wanted to be just like them.

'Why don't we do something like this at Arcadia?' he said.

We all knew why not. A musical like that wouldn't be flashy or impressive enough for Arcadia. They always stuck with the classics. There was no way we'd ever change their mind. But Will never let up about it. He talked about it. Dreamed about it. Complained about it. But I didn't know he was actually *doing* something about it until he called me this morning to tell me.

'What?' I'd croaked into the phone. I still had ten beautiful minutes before my alarm went off, before I had to get up and get ready for work. Will had ruined that.

'Good morning!' Will was always wide awake and energetic in the morning. I grumbled something and then he proceeded to remind me how it had been all my idea to wait until Year Twelve to put on his musical.

'What musical?'

'The musical I've written.'

'You've actually written it?'

'And we're going to put it on, at Arcadia, and I know there's not a heap of time so we have to start today –'

'I have work, Will.'

'I'll see you there.'

Will's musical might have become our punchline but that whole time, Will knew what he was doing. The joke was on us. You would think I'd have learnt by now not to underestimate William Yoon.

*

Every Sunday from eight to five I work at the local supermarket. Nan got me the job a couple of years ago – she works here too so it's totally favouritism. It's OK for a casual job. There are heaps worse things I could be doing, plus the pay is all right and the people I work with are pretty nice. Except for Marshall, who is the supervisor on Sundays and takes the role way too seriously. He also calls me Princess, which I hate. But I can't complain because that would just

56

prove him right, wouldn't it? Only a princess would complain about being called a princess. I just ignore him. Or try to.

'What's wrong, Princess?' he smirks as he leans over the counter. Today I am working the deli shift, which I also hate.

'It's one o'clock,' I say.

'So?'

'It's my lunchbreak.'

He pulls away from the counter, stands back with his arms folded across his chest. Stares me down.

'Can I go? Please?'

He huffs, rolls his eyes and makes a big deal over it. You'd think I was asking him for a pay rise and not for the scheduled lunchbreak I am entitled to. It's always like this with Marshall. The power goes to his head. I look at him blankly while he *umms* and *ahhs* about it. Finally, he does this stupid bow and says, 'Of course, Princess, off you go.'

'Leave her alone, Marshall, you bloody dickhead,' Justine shouts at him from the chicken rotisserie.

Marshall turns bright red and makes a quick exit. He wouldn't dare cross Justine. No-one would. She gives me a wink. Justine always has my back.

My lunch break is forty-five minutes and I always take it in the coffee shop opposite the supermarket. The supermarket is part of a small shopping centre so there's not a lot of choice. There's only our store, the coffee shop, a really random two-dollar shop, newsagent, butcher and bakery. That's it. The coffee shop is the heart of it, and at one o'clock you usually have to fight for a table. Except today Will and Aubrey are already there, waiting, seated at one of the plastic tables and looking at their coffees like they don't quite trust them.

I wish I wasn't wearing my work uniform. I'm embarrassed about them seeing me in it. I mean, we wear a school uniform every day, but there's something about the Arcadia emblem that makes that uniform special. You've been *chosen* to wear that uniform. That uniform stands for something exceptional. It gets noticed – for the right reasons. In this uniform, you don't get noticed unless a customer wants to shout at you about something.

My work uniform is black pants and a polo shirt in a disappointing maroon colour, made out of the kind of fabric that sticks to your skin and shows up every sweat patch, even if you're sure you're not sweating. The ugly maroon plus the fluorescent lights turn my skin sort of grey, which makes me look like I'm sick. I feel sweaty and gross and I wish Will could have waited until Monday to talk about this.

But it's Will. And patience isn't really his thing.

They see me and wave brightly, trying to cover up how out of place they feel here. As if they hadn't just been whispering about how crappy the coffee shop is compared to the amazing cafes in their neighbourhoods. I get it. I do. Still, at least they visit me here, in this neighbourhood no-one else from Arcadia would be caught dead in. The others say it is too far away, but I know that's just code. Where I live is not a place they'd like to be seen. It's beneath them. This place isn't pretty enough or arty enough or wealthy enough for them. That's the truth.

Before I even have a chance to say hi, Will starts talking really, really fast about NYU and a course on writing musical theatre and how it's a really incredible opportunity and that it's kind of perfect because it's an American winter school thing, held over our summer, so he'll be back in time to start uni and it won't mess up the whole plan for his medical degree.

'It's really competitive, heaps of people from all over the world apply but they only accept twenty writers – and I need to show them something for the application, they need to see what I can do and I want them to see this, my musical, I mean they won't *see* it, but I'll send a recording or something, and anyway, no pressure but this is my whole future, right here ...'

'You're going to New York?' I'm trying to keep up with everything he's saying, but I can't get past this New York thing – why hasn't he mentioned it before?

'Not now but hopefully, yeah ...'

'Everyone's leaving,' I say. 'You're going to New York, Aubrey's going to Singapore –'

'And you have been invited, you *could* still come with me,' Aubrey says, pursing her lips. She's still annoyed with me about it.

Aubrey recently sprung her gap year plan on us. It was pretty unexpected. She'd always seemed to know exactly what she wanted to do when she left school: a double degree in Arts/Law. That's what she's told everyone since Year Seven. But now, she's changed her mind. It makes me anxious that someone as sure and steady as Aubrey can suddenly feel so uncertain about her future that she's running away on a gap year. If Aubrey doesn't know what she wants to do, how is there any hope for me? I mean, I want to be an actor, I've always said I want to be an actor, but Aubrey always said she wanted to do Arts/Law and, bam, just like that she changed her mind. What happens if I change my mind? What happens if it doesn't work out? Where can I run to?

I can't go and figure it all out in Singapore and Europe like Aubrey's planning to do. She invited me to stay with her grandmother in Singapore and I got excited and got ahead of myself and thought if I saved hard enough I'd be able to pay for my flights. But then I did the maths and fell back to earth. Because it's not just flights, but also a passport, and food, and all the amazing plans Aubrey was making for us, all the places we'd see, the things we'd do. And so I had to tell her, *Sorry, I can't come,* and she said, *You can, because I've got you* – which is generous and kind, but makes me feel really awkward. I don't want other people paying my way. I've tried explaining it to her, but she just rolls her eyes and says I am making excuses because I'm scared. Which I am. I've never even been on a plane. But it isn't just that. I have responsibilities to *my* grandparents, a job I need to hold onto. I can't just go away for a month like that. Although, part of me worries that I'm going to be stuck here forever, while all my friends scatter across the world and do amazing things. I don't want to be left behind and forgotten.

'Or you could come with me. To New York,' Will says. 'It'll be a long shot, me getting into the program, but I reckon I'll head over anyway, see some shows … You could check out the programs they have for actors, and we could get a cheap flight to LA, visit your mum. It would be awesome.'

'Yeah,' I say, 'I don't know …'

'I asked her first, Will,' Aubrey says.

'You should come, too. Think about it! The three of us in New York City!'

'I'm not going anywhere,' I say. Because I can't imagine it. I can't imagine being able to go anywhere like that.

'But your mum is there,' Will says. 'Don't you want to see her?'

I shrug. I hate it when the conversation turns towards Mum.

'I hope she had a good reason for being a no-show last night. Again. I'm sorry, Edie, but I'm just so mad at her. I can't help it,' Aubrey says. 'She lets you down all the time.'

'She had some emergency with a producer or something. It's my own fault. Nan warned me not get my hopes up. I mean, LA is a long way away. It's not so easy for her to get to stuff. I get it.'

My friends look at me with their sad, concerned faces and it kills me, lying to them like this. The whole LA story is getting way out of hand, but it's been going on for so long I don't know how I could ever tell them the truth. Or deal with what they'd think of me if I did.

'Anyway' – I change the topic – 'we're not here to talk about me. Will? You wanna tell us more about this musical?'

But Will doesn't get a chance, because I see Ronny lumbering towards our table, a mean look on his face. Ronny gets very upset when people sit in his coffee shop without buying anything. A couple of coffees will get you about fifteen minutes here without his famous side-eye, and it looks like our time is up.

'Have you guys ordered lunch?' I must sound frantic, because Will and Aubrey exchange confused looks. 'What do you want? Chips? A sandwich? They do burgers. You want a burger?'

They're both just staring at me now. I stand up as Ronny reaches the table.

'Ronny, Ronny, Ronny,' I smile sweetly, 'just coming to order one of your amazing chicken sandwiches.'

He narrows his eyes. 'Just a sandwich?'

'And …' I give Aubrey a little nudge.

'Um, chips? Hot chips?' she says.

'Great!' I sound way too happy. 'Will, what do you want?'

'Nothing. I'm not really hungry.'

Ronny folds his arms. His lip twitches. He is going to go off. I've seen him do it multiple times. It's not pretty.

'My friend here will have the burger with cheese, please,' I say quickly. 'And a side of chips. Please.' I grin inanely as Ronny scribbles down the order.

Once he has gone, barking orders to the kitchen staff, I relax. Aubrey and Will are still staring at me.

'What the hell was that?' Aubrey says, looking around to make sure Ronny can't hear her. 'This place is weird.'

'It's quirky,' I say, 'but the food is all right. I promise. Way better than the coffee.'

'It'd want to be,' Will laughs.

Will tells us his musical is about a superhero called Jack (played by Will) who has to hide his powers from the girl of his dreams, Lily (played by me). He describes his yet-to-be-titled show as Marvel meets Bo Burnham. I sneak a look at Aubrey and she shakes her head, ever so slightly, and we try not to laugh. It is just so Will. Comparing the *first* thing he has written to the most popular movie franchise of all time *and* to the work of a super-famous comedian-actor-filmmaker with literally millions of YouTube subscribers. On anyone else, this level of overconfidence would look gross. It would sound egotistical and arrogant and ridiculous. But somehow, Will gets away with it. It's just who he is. Who he's always been. William Yoon: overconfident, full of big plans and ideas and this genuine enthusiasm for, well, everything.

We're pretty different. I worry about what people think and I get embarrassed and although I love taking centre stage in a show, in real life I'd prefer to hide in the background. Which is sort of how we became friends in the first place. I'd completely embarrassed myself trying to ice-skate. We were on a Year Seven camp activity Aubrey had signed us up for. I hadn't wanted to do it because I knew I couldn't, but Aubrey gave one of her 'little steps' pep talks and suddenly, there I was, stuck to the edge of the skating rink while everyone else was zooming around like this was the easiest, most natural thing in the world. I had no idea how they moved like that. I could barely get one foot in front of the other while clinging to the railing. And then he was there – Will. Also clinging to the railing. But he was making this big slapstick comedy routine out of it. Like Mr Bean on ice-skates. It was hilarious. I laughed until I lost my balance and slipped, bang, hard onto the ice. Normally I would have died of embarrassment, but I didn't. It just made us both laugh even more. We helped each other out of the rink, drank hot chocolate together on the sidelines, and became best friends. That's how it all started.

The three of us became inseparable.

'So, the thing is, the reason I wanted to talk to you both is cos, well, there's not a whole heap of time to get it done,' Will says. 'We need to put it on by July.'

'July?' I say it a lot louder than I mean to. A few people look over at us. 'That's not enough time. Not for a totally new musical. Is it?'

I look to Aubrey for some back-up. She understands rehearsal schedules better than anyone. She knows how long it takes to get a show up. She isn't delusional. 'It's tight. But it's not impossible.'

OK. Maybe she is delusional today.

'Three months? Really? You think we can do this in three months?'

'Sure,' she says. 'It's going to be pretty low-key, right? Like a stripped-back thing. That's what I have in mind, anyway. We can keep it simple in terms of production values.'

I wonder how much the two of them worked out between themselves before I got here. The writer and the director plotting behind my back to ambush me into agreeing to a ridiculous three-month rehearsal schedule. I mean, if *all* we were doing was Will's show it would be fine. More than fine. But we still have school and exams and homework and jobs and *Romeo and Juliet*. The final play for our time at Arcadia. I always do the play. Never the lead – that's Imogen's territory – but I'm always in it. It's part of my scholarship. Plus, I enjoy it.

'What about *Romeo and Juliet*? Are we just not going to do our final play? What's Mrs B gonna think?'

'I'm not doing it,' Aubrey says. 'I'm sick of this school always doing old stuff. Wow. Way to go Arcadia. Let's do Shakespeare. Again.' She scrunches up her face like even the word *Shakespeare* makes her want to gag.

'You don't want to try out for Romeo?' I ask Will, who

laughs so loudly I can feel everyone in the coffee shop stop and stare. 'What? What did I say?'

'No way would they cast me as Romeo. I'm the funny guy, remember? Not romantic lead material.'

'I think you could do it.'

I say it because I believe it. Will would be a wonderful Romeo. Sure, he is a great comedic actor, but he is also a great actor full stop. And he is cute. Which is super important when you're Romeo. I mean, there's no way anyone can quite live up to late 90s Leonardo DiCaprio level cute, so it's not fair to even try to compare. But still. Will has something that gets the girls in Year Seven giggling and whispering every time we walk by. Or whenever they walk by us. Again and again and again.

'You know Arcadia Grammar would never cast an Asian Romeo,' he says.

'But –'

'They let me be Aladdin, and for that I will be forever grateful. My one and only leading role,' he says, pretending to be all teary-eyed about it. Except, maybe he isn't pretending. Maybe he is upset. 'They never did shows for me. I never saw myself in any of those characters. The characters were always white. And they were always cast like that. White leads. So, I just … stopped trying. They were never gonna choose me anyway.'

With a sudden, sinking feeling I realise he's absolutely right. But I had no idea he felt that way, and I feel so stupid. Why hadn't I seen that before? Why hadn't I realised? I always thought he was just over the traditional shows. Sick of putting on stupid accents. Bored of the Broadway classics. 'But ...' I go to say something, but I don't know what to say. *That's shit? I'm sorry?* It all sounds so empty and dumb.

But I say it anyway. 'Sorry, Will. That's so shit.'

'It's total shit. I mean, *Aladdin* is messed up anyway, right? That whole *Arabian Nights* thing is straight-up racist. But then to cast me as Aladdin? Me? Cos I'm the closet thing they could find to an Arab in our year group? Did they just look around and think, *Uh, Will's not white, he'll do*. It's shit.'

'And I was Jasmine,' I say quietly.

'Surprised they didn't force me, "the Hadid girl", to take the role,' Aubrey says. 'I mean, I can't act but at least I wouldn't have needed that awful wig.'

'That wig! I'd forgotten about the wig,' Will laughs.

'Did you want to play Jasmine?' I ask Aubrey. I don't know why I never considered she might have wanted the part until now.

'Are you joking? Princess Jasmine?' She pulls a face like she's eaten something really bad. 'I'm a stage manager, not an actor. Besides, Mum would have killed me. She instilled in all of us from a very young age that Aladdin is bad. And wrong. And I thought about giving you guys the same lecture but you were so excited, and I always kinda thought you'd work it out for yourselves. Which you finally have!' She smiles. 'I'm surprised it took you so long.'

'Sorry,' I say.

'It's got catchy songs,' Will adds.

'It does,' Aubrey sighs.

'Screw Arcadia. We're doing our own musical,' Will says. Aubrey cheers, 'Yes, we are!'

Ronny approaches our table, and we watch in silence as he slams our plates down in front of us. It is quite a skill the way he ensures everyone gets the wrong order. We don't correct him, just smile and stammer a quiet *thank you* as he grunts at us. I have no idea why Ronny chose to get into hospitality. And I will never, ever ask him. Once he goes, we swap plates. I steal one of Aubrey's chips, Aubrey takes the pickle from Will's burger, Will waits for me to hand over the cheese from my sandwich. It's how we roll.

'I can't do it without you, Eds,' Will says, but he won't look at me. He is staring at the untouched burger in front of him. 'I think this could be as good as StarKid stuff but we need our own Darren Criss – and Edie, you are our Darren Criss.'

I burst out laughing. Darren Criss? Award-winning, uber-talented, super-famous singer-songwriter-actor, amazing Darren Criss? 'Sorry, Will, but we really don't look anything alike and we have a completely different range and style and –'

Will looks at me with complete seriousness, which isn't something you see all that much in Will. His dark eyes are super serious and intense. It stops me. Dead.

If Will and Aubrey aren't doing *Romeo and Juliet*, then Will's musical might be the last chance we have to do something big together before we all separate; my best friends travelling and going on to bigger and better things, and me doing something I haven't figured out yet. Thinking about a future without them makes me want to cry, so I'm going to hold onto the precious moments we have left – and that includes Will's musical. I can't miss out on this, even if it does mean not doing the play. I just hope not being in

Romeo and Juliet – not even auditioning for it – won't mess up my scholarship.

'I'm doing your show,' I say. It feels like the right decision. No, it *is* the right decision. I know it.

'You sure? Cos you don't really sound so sure.'

'Of course I'm sure. I just feel bad for Mrs B.'

'She'll get over it,' Will says.

'I know,' I say and take a bite of my sandwich. I'll be leaving Arcadia and will soon be forgotten by Mrs B, just like all the other Year Twelves who didn't meet their potential and now work full-time in some soul-destroying office job while reminiscing about the days they were the lead in the school musical. I wonder if they sing by the photocopier, break out into a little tap routine in empty meeting rooms, stare into the computer screen and see the lights of the stage reflected back at them.

'I think you've made the right choice. I mean, *Romeo and Juliet* has nothing on this musical,' Will says.

'You're saying you're a better writer than Shakespeare?' I throw a chip at him.

'HEY!' Ronny shouts from the counter.

We wave our apologies. I pick the chip up off the floor.

'The script's not quite ready for you to read yet, but trust me. It's funny. It's brilliant. You're gonna love it.' Will shoves the burger in his mouth. Being humble is not always his strong suit.

'Are you done now, Will? Cos we really, really need to talk about last night's pool incident,' Aubrey says.

'Do we have to?' I say.

'Um, yes, yes we do.'

SIX

I hate the first Monday back at school after a production. It feels like the colour has been drained out of everything. Everyone is in a bad mood and the teachers aren't as likely to give us extensions on homework or postpone tests.

Dr Lee wants to know what's wrong. She's standing in front of me, tapping her pencil on my desk and giving her best I'm-Very-Concerned-About-You face. There's nothing wrong. I'd just forgotten about the revision test. Not that I can tell her that. She takes it pretty personally the way our school gives the Arts more attention than science. If I tell her I forgot about the test she'd just start one of her lectures. Again.

I'm good at biology. I'm good at all my non-performing-arts classes. Not great, but good enough. So I know I'll do fine on this test, even though I didn't study as much as I should have. Or at all. But it will be fine. I am all set for a solid B. Or B minus. I'm happy with that. Dr Lee, however, is not. She has very high standards.

I hand her the test I only just completed in time and tell her I'm a little tired, hoping that's enough and she'll move on to the next person. She doesn't move on. She flips my test open and shows me a page I have missed. A whole page. She taps her pencil on it as if it will magically fill with all the writing I should have done on it.

'Sorry,' I say quietly.

Dr Lee shakes her head and moves on. Looks like that solid B minus might not be so solid after all. Still, a C is all right. It's a pass and that's all I need.

A voice crackles over the PA, demanding I go to the office and see the principal: *Edie Emerson to Mr Healy's office*. Everyone turns to look at me and starts joking around about how I'm in trouble, like we're back in Year Seven or something. Dr Lee just shakes her head again and tells me to go.

I've spent the last six years waiting for my scholarship to be revoked, worried that somehow this whole thing was a big mistake and we'll end up owing the school thousands in tuition fees. And maybe this is it. I have never been summoned to the principal's office like this before. Over the PA. Removed during class. That's not how Old Man Healy does things. He is an approachable, usually kind principal; sure, he puts me through cringeworthy meet-n-greets with donors, but he also takes the time to walk through the grounds and actually talk to the students and get to know us. If he needed me, he'd just find me during the lunchbreak, like he usually does. Something must be wrong. Maybe, somehow, he already knows I won't be auditioning for *Romeo and Juliet*. Maybe he has a sixth sense for sniffing out students who are about to screw up their scholarships.

Other scholarship students haven't made it through the whole six years. Blossom Reddy was asked to leave after Year Nine when she lost interest in violin and didn't quite live up to the child prodigy label they'd plastered on her. And Luka Corlic's scholarship was cancelled after he busted his knee and couldn't keep dancing. Of course, the school said they had to leave because of bad behaviour or too many 'unexplained' absences or something else we all know was just a crappy excuse to justify a pretty crappy decision. Arcadia Grammar is all about its image. And money. If you're not adding anything in one of those areas, preferably both, then it's *goodbye*. So even though my logical brain is telling me there is no way Mr Healy would be saying goodbye to me now, not when I'm in Year Twelve and the end is in sight, there's a part of me that's shouting: *But you never know!* My anxiety likes to remind me this is always a possibility.

I'm nervous, really nervous, when I get to reception. So nervous I barely have a voice to tell Shelley, the receptionist, I'm here.

'You can go in now,' Shelley smiles, and waves me through. Shelley never smiles. This is not a good sign.

Mr Healy is a huge *Phantom of the Opera* fan. If you didn't know that about him before you visited his office, it might freak you out a bit. His office is full of memorabilia from the show – there's heaps of those Phantom masks everywhere, and that creepy music box from the show with the freaky monkey perched on top playing the cymbals, and a bookshelf full of old theatre programmes and books about the show and signed posters and figurines and a *Phantom of the Opera* coffee mug. It's a lot. Oh, and he played the Phantom. Once. A hundred years ago. In a university production. He got to keep the cape. We know this because he likes to wear the cape. Usually during our whole school assemblies.

Today it looks like Mr Healy has received a new delivery of merchandise. The chairs in his office are swamped with cushions, all featuring quotes from the show. I move a cushion that says 'Close Your Eyes and Let The Music Set You Free', which doesn't feel like the sort of thing I want my high school principal telling me. It's creepy.

'You would have made a delightful Christine,' he says as I sit down. He always says that. He's been trying to convince Mrs B to do an Arcadia Grammar production of the show for years. But she's always been able to avoid it. And now it's too late – for me, anyway. I am sure there will be some other student who gets to play the role at some point, and Old Man Healy will forget all about me.

Anyway, if he's talking about *Phantom* he must be in a good mood, and if he's in a good mood then surely I'm not about to be kicked out.

'You disappeared very quickly the other night. Like the Phantom in the finale of the show! He's gone, just like that.' Healy snaps his fingers. 'That was you.'

'Sorry, sir, we had the party and –'

'Don't apologise. The afterparty is a vital part of the theatre experience. The closing night parties I attended back in the day ... you wouldn't believe the things we got up to,' he laughs. I really don't want to think about what Old Man

72

Healy got up to 'in his day' but I also don't want to be rude, so I laugh with him. He dabs his eyes with his Phantom handkerchief. 'So, you're probably wondering why I asked to see you?'

My mouth is dry and my stomach is churning. I need to calm down. There's no way Old Man Healy would kick me out. Not now. There have been too many good signs – the laughing, the Phantom references, the mint he is now offering me. He doesn't offer those mints lightly. I take one, gratefully.

'You remember the Winters? That charming couple I introduced you to on closing night?'

I nod, even though I wouldn't call Mr Winters *charming*.

'Their son is a late enrolment, very keen on being a part of the school production, and Mr Winters specifically asked that you'd help him out. Give him some coaching,' he says. 'Mrs Winters said she thought you had spunk and a good work ethic.'

'But –'

'The Winters family is offering our school a very large donation, which would enable us to extend the scholarship program. We'd be in the position to afford this very special opportunity to even more young people like yourself, Edie. I thought you, of all people, would support that.'

I think I support that. I mean, who wouldn't want to go to Arcadia Grammar? It's amazing. I think about the high school I would have gone to if I hadn't got this scholarship. They don't have a performing arts centre, so when they put on a play they have to convert the gym into a theatre. There's no school band, no extra-curricular dance or music or drama classes. They don't have a swimming pool or lecture theatres or an international exchange program with their sister school in Tokyo. But I do wonder why people like the Winters keep giving money to a school like Arcadia when it already has everything it could possibly ever want and other schools have, well, nothing. Maybe they could share it out a little more evenly. I'd support that. In a second. Not that I'm about tell Old Man Healy that. He wouldn't get it.

'And I hate to bring it up, Edie, but, well, it is the least you could do. For the school. Isn't it? After everything we've done for you?' Old Man Healy pulls this sad-puppy-dog face, but I can see the *gotcha* look in his eye. Nothing like a bit of emotional blackmail on a Monday morning. 'All I'm asking is for is a little help with the play.'

I ignore the nerves that are bubbling up from my stomach into my throat. 'Sir' – I can hear my voice wavering, but I keep going – 'if it's OK with you I was thinking that maybe I wouldn't do the play this year.'

That's not quite what I rehearsed but at least I've said it now.

'Of course you're doing the play,' Healy laughs and then stops, quickly, when he realises I'm not joking. 'You have to, Edie, it's in the agreement.'

By 'the agreement' he means my scholarship. And he is right. Technically. The scholarship clearly states that I must 'audition for and commit to perform in the annual musical and annual play, and other productions as required, in any role as decided by the audition process'. I've never questioned that clause in the scholarship contract. At the time it was exciting. And I never thought I wouldn't want to do an Arcadia production.

'There's another opportunity I'd prefer to take,' I say carefully.

'What "opportunity"?'

'Will has written a musical and we want to –'

'No, no, no, no, that is not a sanctioned Arcadia Grammar production.'

'Yes, but we thought that –'

'No, no, no, no. We don't do *new* shows, Edie. We stick with the classics. The works that have held up to the test of time. That's what we do,' he says, 'and I would be thrilled to see you take one last lead role at Arcadia. If Imogen hears about this, I will deny it … but I believe you will make a far better Juliet than she ever would.'

'Sir,' I say politely, 'I can't do it. I'm sorry.' But even as I say it, I'm worried. What if he decides to kick me out after all? I try out the line Aubrey told me to say if Mrs B questioned my decision: 'It's too much for me to take on the play on top of everything else right now, and I want to leave Arcadia with happy memories and good grades. Isn't that what you want for your students?'

He takes off his glasses and rubs his eyes, pinches the bridge of his nose like Nan does when she is getting a headache. I wonder if I am causing him a migraine. Probably. I think I sometimes have that effect on people.

'Well,' he sighs. 'I'm not going to force you to do *Romeo and Juliet*. I could. It is in the agreement. But I won't. Which isn't to say I'm not very, very disappointed.'

'Sorry, sir,' I say, feeling relieved, but also awful. This tight knot twists in the pit of my stomach. Aubrey tells me I'm too much of a people pleaser, that I need to say what

I want and if someone doesn't like it I have to let it go and move on. Which is easy for people like Aubrey. I bet Aubrey wouldn't have apologised to Mr Healy. I bet she would have said something like, *It wasn't my intention to disappoint you, Sir,* and, *Your feelings are valid but they are not my responsibility.* Something like that. I can't say those things. Instead, I just say *sorry,* for the second time, and Mr Healy sighs again as he puts his glasses back on. I start to wonder if he was faking a migraine for sympathy. I wouldn't put it past him.

'I am still hoping you will agree to assist this young man with his audition. Would you do that? For me? For your school?'

'I think Imogen would be –'

'They have specifically asked for you, Edie.'

'OK, I'll do it,' I say, because what choice do I have, really?

'Wonderful, wonderful. And let's just see where it goes. You may change your mind and decide to audition anyway,' he says as he ushers me out of the office.

'I'm not going to change my mind.' I try to channel Aubrey as I say it. Stay strong. Be confident.

'We'll see about that,' he says.

As we leave Old Man Healy's office, I hear a familiar laugh. That confident voice. The realisation slowly rolls over me. No. Fricking. Way. Of course, the Winters' son – the person I just agreed to coach – is that arrogant jerk from the afterparty. Noah. *The* Noah. Cute. But still a jerk, which is a complete waste of cuteness. He is standing by Shelley's desk, chatting away to her, and she doesn't even look that annoyed about it. There is something about his face that just makes me want to argue with it.

He smiles broadly. 'Edie!' He says it like we're old friends.

'You already know each other?' Mr Healy's eyes light up. 'Perfect!'

Yeah, sure, this is gonna be perfect.

*

I'm late for Drama and Old Man Healy insists Noah should tag along. I don't know if he's officially in the class or if Healy just wanted him out of his office. It feels a little late for someone to be joining us now, this far into the school year. I have no idea why Noah Winters has decided to enrol at Arcadia Grammar and no intention of asking him. I just want to get to class; Mrs B has major issues with tardiness, and annoying one teacher per day is my absolute limit, so I have to keep moving. But Noah doesn't seem to care. He is taking his time, stopping to peep inside classrooms, reading every single sign and poster we pass, carefully inspecting the student artwork that hangs in the hallways like he's some serious art collector. I keep having to tell him to hurry up, move it, like a stressed-out mum trying to get her toddler out of a toy store.

And then it hits me. This is all new to him. Not just Arcadia Grammar, but high school itself. It's so obvious. Noah Winters has never attended a school before. I stop. Noah is so engrossed with checking out the lockers that he almost collides with me.

'This is brilliant,' he says.

I have so many questions, but no time. I grab his hand and literally pull him towards the Drama studio.

The tragedy and comedy drama masks that hang above the door are mocking me. I can see it in those disturbing empty eye sockets. A closed door is Mr B's way of telling you that you're late and there will be no Drama for you today. It means we have to sit outside for ninety minutes, and then get Mrs B's infamous I'm-Very-Disappointed-In-You talk. Her eyes will fill with tears and she'll get that wobble in her voice. It's a lot.

'You can let go now,' Noah says, and I quickly release his hand. I didn't realise I was still holding on.

'Sorry.' My face is burning hot.

'So. This is Drama?'

I nod and am about to explain the closed-door situation when he just opens it and walks right on in like it's no big deal. But it is. Or it will be. I can't believe the audacity of this guy. Opening doors like he owns the place! I follow him into the studio.

Mrs B's Drama studio is my favourite place at Arcadia Grammar, which is a big call for a school as beautiful as this. There's an actual rose garden, an outdoor amphitheatre carved into a hillside, the most incredible library I have ever seen. But it is this room that is my favourite. Mainly because it was the first place I felt truly at home, truly myself, at Arcadia. I mean, attending a school that has manicured lawns and water features is just a little intimidating. I wasn't really prepared. Particularly for the number of people who didn't find it intimidating at all. The rest of my class acted as if Arcadia were just like any other school, and they weren't the luckiest people in the world to come here – it was just normal, expected, a natural step in their very fortunate lives.

I couldn't keep up with them. In French class they already knew the language because they holidayed there in the summer. Their private tutors had already worked with them on complex concepts for Maths or made them read the right books for English. And they had been attending exclusive dance studios and music classes for years and years, so they were confident and polished in Music and Dance. I was out of my depth. Who did I think I was, trying to fit into a place that was so obviously out of my league?

And then I walked into Mrs B's Drama studio and suddenly all the voices in my head went quiet. Walking into that room was like walking into a warm hug. It felt like it back then, and it stills feels like it now. In one corner is what she calls the 'Actor's Nook' – a carpeted, cosy space littered with beanbags and cushions, bookshelves full of plays and musical scores and actor-theory texts we always promise her we'll read one day but never have. In the other corner sits her desk, plus tables and chairs for us, and on the walls are posters from all the old productions going way back to the 80s. And then, there is the practice area – a big open space for the physical work we need to do. It is quite a place. And I love it. But what really makes it the best place in the school is the fact that Mrs B is there. That's what made me feel like I belonged at the school – it was her, not her fancy studio. She'd learnt all our names before we'd even stepped through the door. She spoke to us like we were actually interesting human beings and not the annoying Year Sevens everyone else seemed to see us as. When she asked a question she actually listened to our response. She taught with such passion that even if you weren't too sure about Drama, after a ninety-minute class, you were all in. One hundred per cent. But most of all, she really cared. And that was the first time in my first week at Arcadia that I'd felt really safe. I think I'll always associate Mrs B and her Drama studio with that – the feeling of safety, of acceptance – when I step inside.

Even when I'm running super late and know she will be very disappointed about it.

'Noah Winters!' Mrs B claps her hands and rushes over to greet him.

OK. So, not the lecture I was expecting ...

'Sorry we're late –'

She stops me mid-apology with a bright smile. 'Not to worry!'

I look at the rest of the class, who seem just as confused as me by this reaction. I catch Will's eye. He shrugs. I remember us sitting out by the closed Drama door once, in Year Eight: me bawling my eyes out at the thought of letting Mrs B down, and Will trying to lighten the mood with stupid jokes.

'So thrilled to have you with us, Noah Winters,' she says, using his full name again. What's that about? 'Everyone, everyone, listen up. This is Noah Winters!'

She says it like we should all know who he is, like his name should mean something to us. Everyone says hello. Everyone uses his full name. *Hello, Noah Winters*, they chorus.

'Just Noah is fine,' he says.

'Aren't you the guy who pushed Edie into the pool?' Yazi shouts from the back of the room. And it's on. The class erupts. They reach for their phones to find the evidence, searching for the video to show each other. Yazi finds it first and shows Makayla, who laughs like it is way funnier than it really is, and then Kellen joins in with his big stupid laugh and even Mrs B takes a look at Yazi's screen and laughs too. It really wasn't that funny. The whole class has lost the plot.

'That was you?' Will stands. He is not joining in the let's-humiliate-Edie game. He actually looks pissed off. Which is not a look I am used to seeing on Will's face.

'In my defence, they did tell me to aim for Diego,' Noah laughs.

'Still not cool, man,' Will says.

'*Man*? Who says *man*?' Noah is still laughing but there's an edge to it now, a cruelty to the laughter I've not noticed before.

Will takes a step forward. 'You got an issue, man?'

It all feels so fake. It's like Will's acting the part of some cowboy in a terrible old Western film. And I hate it. This is not my friend. He is not this person.

I step between them. 'Noah, this is Will, my best friend who does not say *man* and is not a jerk. Usually. Will, this is Noah. He pushed me into the pool but he's apologised, many times, so maybe he isn't a complete jerk. Who knows?'

I wait for Will to say something funny or for Noah to break into one of his charming smiles. They don't. They just stare at each other. I give Will a gentle shove to snap him out of it. He takes the hint: mumbles something that sounds like *hi,* and then they shake hands. Quickly. Like little kids who are scared to catch cooties. It's ridiculous.

We've interrupted Mrs B's lesson on the Meisner technique. He was this acting teacher in America in the 1930s through to the 1990s who taught heaps of famous movie stars and theatre actors; people still practise his technique today. Anyway, Mrs B loves him and wants to teach us his technique because, she says, it will get us out of our heads when we act. When she says this, she looks right at me. I know why. I am way too much in my head. It is why I stuffed up on closing night. Mrs B has told me before I need to stop worrying about being perfect, about getting it right, and trust myself more. But I *want* to be perfect. I *want* to get it right. Imogen says that is why I will never really make it. She didn't say it to my face, but I overheard her once. 'Technically she is perfect but I find her performances quite dull,' she said. I never let on that I heard her but I'll never forget what she said. That sort of stuff stays with you forever.

'Meisner says your instincts are more honest than your thoughts,' Mrs B explains. 'So, we're going to keep exploring that idea by learning to trust our instincts. In this exercise I don't want to see any acting; no comedy routines, no trying to get a laugh. None of that at all. William Yoon, I'm looking at you – you got it?'

'What did I do?' Will pretends to be completely outraged, which makes everyone laugh.

'That!' Mrs B says. 'That, right there, is what you do. OK. Partner up, please.'

Usually I partner with Will. We do most things in Drama together, except when Mrs B forces us not to. I turn to him, like I always do, but Yazi has grabbed his arm and is pulling him towards the back of the room.

'Looks like you're stuck with me,' Noah says.

'You gonna be nice?' I ask him.

'I'm always nice,' he says.

We each grab a chair and sit facing our partner. Mrs B wanders through the room, between the pairings, as she explains, 'All you do is make an observation about your partner. Don't overthink it. Something simple and true, the first thing that comes to you. I might say something like, *You have curly hair*. The other person then repeats the line, *I have curly hair*. And you keep that repetition going. Don't force it. Just see where it takes you.'

We often do some really weird stuff in Drama. Like one time we had to pretend to be babies and crawl around on the ground making goo-gaa baby noises, and another time we had to act like different animals and Mrs B made us really get into it. So this Meisner stuff doesn't sound too bad.

'Edie? How about you and Noah Winters get in demo-mode?' Mrs B says, pausing by our chairs. 'Just to help me demonstrate how to do this exercise.'

I don't mind demonstrating things for the class. I've done it plenty of times. We all have. Everyone gets a turn in 'demo-mode', and Mrs B always ensures a new 'volunteer' is pulled up in front of every class. So, it's not surprising she is choosing Noah.

Noah, however, looks like he wants to die. He catches my eye and shakes his head, mouths *NO WAY* at me. I could help him out. Suggest Imogen and Makayla instead. Imogen would love that. She's always keen to be picked for demo-mode. He looks desperate, like a man clinging to the edge of a cliff, pleading for someone to pull him to safety. I could do that for him. Mrs B would understand. But then I remember the pool. The arrogant swagger. The bravado. I ignore his desperation as I say cheerfully, 'You're not scared of a little

83

Meisner, are you, Noah Winters?' I feel like I have just won a point in a game I didn't know I was playing, but am kind of enjoying anyway.

'No. This'll be great.' There's a nervousness in his voice that he is trying to hide. 'Let's do this.'

My stomach twists in a pang of guilt. Maybe I'm being too mean. It's his first day, and to throw him into something like this, in front of a heap of people he doesn't know, is probably too much. But he is suddenly all dazzling smiles, beaming at the class as they gather around us to observe. He looks at me, raises an eyebrow, then shakes his head at me like I should have known better. Of course he is fine, confident, in his element; he is Noah Winters.

The way Mrs B explained the exercise made it sound really simple. Doing it is entirely different. Noah and I look at each other. Direct, unbroken eye-contact. And, just like that, I become very, very aware of myself. The way I breathe. How often I blink. My dry lips. There is a warmth growing in my chest that's starting to rise up my neck and to my face and I hope, hope, *hope* I'm not turning bright red right now. I look down to my hands, twist them into knots on my lap. What the hell is wrong with me?

'Maintain eye contact,' Mrs B says gently.

I look back at Noah. He has not taken his eyes off me. There's something in that look that makes me smile, ever so slightly.

'You're smiling,' he says.

'No, I'm not.'

'Repeat the words, Edie,' Mrs B coaches from the sidelines. 'Listen, react, repeat. That's all you have to do.'

I try to focus again but I'm distracted by Noah's eyes. Why is it always the eyes? It's such a cliché and I'm hating myself, just a little, for even going there right now because the girls in stories and songs and poetry are always falling for the boys' damn eyes. It's so stupid. And I always thought it was a load of crap. Until now – now that I'm looking, really looking, into Noah's hazel eyes. Are they hazel? Maybe green? Hazely-green? Is that a colour?

'You're smiling,' he says again.

I didn't think I was. I thought I'd managed to rearrange my face into something more neutral, but I can't argue – I have to repeat what he said – so I say, 'I'm smiling.'

'You're smiling.'

'I'm smiling.'

And now I know I am. I can't help it. A big, goofy smile sneaks up on me. And it affects the way I repeat the line. I hear Mrs B softly say, *Good work, good work,* but I keep my focus.

'You're smiling.'

This time I notice his smile looks different. More real than any other he has offered me. Kinder. Cuter. Smiling with his whole face, his eyes. It catches me off guard and I say, 'You're smiling.' Turn the repetition back to him.

He smiles broadly, tilts his head ever so slightly. 'I'm smiling,' he repeats.

'You're smiling,' I say and think we're onto something here. Mrs B is quietly saying, *Good, keep going.*

'You're beautiful,' Noah says. Breaks the moment. I freeze. He can't be serious, can he? I wonder if Noah's sole purpose is to embarrass the hell out of me. What am I supposed to say to that? I say nothing.

'Keep going,' Mrs B says. I shoot her a look. She shrugs innocently. I think she's enjoying this.

I stare back at Noah, waiting for him to wink at me or turn on that annoying grin. But he doesn't. He looks very, very serious. Like he has just told me the most important thing in the world. My stomach swirls and soars, the way it does before I step onstage. But I'm not stepping onstage. I'm just sitting here, in front of this guy I barely know. And the stuff I do know isn't great, is it? What's wrong with me?

He clears his throat. 'You're beautiful.' He says it quietly. I have to resist the urge to lean closer to him.

'OK, Mrs B,' I say, forcing myself to break eye contact, 'I think we all get the exercise now.'

Everyone looks a little disappointed, like they wanted to see how this show would end. Will pulls a face at me, mouths, *What the hell?*

'All right. Everyone, let's thank Edie and Noah Winters, please. Good job.' Mrs B leads the class in a round of applause. Noah stands and takes a little bow. It's totally awkward, but kind of endearing.

'We don't bow in class,' Imogen tells him. 'It is distasteful and a little tacky.'

'Is it?' he says, completely unfazed. Wow. Absolutely nothing embarrasses this guy. He takes another bow because there are some people still clapping and staring at him, adoringly. I get it. Objectively, there is no denying the guy is good looking, and he says all the right things – but actions speak louder than words, right? And the only action I've seen from him is pushing strangers into pools for a laugh. Which not only makes him a jerk, but kind of stupid, too. Doesn't it? And dangerous. I could have died. He could have killed me. Not that anyone seems too worried about that now. They're all so into him. Makayla is asking if we can swap partners and is standing very close to Noah, poised to grab him the minute she gets the all-clear from Mrs B. Which she does. The word *fine* has barely left Mrs 'B's mouth before Makayla has latched onto his arm.

I look for Will, thinking that maybe Yazi has chosen someone else, too. She hasn't. They are sitting together. Will is saying something that's making Yazi crack up, her laugh fluttering over the room until Mrs B kindly asks us all to focus.

I make my way to Imogen, who is already seated, staring at the empty chair in front of her. I wonder if she's started the activity already, making observations to the chair and waiting for its response – *You are plastic, you have legs, you are a chair*. She looks up at me and I feel a little bad for her. She's like the kid who is always chosen last in PE, the one no-one wants on their team, which is weird when you consider she is really the star player.

'I am very experienced in this technique, Edie, are you sure you want to partner with me?' She says it as if I had some sort of choice in the matter. Like I'd specifically chosen her.

I sigh. 'Of course, Imogen,' I say. Because I don't have a choice either. No-one grabbed my arm and whisked me away to be their partner. No-one chose me.

SEVEN

Noah wants to know where the cafeteria is. I tried to sneak out of Drama without him, but here he is, by my side. I can't shake him.

'What are you talking about?'

'It's lunchbreak, isn't it? Don't you all go to the cafeteria at lunch?'

'You have watched way too many American movies,' I laugh. He looks confused. 'We have a canteen, and a cafe, which is not that great, but no cafeteria – not the kind you're thinking of. No tater-tots. No food fights. No cheerleaders at the popular table sitting with the quarterback or whatever.'

'Oh, yeah, I know that,' he says unconvincingly.

'First time at a real high school?'

'It's that obvious, huh?'

'Yep.' I look at him as he watches the busy, noisy hallways, and realise he is actually nervous. He'd never say it. He'd never show it. But I can see it in his eyes darting all over the place, hear it in the slight hesitation of his voice. Despite the fact he's a jerk, I feel bad for him: it must be hard to start high school for the first time ever in the second term of Year Twelve. 'Wanna split a sandwich?'

I take him on a whirlwind tour of the school, pointing out the major landmarks he might need to know and explaining that Arcadia is most definitely not like other high schools.

'And this is the rose garden and, look, I have to say it –'

'Arcadia is not like other schools,' he deadpans.

'I don't want you walking into other schools asking about their rose gardens,' I tell him. 'It's not a thing.'

Not many people sit in the rose garden at lunchtime. I come here when I need some space, a moment to breathe, a place to hide. Which used to happen a lot in Year Seven, but the more I got used to Arcadia, the less I needed this spot. Looking at it now, though, I realise I should come here more often. It's really beautiful, this maze-like garden of winding paths and flower beds full of colourful roses.

'You still up for sharing that sandwich?' Noah asks as he sits on a bench.

'Here?'

'It's nice,' he says and motions for me to sit next to him.

The soft perfume of the roses fills me up. The sounds of the school seem to drift away. And it suddenly hits me: I have taken Noah to a super romantic spot which, when I think about it, is weird for a school to even have. I mean, schools should be doing all they can to stop any sort of romantic feelings between students, right? Like, our uniforms are the most unsexy things imaginable – except, looking at Noah now, I'm noticing how good he looks in a shirt and tie, which is not something I have ever thought about anyone at this school, and I wonder if he meant it when he said I was beautiful, and ... what is *wrong* with me?

'Lunch,' he says and tilts his head.

This is starting to feel like a weird, but kind of cute, first-date picnic or something, which is not what I was planning on. I imagine sitting close to him, letting my head fall onto his shoulder, feeling his arm around me, lifting my face towards his ... 'I need to show you the cafe,' I say quickly. 'You can get a coffee. Do you like coffee? I think I need a coffee.'

'You said the cafe was bad,' he says.

'It's not *that* bad,' I say. 'Come on.'

As we walk towards the cafe, I give him my sandwich and tell him to eat it all because I have lost my appetite. Completely.

'You want to know why?' he says between mouthfuls.

'Why what?'

'Why I haven't been to school,' he says.

'Only if you want to tell me,' I say.

'Usually, people ask me straight up,' he says.

'Usually, people don't know how to mind their own business,' I tell him.

He goes quiet then, and I turn to look at him in case he is choking to death. Which he isn't. He shrugs. Smiles. 'Great sandwich,' he says, popping the last of it into his mouth. 'Thanks.'

The cafe is only for senior students. I was so excited when our chance finally came to use it, and then I tried to drink a coffee and realised the dream was far better than the reality. As I open the heavy door, a wall of noise hits me. The place is packed, which is a relief. More people to distract myself with, and no more staring stupidly into Noah's eyes, because that is absolutely not me. Especially not with someone like Noah. There are people sitting on tables and talking loudly, someone is playing acoustic guitar in the corner, and others are crowded around a screen screaming with laughter.

'You wanna coffee or something?' I shout at Noah over the noise. He has this weird expression on his face that I can't read. 'Hey,' I say, 'you all right?'

He nods, but I don't know if I believe him. He leans closer, whispers in my ear, 'It's just so loud.'

'Yep,' I grin, 'welcome to high school.'

I lead the way through the crowd to the counter. It sounds like a lot of people already know Noah. There are heaps of *hey*s and *Noah Winters!* and people looking genuinely pleased to see him.

'You're popular,' I say as we wait in line to order.

'Just Tara's friends, that's all.' He says it like I should know what he means. Tara's friends? Why would he know Tara's friends? And then it slowly becomes clear. Noah is dating Tara. Why else would he be at her party? Why else would he have come along to see *Sweet Charity* in the first place? It makes perfect sense. I am such an idiot.

'Tara's so great,' I say.

Noah shrugs. 'She can be a real pain in the arse, actually.'

'Wow. Really? That's how you talk about your girlfriend? Nice, Noah, really nice.'

He starts laughing. 'She's not my girlfriend, she's my cousin.'

I feel myself turning bright red and am very grateful that it's our turn to order. I watch Noah charm May at the counter, asking her about the cakes and pies as if she's a world-class pastry chef, and when he finally makes a selection (a flat white with almond milk *and* a brownie, because obviously eating my lunch wasn't enough for him) he adds my order to his own and goes to pay for the lot.

'Don't do that,' I say. 'I can pay my own way.'

'But I want to. I mean, I at least owe you a coffee, don't I? After everything –'

'I've got a line here, kids,' May says. 'Argue about it later.' And with that she snatches Noah's credit card from his hand and taps it herself, giving him a wink.

We find a couple of spare seats at the share table and I'm about to explain to Noah exactly why I don't need him to pay for my coffee (and a chocolate-chip cookie because I may not have an appetite, but I can't not have one of those) when I notice Aubrey. She's sitting with Lexie, as usual, along with Lexie's friends, who are probably also Aubrey's friends now. The serious dancers. I wave at Aubrey, but she doesn't see me. She's too caught up in whatever it is Lexie is saying. It must be very clever and very funny, judging by the look on Aubrey's face.

'Who's that?' Noah asks.

I pull my focus back to him. 'My best friend.'

'Which one?'

I point her out. She is still staring at Lexie, nodding and smiling at everything she's saying.

'If she's your best friend then why is she over there?'

'Because she can do what she wants,' I snap and then instantly regret it. I grab a teaspoon and stir the sad foam into my coffee.

I've been worrying and wondering for a while now if Aubrey is still my best friend. Or is it just the thing we say because we've been saying it for so long? It's like an automatic response. The same way you say *good* when anyone asks you how you are. I'm not good and I don't even know if my best friend is still my best friend. Not that I'm about to say all this to Noah.

'So, what kind of help do you actually need for the audition?' I say instead. 'I mean, it's not hard. I don't get why your parents think you need coaching for it.'

'It's not them who think I need it. It's me. I've never auditioned for anything before. I've never acted in anything before. Not really. And I want to do it properly.' He breaks the brownie in half and holds the smaller piece out to me. 'Swap you? Half for half?'

'No,' I say. 'If I wanted a brownie I would have chosen a brownie.'

'Harsh,' he says and pops the full half into his mouth.

I hear Will's laugh and turn to see him in a very animated conversation with May, who also lets out a big laugh. She hands him a coffee, which she probably gave him for free. Will is everybody's favourite.

'I hate that guy,' Noah says.

OK. Perhaps he's not everybody's favourite after all.

'That's ridiculous,' I tell him. 'You don't even know him.'

'Know who?' Will is standing beside me, coffee in one

hand and a chair in another. He positions the chair up close to me and sits. It looks like the two of us are about to interview Noah for a job. Or interrogate him. Looking at Will's face, interrogation may be a better word.

Noah passively drinks his coffee as if Will hasn't even spoken. Will takes a sip of his long black. It's tense, all this silent coffee-drinking. I don't like it.

'So, um, Will's written a musical. It's going to be really good. Better than good, actually. It'll be brilliant and funny and – and ... poignant.' *Poignant?* Who says that? Me. That's who. Right now. Gushing over Will's musical, which I haven't even read yet. I'm sure it *is* good, but not in the earth-shattering way I'm describing it. But I've started now, and I can't stop. 'It's probably going to change the direction of musicals in this country.'

'I don't think so, Edie,' Will says. But he looks pretty pleased. Like perhaps, maybe, a tiny part of him believes this could be true.

'If Edie's in it, I'll come see it,' Noah says.

'Of course she's in it,' Will says.

'Don't know where she gets the time. *Romeo and Juliet* plus this musical. Sounds like a lot for one person.'

Will shoots me a look.

'I'm not doing the play,' I say quickly. 'I'm helping Noah with his audition, but I'm not auditioning.'

'Not yet,' Noah smirks.

'What the hell does that even mean?' I say.

'Yo! Cody! Wait up!' Noah leaps from his seat and jogs towards Cody. He puts his arm around him like they're old buddies, and disappears. I feel as if I can finally breathe again.

Will is still giving me that look. I ignore him. Or try to.

'Why are you helping him?' he says.

'Mr Healy asked me to.'

'And?'

'I have to.'

'No, you don't.'

He doesn't understand what it's like, being here on a scholarship and feeling as if I owe my whole existence to the generosity of others. A generosity they could just stop, at any point. They could just say, *Nope, we're not helping her anymore*, whenever they wanted. On a whim. What if they don't like my performance? Or I get poor grades? Or refuse to help their son with this audition for the school play? That could be reason enough to stop helping me, and other people like me. And if they do withdraw that helping hand, what will happen to me? Will can't understand that. Why would he?

The bell rings and everyone starts packing up and heading off to class. I notice Noah has left all his rubbish on the table. Thinking someone else is going to clean up after him, I suppose. And I do. Pick up the wrapper and the empty coffee cup and place them in the bin on my way to class.

EIGHT

'He said no?' Will has stopped, dead, in the middle of the corridor, completely oblivious to the hold-up he is causing behind us. The final bell has sounded and everyone is trying to get out of school as quickly as possible, jostling past us.

'He said it wasn't a *sanctioned* production.' I try to pull him along, get him moving again. I can't miss my bus.

'But he didn't say no?'

'I can't remember – I just remember the part about it not being sanctioned.'

'Well, let's get it sanctioned.' And suddenly I'm the one being pulled along. Not towards the exit, but towards Old Man Healy's office.

I should have expected this. What was I thinking? That I could just give Will this major bit of news and he'd shrug, say *OK*, and move on? That we would calmly discuss it and work out a plan? Do I know my friend at all? Of course he wants to sort this out with Healy – right now. Will does not wait.

Aubrey is at her locker, locked in some deep conversation with Lexie. Will doesn't say a word, just takes hold of her arm and starts pulling her along too. She scrambles to keep up.

'What the hell, Will?'

'Healy said we can't do Will's musical,' I explain. 'It's a whole thing …'

Shelley says Mr Healy is very busy and that we can make an appointment for next week. Apparently there is no way she can fit us in before then because he has a very tight schedule, and we need to understand that she can't just have students turning up like this when she works so hard to maintain a very carefully coordinated diary.

'We will wait,' Will says.

'William Yoon,' Shelley says. 'You will not wait. You will leave. Now. Like every other student at the end of the school day.'

Will sits, picks up a magazine from the side table and starts flipping through it, like he hasn't heard a word Shelley said. I look at Aubrey, who shrugs before taking the seat next to him. I sit on the other side. The sound of a saxophone from Shelley's smooth jazz playlist wafts through the waiting room.

When we hear Mr Healy's door open we all look up from our phones, but it's not Healy leaving his office. It's Imogen. She stops at Shelley's desk and says something I can't quite hear. Shelley reaches out and pats her hand. Is Imogen crying? Imogen only ever cries onstage. In fact, that's the only place where I see any emotion from her. She's always so … put together. Aubrey calls her the Ice Queen. I've always thought she's just more sophisticated and mature than the rest of us. Or at least that's the image she's carefully crafted over the years.

She avoids eye contact as she walks past us, but I can't just let her go. Not when she looks so sad. I follow her out to the corridor.

'Imogen?'

'Oh, Edie. Hello. I didn't see you,' she says and smiles brightly. She's a good actor, but it's still obvious she has been crying.

'Are you OK?'

'Fine. Thank you.'

There's something about the way she is desperately trying to hide how *not* fine she is that makes me feel so bad for her. I wonder if she has anyone to talk to. I don't think she has any friends. Maybe that's why she's been talking to Old Man Healy. 'Look, if you ever need to talk or whatever, I'm here –'

'I have plenty of people to talk to, thank you.' She turns away quickly and strides down the corridor.

I wander back into the waiting room.

Aubrey gives me a weird look. 'What was that about?'

I shrug. 'No idea.'

I take out my phone. I have missed my bus and am about to miss the late bus. This is getting ridiculous. I don't know why we couldn't make an appointment to see Mr Healy within school hours. Now I won't get home until super late, and I have a heap of homework to do. Why does Will have to be so damn impatient?

'Shelley?' I say sweetly. 'Could we please, please, please just get five minutes with him? Please? Pretty please?'

Shelley sighs very loudly and dramatically before getting up from her desk and marching into Healy's office.

Moments later the three of us are in his office, sitting among the *Phantom* cushions and politely declining mints.

'Well' – Mr Healy sits back in his chair – 'this is a pleasant surprise. I thought I had a budget meeting with the science department and, no offence to Dr Lee, but I'd much rather chat with you three. So, how are we? Excited for *Romeo and Juliet*? I assume you'll all be a part of it, your final Arcadia show.'

I frown. He knows I'm not auditioning.

'Sir,' Will interrupts. 'I've written a musical and I want to do it here. It won't interfere with school, or the play, or anything like that. We're completely self-sufficient. I mean, except, we need space and sound gear and stuff like that, which Arcadia has and we could use, I mean, if that's OK with you.'

Mr Healy shakes his head, takes off his glasses and starts cleaning them. We wait. I know he's trying to find a way to let us down gently. We should have come in here with a plan. Or, at least, a clearer idea of how we were actually going to make this musical work. Aubrey could have written up one of her perfect rehearsal schedules and we could have gotten Mrs B onside for a little extra support, maybe performed a song, presented Mr Healy with a copy of the script. That kind of thing.

'I already explained this to Edie, and I thought I'd made myself very clear.' Healy looks at me pointedly. 'William, I'm sure you understand. Arcadia has such a busy calendar and we simply couldn't add anything else to it. Not now. All our productions have approval from the School Board and there just isn't the appetite for new shows. It's a bit of a risk, you see, staging a new musical.'

'Will's musical is amazing. Like the next StarKid and Bo Burnham all rolled into one,' I say.

'I don't know what any of those things are, but I am sure it is amazing. However, that doesn't change my position.'

'Mr Healy,' Aubrey says calmly. 'I hear your concerns, but let me explain –'

'I said no,' he says.

'I don't get it,' Will says.

'If I say yes to your show, William, it will just open the floodgates. Everyone will pour in with their original plays and musicals and monologues demanding their own season. Can you imagine? There will be no quality control, not to mention the drain on our resources. It can't happen. Not on school time. Not on school grounds. I'm sorry.'

*

As we leave Healy's office, Aubrey and I try to tell Will we can do the show outside of school. That Arcadia can't control what we do after school or on weekends. We come up with plans to rehearse at his house, Aubrey's house, even my house if needed. We say we could rent a space for the show. A small theatre, a hall, a circus tent. Or we could use Tara's mansion. There's bound to be room in there to create a theatre. Actually, she probably already has one.

'But if we do that, then you'd have to give her a part. She'll want the lead, of course,' I say.

'You don't want to do the show anymore?'

'I'm not saying she could have *my* part. She'd have to take yours.'

He doesn't find this funny. And he's probably right. But I don't think it's as serious as he's making it out to be. We can still do the show. It might be a little more difficult, but it's not impossible.

'I'll write up a rehearsal schedule – it's fine, we can do this.' Aubrey sounds like she is back in stage manager mode, solving all our problems in her calm and measured way. 'What nights can we use your place?'

'I haven't told my mums,' he says.

'Well, you'll have to. Because we need the space. We can't expect people to travel all the way out to Edie's house. No offence, Edie.'

I'm not offended. It's actually kind of a relief. I don't know if I want a heap of people from school seeing my home. Not that I'm ashamed. I just know they'd judge.

'Why don't your mums know about this?' I ask Will. Jeanie and Wanda are the most supportive and wonderful mothers anyone could wish for. In fact, I have often wished they were my mums. It doesn't seem fair that Will has two of the best mums going around when people like me can't even manage to get one. Anyway, I can't imagine why Will wouldn't have told them about this. He tells them pretty much everything.

'I'm meant to be focusing on my future, and my future is medicine. You guys know that,' he says. 'Doing this musical, going to New York ... that's not part of the plan. They wouldn't approve.'

'So, what are you planning to do? Call them from New York?' Aubrey says.

'Yeah. No. Maybe. I don't know.'

'You need to talk to them,' I say.

'I know, it's just – it's different for me. My mums aren't like your grandparents, Edie. They have expectations.'

'What the hell does that mean?'

'It's not – I just mean, there's this expectation that I'll do medicine. They have a plan – a very clear, detailed plan for me, which means I'm under a lot of pressure here. But you? You can do whatever you want and your grandparents will back you one hundred per cent. It's different for me.'

Will's always said he's going to study medicine, so I don't get why he's suddenly freaking out about it. But I don't say anything, because I don't want to argue with him about who's under more pressure or who has the least supportive family. I just let him and Aubrey work out some kind of schedule, which I'm not really listening to because I can't stop thinking about what else he said. I know I'm lucky to have Nan and Pops. I know that.

When I first decided I was going to try to get into Arcadia Grammar, Pops said I needed to get serious about my practice. *A school like that requires discipline*, he said, and started looking into private tuition. He was worried I was going to be left behind. He somehow managed to book me in for six weeks of classes with Ms Erica Tree. Pops told me she was the best, and listed all the wonderful things her students had gone on to achieve; roles on Broadway and the West End, a Tony-award nomination, admissions to the best musical theatre schools around the world. I knew classes like that were expensive, but when I asked Pops how we could it afford it he just said, *I have my ways.*

I was very nervous on that first day. I didn't think I could get out of the car. A boy strode out of Ms Tree's house, where she ran her studio, with music books tucked under one arm. He looked so confident as he crossed the front lawn. Like maybe he was famous or would be famous soon. He had the right clothes, the right sneakers, the perfect haircut. I watched as he got into the shiny new car that was awaiting him on the street, and suddenly felt very aware of my clothes, my hair, my lack of music books, the old car I'd turned up in.

'Maybe we should just ask for the money back,' I offered.

Pops shook his head.

'I don't think I can go in there,' I said weakly.

'I know you don't think you deserve this. But you do. You have just as much right as that Justin Bieber lookalike,' he said, motioning towards the boy I'd been watching, who looked nothing like Bieber. 'You're an original, Edie. You're going to be different from those other kids at Arcadia, and that's a good thing. Never think different is *less than*. Because it's not.'

Pops never questioned whether I'd make it into Arcadia or not. To him it was a given. I was already an Arcadia student the moment I mentioned I was thinking of trying for the scholarship. He always believed in me.

Pops drove me to every session. He would wait in our car, parked in Ms Tree's long driveway, and spend the thirty minutes of my class reading the newspaper and eating liquorice. The classes were good. Great, in fact. Ms Tree

103

was all about technique, which was something, she told me kindly, I did not possess. But she promised she could help.

'However, you must promise to do your homework and practise every single day, even on the days you don't feel like it. *Especially* on those days,' she said.

I promised. I fell in love with her and her lessons. Her techniques and processes and discipline helped me a lot. I don't think I would have gotten into Arcadia without her. But my favourite part of the lesson was always singing with Pops, at the top of our voices, on the long drive back home.

Will never had to worry about any of that. He just decided he wanted to go to Arcadia and – bam – his parents could make it happen. They had the money. He had the confidence. So it happened.

'They let you enrol at Arcadia,' I blurt out. Aubrey and Will stop talking, and look at me strangely. 'Jeanie and Wanda let you come here. Not some super academic school like your sister went to. This school. A *performing arts* school. So they must support you, Will. Just talk to them about it.'

'It's not that simple –'

'Maybe not. But if you don't talk to them you'll never know, right?'

NINE

Farah Carbasse is the stuff of legend at Arcadia Grammar. People whisper her name in awe. She is famous here. Not anywhere else, yet, but it's only a matter of time. Farah Carbasse managed to get offers from every drama school she auditioned for, straight out of high school. And she auditioned for all the top-tier schools in the country. And the UK. And the States. Every. Single. One. And every single one wanted her – or so the story goes. It's a good story. She chose to go closer to home because, according to the legend, she felt it was important to support the local industry. And, as she said in a recent article entitled 'The Next Big Things', for *Vogue*, 'The training here is world-class and minus all those other distractions so I can solely concentrate on my craft.'

I don't know Farah very well. We did some shows together but I was younger than her and so I was ignored by the senior students. They always seemed so much older and more sophisticated and really annoyed that there were juniors backstage, messing up their dressing rooms, getting in their way in the wings. Farah seemed nice enough, though. She seemed to float through the school like some kind of Disney princess, bestowing her gentle smile on all her adoring subjects. Everyone was kind of in awe of her. And there's a lot of excited chatter now as we sit in the lecture hall and wait for Farah's entrance. She's speaking as part of this ongoing series the school is doing with alumni. Getting them to come back and tell the Year Twelves how great their lives turned out post-Arcadia, and to encourage us to make similar, great life choices. It's supposed to make us feel confident, but all it does is fill me with anxiety.

I'm keeping an eye out for Will and Aubrey, desperately trying to save the empty seats on either side of me for them, but as the lecture hall fills up it's getting harder to shoo people away.

'Anyone sitting here?' Imogen stands over me.

'I'm saving them for –'

'Delightful. Thank you, Edie.' She sits down and smooths out her skirt across her lap. Rolls her shoulders back. Settles into the seat. I should ask her to move, but it's not worth it. I know she'll only say no and then act all hurt about it. 'I simply couldn't bear to sit in the front row, like some kind of Farah devotee. Look at them down there. It's incredibly embarrassing.'

When I said *everyone was in awe of Farah* I forgot the one person who wasn't. Imogen. I don't think Imogen has ever been awe of anyone. It's not her style. Particularly not when that person is someone she had to share the spotlight with on stage. During *The Crucible*, we would gather in the wings to watch Farah play Elizabeth Proctor and sigh in reverence over that big emotional scene she has at the end of the play. But Imogen declared the performance *absolutely dull and devoid of nuance* and when Farah overheard this she laughed and called Imogen *sweet* in a way that could only be interpreted as the opposite. They didn't speak to each other for the rest of the run. It was a whole thing.

Kellen is asking me to move my bag so he can sit down, and I do. I scan the crowd for any sign of Aubrey or Will. I hear someone shout, '*OVER HERE!*' and see Lexie waving madly from the front row to the back of the hall, and then Aubrey sprinting down the aisle towards her. It's fine. It's more than fine. I don't even have a seat saved for her anymore. Where else was she going to sit? I bite the inside of my cheek. Twist the rings on my fingers around and around. Ignore the lump in my throat, which feels like it may suffocate me. It makes sense for Aubrey to want to sit with her girlfriend. It's normal. It's part of growing up. And moving on. I try to relax my jaw the way we do in singing lessons. Take a deep breath, in through the nose, out through the mouth. Aubrey hugs Lexie. They sit in the front row. Together.

Imogen says, 'Well, that's a little over the top, don't you think –'

Will interrupts whatever it was she was going to say, his head poking between us from the seats behind ours. 'Hello Imogen,' he says, and she turns away as if he has somehow insulted her. 'Sorry I'm late, Eds. Let's debrief after.'

We usually debrief during these talks, not after. Whispering comments. Shooting each other funny looks. Sometimes the presenters can be super patronising (one guy kept calling us 'kids' and telling us how proud he was of all of us) or really heartfelt (another kept crying because 'Arcadia is such a special place') or really, really overwhelming (one explained all the degrees she'd gotten and the hours she'd committed to study and the time spent in unpaid internships in order to 'climb the ladder' and I thought I was going to have a panic attack just listening to her), so you need to get through them any way you can. But today I won't have Will or Aubrey for that. Instead, I have Imogen.

Will leans back into his chair behind me, and I turn to Imogen. 'What were you saying?' I ask her. 'Something about Lexie and Aubrey being over the top?'

'Oh, no, it was nothing.' She crosses her legs. 'It looks like it is about to start.'

Old Man Healy makes an introduction, calling her *future-Academy-Award-winner Farah Carbasse*, and the room explodes into applause as she strides onto the stage. She moves downstage and puts her hands together as if in prayer, then bows her head. Imogen makes a weird noise and I glance over, hoping she will have more to say about it, but she just keeps looking straight ahead. Farah shakes Healy's hand before taking her place behind the lectern to deliver her presentation.

'Some people ask me why I chose to pursue a career as an actor. And I always say, I didn't choose acting. Acting chose me. It's my calling. It's what I was born to do. Believe me, if there is anything else you think you'd prefer to do then I would recommend you do that. The life of an actor is difficult. Soul-destroying at times. Heartbreaking at others.

There is no straight line to success. Most of us do not make it at all.' The crowd is hushed, hanging on her every word. 'But I can't not be an actor. And these past years, training at one of the most challenging, serious, well-respected and rigorous drama schools in the world, has made me realise I will make it.'

Farah goes on to tell us about her time at Arcadia and how it prepared her for all those auditions. 'If you're really serious,' she says, 'you will audition everywhere. For everyone. If you are truly serious, truly committed, you won't let a little ocean get between you and your dreams.'

I'm serious and committed. Truly. But I can't imagine being able to jump on a plane to audition for a drama school I can't even afford to attend in the first place.

She explains how drama school works. How she is there from early in the morning until late at night and how you have to give it your full, undivided attention, but it isn't a sacrifice when it's something you are born to do. 'It is a privilege,' she says. 'And, look, I'm aware that I'm in a very fortunate position. My parents are supporting me throughout this journey. If you don't have that kind of support, then perhaps drama school won't be the right option. It is very difficult to work while you're at drama school – so I'm told. But there are things in place to help students like that. We can discuss it later, if anyone is interested to know more. For now, let me take you through some of the highlights from the last three years ...'

I'm sure no-one at Arcadia has had to consider how they will afford uni. It's not something that keeps them up at night. Why should it? But it's all I can think of now as Farah starts a slideshow presentation of images from her drama school productions. I wonder if I can ask her about it. How other students have managed. Balanced drama school with a job so you can, you know, pay rent and buy food. Maybe I can get some time with her alone. It's not like people aren't aware of my situation, but it still makes me feel embarrassed to speak up about that kind of thing.

There's a Q&A session following the presentation. Old Man Healy sits onstage next to Farah like he's Oprah Winfrey or something.

'Can you tell us more about how drama school works?' Noah asks. I feel my face grow hot at the sound of his voice. I don't dare turn around to look at him.

'You want to know about the financial stuff?' Farah asks.

He laughs. 'No, that's not an issue for me. I just wanted to know about the hours. I mean, Farah, do you have any time for yourself at all?'

Is he flirting with her? She giggles. Actually giggles. I want to vomit.

Not all the questions are that bad. People ask about the value of taking a gap year and gaining experience before attending drama school, someone asks about degrees you could add on to the acting degree, and Phoebe wants to know if it's necessary to attend auditions in person when we're so used to using Zoom and stuff now because 'you have to think about the climate'. To which a lot of people cheer.

Then Imogen rises from her seat. 'Farah,' she says sweetly. 'Is there any proof that you were offered a place at every drama school you auditioned for? Or is that just a rumour you started to make yourself sound more interesting than you are?'

Old Man Healy gasps like he's in a pantomime. Farah looks like she is in physical pain as she tries to keep the smile plastered on her face. Everyone else goes really, really quiet. I can't believe Imogen just said that.

'Of course I have proof,' Farah says with a nervous laugh. 'I didn't think I'd need to bring it with me, obviously. Do you have a real question, Imogen?'

'I look forward to seeing that proof when you can provide it, Farah,' she says. 'And yes, I do have another question. Thank you. I am interested in any tips or advice you have for how to financially support oneself through the demands of drama school. I understand your experience is limited to the Australian context, but it will be useful, even though I will be furthering my acting training in New York City.'

I look at Imogen in surprise. She doesn't need that sort of information. She must only be asking this because of me. But since when has she cared about me? About my situation? Imogen doesn't acknowledge me, though. Even when I lean over and whisper, *Thank you,* she keeps her attention on Farah.

'It's not impossible,' Farah says. 'But it's hard. Sadly, many of my drama school friends have had to drop out. If you can get support, take it. There are often scholarships and grants available for students who need it. Some people try to work over the holidays and save like crazy, eat a lot of instant ramen, that kind of thing. It's sad.'

That's it? That's the best advice she can give? Work all holidays and live on noodles? And to say working is *sad*. Sad?

For most people, it's life. What's sad is Farah's attitude – she's so out of touch with reality.

'If I can be completely honest: don't go to drama school if you don't have someone paying for you. Find another way to become an actor,' Farah says before moving on to another question.

Find another way? What does that mean? What does that look like? I know not every actor goes to drama school and not everyone who goes to drama school becomes an actor. But I want to be a musical theatre actor who trained at drama school. I can't even imagine what else I'm supposed to do when I leave here.

Imogen slips out just before the session comes to an end. Probably to avoid all the Farah fans who want to yell at her for being mean to their idol. Will asks me if I'm OK as we walk out together. I thread my arm through his and tell him I'm fine, but I don't know if that's true. I thought today's session was going to help me figure out my post-Arcadia life. Turns out, I feel even further from a solution now than I did before walking into the lecture theatre.

TEN

Noah might be new to the whole high school thing but that doesn't seem to stop him from acting like he owns the place. It's infuriating. Some of us have been here since Year Seven. Struggling. Trying desperately to fit in. Doing all the right things. And then this guy rocks up and does whatever the hell he wants, when he wants. And everyone loves him for it. It is beyond infuriating.

He says *hey* to everyone he passes in the corridor. Every. One. He doesn't stop to talk to them or even ask how they are, he just says *hey* with this little raised-eyebrow thing and you're meant to feel flattered he even noticed you, let alone acknowledged your existence. And, frustratingly, that's how everyone acts. Like he is some kind of superstar. Like Chris Hemsworth himself is walking the school halls, saying, *Hey, no autographs, no photos please, but here, take my dazzling smile.*

And, for some reason, he's allowed to use the PA, which, as far as I know, is strictly for Shelley's use only. But nope. Noah uses it now. The other day he announced he'd bought the whole school ice-cream. Free ice-cream? What is this? Some sort of weird political campaign, buying votes with free ice-cream? The whole school went nuts over it. A convoy of Mr Whippy vans turned up, tinny music blaring, queues quickly forming as everyone – teachers included – lined up for their favourite flavour. Lunchtime was extended by twenty minutes and Noah was declared a hero. I literally heard people calling him that. A hero. Just because he's some rich kid who can bribe everyone with ice-cream.

And it's not just ice-cream and the way he says *hey*. He bounces a basketball indoors even though there are signs everywhere that clearly state he shouldn't. He sets up his speakers at lunchtime to play music wherever he and his friends have decided to hang. And that's the other thing. We all have our spots. Carefully selected locations we have sat in with our friendship groups since Year Seven. Aubrey and Will and I sat by the wall near the library until Year Ten, when we upgraded to the fountain because the group who used to sit there had graduated. We waited our turn. We didn't just assume we could sit wherever we wanted. But Noah does. Even in class. One day he'll sit down the front, next time he'll choose the back row, and he doesn't care who he displaces. You just have to deal with it. And he assumes he will get the lead role in the school play because he wants the lead role in the school play.

Like I said, he is infuriating. And frustrating. And selfish.

And I have to work with him on this audition. I have spent a week avoiding it – and him. Which has been quite easy. He's popular, so he's always surrounded by friends and wannabe friends. Until now. Now, he is leaning up against my locker. Smiling and 'hey-ing' at people as they walk past. Ugh.

I stand in front of him. Wait for him to move. He doesn't.

'So, you picked a scene for our audition yet?' he says.

'It's *your* audition. Not *our* audition. And no. That's your job. Can you move?'

He doesn't move. He just smiles like he thinks I'm funny, like what I am saying is some kind of quirky, cute joke. I tell him to move, again, louder this time. He gets the hint. Finally. Shifts a little to the left so I can open my locker. I need to swap out my heavy history textbook for my heavy biology textbook. Why are these books all so heavy?

'Wanna work on it now?'

'Don't you have a class to get to?'

He shrugs. Of course. Noah probably doesn't have to go to class. Probably has some agreement where he comes and goes as he pleases and still gets an A.

'Thought we could choose a scene and –'

'Monologue,' I correct him. 'You need to choose a monologue. That means just you, alone, speaking –'

'I know what a monologue is. I'm not a complete idiot.'

'Aren't you?'

He swings back like I've just sucker-punched him. Someone across the hall giggles. I don't even crack a smile.

'I don't want to help you, Noah. I have to. I am being forced to. Mr Healy is making me. You got it?'

The smile drops, just for a second. And, just for a second, I feel a little twinge. Was I too harsh? Too mean?

'Way to make a guy feel special, Edie.' And that, there.

115

That entitlement. That sense that for some reason my role here is to make Noah Winters feel 'special'. Nope. No way. Any empathy I was starting to feel for him vanishes. I ignore him as I pack my bag. I've got a free period and I'm not wasting it on Noah. Instead, I'm going to waste it on biology, a subject I'm never going to need. I can't even remember why I chose it in the first place.

He follows me to the library. He doesn't say a word, just sits across the table from me. I ignore him. I try to concentrate on reading about biotechnology, but the words are blurring together and I keep reading the same sentence over and over.

I look up at Noah. What the hell is he sticking around for? He pulls a book out from his satchel. An old, battered, dogeared paperback copy of *Bridge to Terabithia*. I don't believe it.

'What?' he says.

'You do realise that book is for children?'

'Yeah. And?'

'Why are you reading it?'

'It's my favourite. I just like to have it close. I dunno. We moved around a lot when I was a kid. And this was the constant, I suppose.' He stares at the book and is quiet for a moment before stuffing it back into his bag like he's suddenly ashamed.

'You should be reading *Romeo and Juliet*,' I say.

'Ah, yeah, right. Don't have a copy.'

'Oh my god. Are you joking?'

'But I've seen the movie. That old 90s one, with Leonardo

DiCaprio and Claire Danes. I know it off by heart,' he says. 'OK, not all of it. Not even close to all of it. Just a couple of lines. But it's a good start, right?'

I close the textbook. It's pointless to even pretend I'm studying. 'You have to actually read the play.'

'Do I?'

'Do you want the part?'

'Are you always this serious?'

'No,' I say. 'Are you always this annoying?'

'People usually find me endearing.'

I laugh then. I can't help it. He honestly believes this is endearing. This act has clearly worked on girls in the past. The grin, the flirty talk, the *Bridge to Terabithia*, the I'm-so-clueless-do-the-work-for-me thing. 'If you're serious about this, you have to do the work. Read the play. Choose the monologue. And then I can help you. I will help you. But I'm not doing the work for you.'

'I don't expect you to. I just – I'd just appreciate your help,' he says. And suddenly he sounds … real? There's none of that bravado. No dazzling smile.

'Why me?' I say. 'Can't your parents pay some big-shot acting coach to help you?'

'Sure, but I wanted you. If that's OK?'

It feels like my heart stops. Whack. Hard in my chest. I don't look at him, just focus on repacking my bag, as quickly as I can, for a fast getaway as soon as the bell rings. Which it should be doing any second now.

'You come alive onstage, did you know that? It's like this light radiates out of you and … sorry, I know it's probably weird but … I couldn't take my eyes off you in *Sweet Charity*. Even when you weren't saying anything at all.'

'Shut up,' I say, laughing it off like, *Yeah, what a weird thing to say*. But it isn't a weird thing to say, it's nice, and I don't want him to shut up. No-one has ever said anything like that to me before.

I avoid his gaze, tell him to read the play, and get the hell out of there. But I can't stop thinking about him for the rest of the day: his confidence, his smile, the way he looked at me when he said *you come alive onstage*, how the rest of the world sort of fades into the background whenever he's around and it feels like the spotlight is shining, brightly, just on the two of us. And as I drift off to sleep that night I realise that, maybe, perhaps, possibly, I am really, badly, truly into Noah Winters.

How infuriating.

ELEVEN

I get to Will's house earlier than expected on Saturday morning. Aubrey and Lexie and I are supposed to be here at ten, so we can start working on the musical. If I was this early to anyone else's house I would hide somewhere, or do a lap, or three, until it was closer to ten o'clock. But this is the Yoons' house. I've spent so much time here it's like my second home. I knock on the door, and Jeanie answers. She smiles warmly, pulls me in for a big hug and chats happily as I slip off my shoes and follow her into the kitchen.

'It's been too long, Edie,' she says as she motions for me to *sit-sit-sit* at the kitchen counter. She stands on the other side and starts listing a whole heap of snack and drink options. I tell her I'm fine but she just scoffs and begins pulling stuff out of the pantry and filling bowls with nuts and crackers and things.

'Is Will around?' I ask.

'He's doing his morning study session. He'll be down in twenty minutes or so. That was the deal. Study comes first,' she explains.

Jeanie and Wanda have always been strict about study. They demanded a lot of Will's sister, Vivi, when she was in Year Eleven and Twelve. I remember her crying and stressing out a lot over those years. Somehow, Will has managed to avoid all of that – until now, it seems.

'So …' I say, 'Will's musical is pretty exciting, isn't it? Can't believe he's actually written it. Do you think those people in New York will like it? I mean, this could be the start of something amazing for him, don't you think?'

Jeanie looks at me blankly. Blinks a couple of times. Pushes a bowl of carrot sticks closer towards me. *Shit*, I think, *Will hasn't told them and I've just gone and opened my big mouth.*

'We love how creative he is – how creative you all are. It's wonderful. And important. I'm not saying it isn't important. But it's a hobby, not a future,' Jeanie says. 'He can do this musical, but he needs to find the right balance. I hope you're finding time for study, too, Edie. This is a very important year.'

'I know.' I crunch down on the carrot stick.

Jeanie's mobile rings and she excuses herself to take the call, which is a relief. I thought she was about to write me up a study timetable or something.

'You're early!' Will appears at the bottom of the stairs. He looks like he just got out of bed; his hair is a mess, his eyes are blurry, and he's wearing pyjamas.

'You've still got ten minutes left of study time,' I say.

He rolls his eyes. Drags himself to the fridge, opens it and stares at the contents until the fridge starts beeping at him.

'Will? You awake?'

'I don't know what I want,' he says and closes the fridge, then leans against the door in exhaustion.

Jeanie is finishing up her phone call as she comes back into the kitchen. It all sounds very urgent and important. She sighs when she sees Will.

'My brain is fried, Mum. Got nothing left. I'm out.'

'That's not the deal.'

'I'll make it up tonight. Do an extra ten minutes. It will be fine, Mum. I'm on top of it.'

'Fine. But we can't make a habit out of this, OK?' Jeanie's phone rings again and she rushes from the room.

'Wow,' I say. 'What time did you start this morning?'

Will grabs a bowl of crackers and starts stuffing them into his mouth like he hasn't eaten for a week. 'Six o'clock. I gotta do six through to nine-thirty, then pick it up again from three o'clock this afternoon through to eight tonight.'

'What? Will! That's hectic.'

'I know,' he says between mouthfuls. 'It's a lot. But if it means I can do the musical then it'll be worth it, right? And maybe once they see it, they'll get off my back a bit. Let me go to New York. Do my thing for a while. Then I'll do their thing.'

I think even if Will wrote the next *Hamilton* there is no way Jeanie or Wanda would get off his back, no way they wouldn't *not* make him study medicine. It's just what they think is best for him, I suppose.

'You know, you're an adult, Will. You don't have to do

121

their thing. You could just go to New York …' I whisper it because it feels wrong to be saying this in the Yoon house.

'I couldn't do that to them,' he says. 'And I want to be a doctor. I just want to do this, too. You can be more than one thing, right?'

We grab the snacks and head up to his room. Aubrey and Lexie are late. Of course. It's to be expected these days. My once always-on-time, overly prepared best friend has become a bit flaky lately. I blame Lexie. Will says I blame Lexie for everything. He's right.

Will's bedroom has never changed. It's like a time capsule. He has the same old desk, covered in scratches and scribbles and dents, that he has had since forever. And the same navy doona cover and the same collection of bobble heads and the same fish tank, although the fish are long dead and the thing just sits there now, waiting for the day he finally gets the turtle he keeps saying he's going to get but never does. The same piano keyboard covered in stickers. The same guitar, also covered in stickers. It was a phase we all went through.

I've sat on this bed, on this doona cover, for years and years. I wonder how many more years we'll do this – hang out in this room, talking about stupid things, sharing our big dreams, wasting time, playing computer games, just hang out. I hate thinking about it but I know we're going to grow up and all of this will end one day. Will I even know when it's the last time? Or it will it just happen? Will it be some unremarkable day that I don't even remember until, years and years later, I realise, *Damn, I haven't seen William Yoon for a while?*

Will sits on the other end of the bed and leans against the wall. I pull my feet up under me. My phone buzzes. It's a message from Noah. A gif of Leo's Romeo looking at Claire's Juliet through the fish tank. He's written: *Act 1 Scene 5 for audition?* I know that scene. The first time Romeo and Juliet meet, and kiss, at the Capulets' ball. It's that love-at-first-sight moment, when they really don't know each other, and everything is an exciting possibility – before the truth hits them and ruins it all.

I try to stop myself from imagining what it would be like to do that scene with him. That kiss. I text him back: *You need to choose a MONOLOGUE. I'm not auditioning.*

'Is that Aubrey?' Will asks.

'No, it was Noah.' I turn the phone upside down. Shove it under my knee.

'What does he want?' There's an edge to his voice.

'It's just about the audition prep. It's nothing. Really.' The phone buzzes. I ignore it. It buzzes again.

'You should probably get that.'

Two messages from Noah and now a third, all just saying, *Please?* I can see the three dots appearing and, yep, there's the fourth message. *Please?* I write back, *NO. CHOOSE. A. MONOLOGUE.* And turn my phone off. He can message as much as he wants but I won't hear it or see it. But I know I'll be thinking about it. About him. Like the idiot I am.

'Edie,' Will says suddenly, his voice sounding strange. He coughs. Looks up at the ceiling. There are glow-in-the-dark stars up there, somewhere. I gave them to him for his birthday one year. We put them up together.

'My stars are all dead,' I tell him.

'What?'

'The glow stars in my bedroom. They don't really glow anymore. How are yours doing?'

'Um, yeah, I don't think mine do either.' He smiles, just that little one-sided grin he does sometimes, so his dimple appears. That dimple has got him out of all sorts of trouble. And probably into a tonne of it, too. The smile, and the dimple, vanish quickly and he runs his hands through his hair before turning back to me. He moves a little closer, then seems to change his mind about something and quickly stands up, sits again and then stands in front of me.

'You all right?' I ask.

'I want you to be a part of this, Edie, cos it's really important to me and you're really important to me,' he says.

'I am going to be a part of it.'

'And –'

There's a knock at the door and, before Will can say anything, in bursts Vivi. 'Oh my god!' she shouts. 'WILL HAS A GIRL IN HIS ROOM!'

It's a joke she's always done, ever since Aubrey and I started hanging out with Will. Vivi finds it hilarious. We used to shriek when she said it, throw something at her, laugh. Now we just roll our eyes at her, like she's a dad with her dumb dad-joke and we have to tolerate it. But today, Will is not tolerating it. He spins around and tells her to *piss off* in a whisper-shout. It doesn't faze her.

'Mum wants you,' she says and wanders into his room, picking up a random book from the pile on his floor and flipping through the pages.

'Right now?'

124

'Yep,' she says. 'This book is mine, by the way.'

'Can you tell her I'm kinda busy?'

'Tell her yourself,' she says as she looks through the pile for more of her books. Will takes a deep breath, as if stopping himself from saying something he shouldn't, and storms out of the room.

When Aubrey and Lexie finally arrive we read through Will's final draft. I keep looking at him in disbelief – the amount of work he's put into this thing, the fact he did it all while maintaining his A-grade average, is incredible. And it's good. Really, really good. But there's heaps of work to turn even a really, really good script into an actual show.

'But it will be heaps of fun,' Aubrey reassures us. 'A lot more fun than violin practice which, sorry Will, I have to get home for right now. I have this stupid solo to play at the assembly next week, and I don't want to completely embarrass myself ...' She pulls a face, but I can tell she's secretly a little excited to be performing again.

'I better head home, too,' I say and turn my phone back on to check the time. Three messages come through in quick succession.

'You're popular,' Will says.

'It's just Noah.' I roll my eyes but can't help smiling as I open the messages. Just more GIFs of Leo and Claire. It's ridiculous. He is ridiculous.

'What does he want?'

'Nothing.' I stuff the phone in my back pocket and start packing up my bag.

As I leave, Will doesn't hug me goodbye.

TWELVE

Aubrey lost interest in violin the same year her dad left. She told us it had nothing to do with her dad even though it obviously had everything to do with him. We all knew the story about how she chose the violin when she was six years old because that was the same instrument her dad had played. But then, after her dad left, she put the violin back in the case, shoved it under her bed and never looked it again because, she said, she was bored with it. So, it's nice to see her back onstage with the band, playing a violin solo, at our Year Twelve assembly. It takes me back to when she had her first ever solo. It was for the final, full-school assembly of the year, which was a massive deal for any Year Seven. She was freaking out and, for once, I was the one reassuring her. Her parents snuck in and stood at the back of the auditorium to watch because Aubrey would have died if she'd known they were there. Holding up their phones, recording the whole thing, proudly. I twist in my seat now to see if Mrs Hadid is there and, sure enough, she is. Recording it on her phone. That same proud expression on her face. I'd love to see that look on my own mum's face again one day.

Will and I shout and cheer for Aubrey at the conclusion of the set. She looks out towards us and shakes her head, having told us multiple times throughout our friendship that people are not supposed to whoop and cheer during classical music recitals. I think she's secretly happy that we make a big deal over it. Or, at least, I hope she is. It looks like she's trying not to smile.

Old Man Healy tells us that Mrs B has an important announcement to make about this year's school play. At this, people start whispering excitedly and Imogen, directly in front of me, sits up a little higher in her seat. I think it's Imogen who starts a round of applause for Mrs B as she approaches the lectern. I love Mrs B as much as anyone does, but clapping like that seems a bit much.

Mrs B looks super embarrassed. 'That's weird, guys, please stop it,' she says.

The room goes quiet.

It looks like Mrs B is trying to work out what to say. She opens her mouth, and nothing comes out. She tries again. Still nothing. I've never seen her like this. Mrs B always has something to say, and she's never afraid to say it.

Cody shouts from the back of the auditorium, 'You can do it, Mrs B!' We laugh. Cheer her on. She gives a shy thumbs up. Clears her throat.

'This is Toby Swan,' she says and motions to someone to come out. This man appears from the shadows, like a tall, thin, ghostly spirit. He takes off a baseball cap – which looks old and worn in a way that only expensive designer wear can look – to reveal a bald head. He's wearing all black. From his scuffed Doc Martens to his long, oversized knitted jumper. There is a very curated, scruffy look about him. Like every hole in his jumper, every rip in his jeans, has been placed just so. The only colour on him is his glasses. Huge, round, red-rimmed glasses. He doesn't smile or nod or acknowledge us in any way. His hands clasped in front of him, he stares as if he is memorising each of our faces, while everyone loses their shit. Like really. Everyone around me is whispering excitedly.

'Toby Swan!' I hear Imogen gasp. There's a lot of gasping going on.

Mrs B does that little hand clap thing to get our attention, something I've not heard her do since we were in Year Seven and getting too rowdy during Theatre Sports. 'OK. It sounds like you are all very aware of Toby Swan's work. So … you'll be very excited to hear that Toby will be directing our school play this year …'

You would think Mrs B had just announced we'd won millions of dollars or something. Everyone loses it. I look at Will and shrug. He cracks up, laughing at me.

'What?'

'He's a huge deal,' he whispers.

'Oh. OK.' It feels like when everyone in the group has some inside joke you're not part of, but you smile anyway so you don't feel left out. I have zero idea what all the fuss is about.

Mrs B is still standing at the lectern. She has this extremely calm expression on her face as she waits for everyone to settle down. I feel awful for her. This isn't the good news everyone seems to think it is – one look at Mrs B can tell you that. It's like she's trying so hard to look neutral and normal, but underneath there is a whole storm. Mrs B loves directing the productions, and she's incredible at it. Why are they taking that away from her?

'This is a very exciting development and a wonderful opportunity – not only for the cast of the show, but for Arcadia Grammar more broadly,' she says. But I don't believe a word of it. It sounds like she's reading a script. 'Toby has a few words, so I'll hand over to him.'

With that, she makes a quick exit from the stage. Mrs B never, ever leaves assemblies early. I think she may be crying, or desperately trying not to cry, and my heart breaks for her. No-one else seems to notice or care, but I can't stand seeing her walk away like that, looking so hurt and dejected. I want to go after her to make sure she's OK but as I get up, a voice from the stage says, 'Leaving already? Wow. That's cold. Ice cold.'

It's Toby Swan, who has now taken the microphone.

'Sorry, no, I just, I just –'

'I just, I just,' he mimics me. Everyone laughs. 'Chill. I was just messing with you. If you need to go, go. No pressure here.'

I mumble another apology before sitting down. I'm burning and sweating and dying all at the same time. Will pats my arm sympathetically, but I can tell he finds all of this just hilarious and he'll pick on me about it for the rest of the week.

'Right, so, yeah, I'm Toby Swan. Director. Theatre-maker. Writer. Actor. Provocateur and trouble-maker,' he says, and someone at the back gives a little whoop. 'I've been invited to direct the shit out of *Romeo and Juliet* for you guys, so that's what I'm gonna do. I love messing with Shakespeare, so let's mess some shit up! This production is gonna blow everyone's minds, you feel me?'

I don't feel him. At all. But everyone else seems to.

Mr Healy thanks Toby Swan for his enthusiasm. He reminds us that inappropriate language is not acceptable at Arcadia, but goes on to say, 'We can forgive artists such as Toby Swan for small indiscretions. He is a visionary. A wunderkind. An internationally celebrated director. I cannot stress the significance of this partnership – what it means for Arcadia Grammar and what an opportunity it is for those students fortunate enough to be cast in *Romeo and Juliet*.'

What *does* it mean? All I can see is a pretty arrogant guy replacing our beloved Mrs B. I explain my position to Will, Yazi and Kellen during our lunch break. Will keeps interrupting me with his Toby Swan impression.

'You just gotta chill,' he says in his best Toby voice. It's a pretty bad imitation, but because everyone keeps cracking up he won't quit it.

It's in the middle of this terrible impression that Imogen appears and sits down with us as if she has been invited. 'You're being incredibly disrespectful, William.'

'Chill, Imogen,' Will says.

She rolls her eyes. 'He is one of the most influential theatre directors of his generation. But sure. Turn it into a joke.'

'I don't care who he is. I don't think it's right. Mrs B shouldn't have been dumped like that,' I say.

'That's quite a reductive, negative way to look at the situation,' Imogen says. As usual, even though I haven't asked for Imogen's opinion, I'm about to get it. 'And I find it surprising. I thought you of all people would be aware of the incredible opportunity this presents. Considering your concerns over drama school and whatnot.'

'What are you talking about?'

'If you're in a Toby Swan production, all sorts of doors are sure to open for you.' Imogen smiles sweetly. 'I am genuinely shocked you didn't know this.'

'How about being a part of the world premiere of a William Yoon musical?' Will says hopefully. 'That's bound to open some doors, too.'

'No offence, William, but Toby Swan is in a completely different league,' Imogen says. 'You're not even close.'

'Ouch, Imogen's bringing the truth today!' Yazi laughs.

*

I don't care what Imogen says; I am worried about Mrs B. I drop in on her on my way to the bus. I find her in the props cupboard in the middle of some big clean out. I walk in on her throwing a heap of broken plastic swords into a bin.

'Everything OK, Edie?'

'I was going to ask you the same thing.'

She tells me I am very kind but that she's totally fine and actually, secretly, quite relieved she won't have to direct *Romeo and Juliet* because she's *had more than enough of that play*, and that she is very excited that we'll be directed by Toby Swan. I'll give her this, Mrs B is a pretty good actor. I almost believe what she's saying.

'This could be a very important opportunity for you, Edie,' she says. 'Working with a director like that – it's not something many people your age ever get to do. God, it's not even something many professional, adult actors get to do. If you want to be an actor you have to seize every opportunity and this, this is a massive one. It could be life-changing for you.'

'I'm not auditioning.'

'Why not? Not because of me, I hope?'

'I – I promised Will. He's written a musical and he wants to put it on. He needs to present it for some big musical theatre program in New York that he wants to do next year.'

'And what about you? What do you want to do next year?'

I shrug. Once, I would have said drama school. But it feels like that dream is vanishing before me, fading away in the reality of logistics and practicalities and Farah's words and my own head telling me it's never going to happen.

Perhaps Toby Swan is my way into this life post-Arcadia. Like Farah said, drama school isn't for everyone; sometimes you have to find another way. Maybe this is it. My other way.

THIRTEEN

I get home late to find Pops asleep in his armchair.

Whenever I see him like that, my breath catches in the back of my throat, and it stays there until I see his chest moving or hear a snore or sometimes even feel for a pulse. He's caught me doing that a couple of times. Today I hear his gentle snoring, and relax. He is alive.

On the small coffee table by his chair is a plate of browning apple pieces, a forgotten glass of water and an untouched crossword puzzle book. I worry about the apple. It's probably all he's eaten today even though Nan has filled the fridge with plastic containers of homemade soup. *Just heat and eat*, she says. He never does. He says he's not hungry. That everything is tasteless. It's awful to see this man who loved to cook and eat slowly fading away. One day I'm scared he is going to vanish completely into the folds of that old armchair.

I throw my bag in my room and head to the kitchen to make the mandatory afternoon cup of tea.

'Is that you, love?' I hear Pops call over the noise of the boiling kettle. I go out to him, give him a quick hug, a kiss on the forehead.

'I must've nodded off. Don't tell your nan,' he says.

I take away the apple, refill his water and get his pills. Even though he's through the surgery and the chemotherapy for now, he still needs to take a heap of pills every day. With food, without food, at this time or that time. It's a lot. But it means he can be home. Here. With us.

I make him have his afternoon tea outside, in the back garden. It's getting pretty overgrown, and I know I'm going to have to stop being lazy and do something about it soon.

Pops holds onto the mug with two hands and looks out over the garden. I put a blanket over his knees. It is still sunny out, but he can get cold pretty easily.

'How was your day?'

'Good, good,' he says. 'I think I watched TV, but I might have just been dreaming. Come on. Tell me what's happening with you. How are Aubrey and Will? They've not been over for a while.'

He's right. They haven't. It doesn't feel like long ago that they were here pretty much every week. But things change. They have to. At least, that's what I'm telling myself. And I need to get used to it, because before I know it my best friends will be on the other side of the world. And I'll be here. Alone.

'I'm trying to figure out what to do with the rest of my life,' I tell Pops.

'Why?' he says.

'Why?' I look at him in disbelief. I can't even begin to explain why I need to sort this out. How I'm running out of time to sort this out. I feel like I'm behind, again. It seems like everyone else knows where they'll be going and what they'll be doing, and then there's me ...

'I'm thinking I might audition for *Romeo and Juliet*, after all.' I'm kind of surprised even though I'm the one saying it. Pops nods thoughtfully. 'They've got this famous director in, and Mrs B thinks it will be a great opportunity, and if I can't go to drama school then maybe this could be a good way in, you know? To the industry. I mean, that's sort of what Imogen was saying. Not that I really listen to Imogen, but she knows about this stuff. And Farah Carbasse, do you remember her, well, she –'

'Slow down. I'm not following. Why can't you go to drama school?'

'It's expensive, Pops.'

'And?'

'And I might not get in. Then what? Then what do I have? If I work with Toby Swan, I may have some options for next year. You know?'

'No,' he says. 'I don't know. I don't know why you're in such a hurry. Your whole life is ahead of you, Edie. There's no rush.'

'You don't understand.'

Pops sighs and stares at those damn weeds. I get up and head into the mess of a garden and start yanking weeds out of the ground. This garden was once perfect. Pops' oasis. He'd be out here every weekend, working away on something.

When he got sick, I told him I'd take care of it, and I did. For a little while. But lately I haven't been keeping up. I pull out a particularly stubborn weed.

'That's not a weed,' Pops says.

'Oh, sorry,' I say. I try to stuff the roots back into the soil, but the not-a-weed won't stand upright. I leave it on the grass, move onto the next weed and hesitate over it, looking to Pops for some reassurance that I'm not about to rip out some beautiful flower he planted there years ago.

'Leave it, Little Ed. Come talk to me,' he says.

I wipe my hands on my school skirt, which I'll now have to wash, and I don't even know if I have another clean one for tomorrow. And suddenly, I just want to cry. It feels like I've been holding in tears all day. All week. All year.

'I was a carpenter because my father was a carpenter,' Pops says.

'Um. OK ...' I say.

'I don't think I ever wanted to be one. It just happened.'

'I thought you liked it?'

'Didn't say I didn't like it, but maybe I should have worked out what I wanted rather than just making my father happy,' he says. 'Figure out what my own dream was and stop living someone else's. You know what I'm saying?'

'This isn't about Mum.'

'I never had time to even consider anything else. It just happened. It was expected. And before I knew it, I was an old man.'

'You're not old,' I say. 'And this is entirely different.'

He stands shakily. I go to help him, but he stops me. Grumbles something about being able to look after himself, which is a load of crap, but I leave him to it. There's no point arguing with Pops. You never win.

'Your mum isn't going to care if you become an actor or not. If you go to drama school or, I don't know, cooking school or no school at all. All that matters is that you're happy, Edie. That's all we want.'

'I honestly don't think Mum gives a shit about me anymore, Pops.'

'Don't say that. That's not true.'

I watch him slowly make his way back inside. Shuffling his feet. Holding onto the door frame for a second to catch his breath before disappearing inside.

*

Sometimes I think Pops forgets things on purpose. It's not like he's doing it to be awful, but it is a form of protection. Because if he let himself remember what Mum was really like, he'd fall into that sadness and anger that turns him into someone he doesn't want to be. Someone I can barely recognise.

I understand the amnesia he has around Mum because I have it, too, sometimes. Maybe even worse, because I'm the one who's created a whole fantasy world in which Mum is some kind of rising Hollywood star, meeting with casting directors, dining with directors, making her mark in pilot season. But she's not. Or maybe she is. I wouldn't really know. We never know where she is, exactly. She's *finding herself* and *getting better* and *doing the work*. Whatever the hell that means. All I know is it's taking her a long time. She's been gone for seven years now. But in reality, I don't know if she was ever really here, with me, even when we lived in the same house. Feels like she's always been somewhere else.

*

I pull out my phone and send Noah a message: *OK. I'm going to audition for R+J.* Imogen's going to lose it when she finds out I'm trying out for Juliet, but I'll deal with her when I have to. She and I had a stupid, childish agreement and circumstances have changed. Besides, if she'd wanted to audition for Charity, I wouldn't have cared. I would have welcomed the competition. Surely Imogen won't be afraid of a little competition from an actor as dull as me? No, the person I'm really worried about telling is Will. He's been so weird about me even helping Noah with audition preparation that I don't know how he will take the news of me actually auditioning. But, like he said, you can do two things – right?

FOURTEEN

As soon as Noah hears I am going to audition he seems way more eager to actually prepare for it. Now he's the one on my back about finding time to work on this thing. Wants to know when we can meet up to practise, if I've read the scene, learned my lines. Sends heaps more texts.

I've tried to explain that I'm auditioning, but not with him. My audition has to be *my* audition. I can't just be some prop that makes Noah Winters look good. I need a killer monologue. Something that will really show my range. Crying is always good. It always works for Imogen. And Juliet cries a lot, so there are a heap of monologues I could do that would be so much better than the scene Noah wants to do. But he won't listen.

He should be listening to the documentary that the substitute History teacher has put on. We told her we'd seen it before, but she didn't care. No-one is really watching it, which she also doesn't seem to care about. Noah, however, missed it last term and probably should be watching it now and trying to catch up. Instead, he has pulled his chair up close to mine and is swinging back and forth on it.

'But everyone is doing monologues,' he says.

'Yes,' I say, 'because that's what you're supposed to do.'

'Who says?'

'It's just the way we do things here.'

'Toby's not from here, so he doesn't know that. Come on, Edie, take a chance. Do something different. What's the worst thing that could happen?'

The worst thing? Oh, no biggie. Just not getting the part and missing out on this life-changing opportunity, and having my career end before it even starts, and being stuck working in the store with Marshall as my boss forever, and never performing professionally, never making it, never leaving my grandparents' house, never doing anything with my life and dying sad and alone. And Noah thinks just smiling at me is going to change any of that? Sure, *he* can go through life smiling and getting whatever he wants. Some of us need more than just a smile.

Suddenly, he pushes the chair away, and it falls to the floor with a bang. Everyone stops – even the substitute teacher looks up from her crossword book – and turns to Noah. He drops to his knees beside my chair. What the hell is he doing?

'Get up,' I whisper to him.

'Edie Emerson,' he announces, speaking to me but also ensuring everyone can hear exactly what he's saying. 'Will you make the happiest man on earth and be my Juliet?'

140

The class erupts into laughter and applause and whooping. I stare at Noah and he stares at me. He annoys me so much I want to scream, but part of me also wants to kiss him. Right now. In front of everyone. I won't. Of course I won't. But it flashes through my my mind, uninvited. I shove it away.

'You're an idiot.'

'Like Romeo?'

'No.'

'I got you this,' he says, and he pulls from his bag a single red rose like I'm the girl he has just chosen on *The Bachelor*.

'Stop it.' I shove the rose away. Get close and whisper in his ear, 'I am not letting you embarrass me again, Noah. Not happening. So just stop it.'

I turn back to the documentary. Or try to. Because now Noah has stood up and leapt onto the desk. Oh my god, what is he doing?

He clears his throat. 'But, soft! what light through yonder window breaks? It is the east, and Edie is the sun.'

What is it with these men shouting Shakespeare at me? First Old Man Healy, and now Noah. I don't like it. I can feel my face getting hot. Can hear the whispers of the class. Their judgement. Their laughter. It's not directed at Noah. No, Noah is cute and enchanting. They're laughing at me. The joke is on me.

'I am not doing the scene with you, Noah. I know you're not used to hearing *no*. I know a rich, spoilt brat like you is used to getting whatever you want when you want, but guess what? I am saying NO. Get over it.'

The whole class has gone silent. Everyone is staring. I feel like I've become the villain in all this even though Noah has pushed me to it. It's too much. I pick up my bag and leave the room.

*

Everyone hears about the scene from History. Of course. They love a good scene and they love to gossip. Three different groups of girls approach me, all concerned that Noah is my boyfriend now and all very relieved when I tell them he most definitely is not.

I join our makeshift group by the fountain at lunchtime. It was always me and Will and Aubrey, but then it became just me and Will because Aubrey was off with Lexie and the dancers. And then Yazi, Kellen, Caleb and Makayla sort of gravitated towards us. I mean, I think it was us. It could just be our prime location that drew them in. Anyway, we've merged into one larger group. Which helps. Because it was getting a little sad – just me and Will hanging out on our own most of the time.

'I need to know everything,' Makayla shouts as I approach. It feels like the whole school is out here today. Feels like they're all watching me.

'There's nothing to tell,' I say as I throw off my backpack. I sit on the edge of the fountain, next to Will.

'What's going on?' Will says.

'Noah Winters did the cutest thing, like totally proposed to her. I mean, not to marry her or take her to the formal, but for their audition. Noah Winters wants Edie to audition with him,' Makayla says, emphasising his name like he's some sort of celebrity, 'even though he *should* be doing a monologue.'

'So, you *are* auditioning for the play?' Will turns to me.

I feel terrible. I haven't told him about my decision because I didn't know how to. I didn't want him to feel rejected, or like his show wasn't enough for me.

'Yeah,' I say, 'it's a good opportunity. Mrs B even said I should. Because, you know, there's that famous director on board. But I can still do your show, Will. I can do both. I'll do both.'

'It's cool. I get it. Stop stressing,' he says. I give him a quick hug. I don't think he realises what a relief it is to hear him say this.

'I'd like to audition with Noah Winters,' Makayla sighs, still lost in thought.

'Be my guest,' I say.

'Noah Winters is hot. And he is *so* into you.'

'He's a dick, and the only person he's into is himself.'

That makes Will burst into laughter.

'Ah, Edie, you sure know how to make a guy feel wanted,' Noah says. He is standing right in front of us. Will stops laughing. 'Can we talk? In private?'

*

Noah is pacing. He says he feels terrible. Didn't mean to embarrass me. That he's sorry. Really sorry. I have never noticed that little flex thing he does with his jaw. Maybe because I've never seen him so serious before. Right now, while he is desperately apologising, he seems sincere and genuine, and there is something about seeing him like that which makes me feel bad for being so harsh with him in the first place.

'I'm sorry, but this audition is too important for me, Noah. I'll help you, but I'm not doing a scene with you –'

'If you really want the part, you should stick with me. I've got an in with Toby Swan. And I know he'll love our scene. I know it. You have to trust me on this.'

'What does that mean? You've got an "in"?'

'Just trust me, Edie. You gotta trust me.' He smiles his real smile. The smile I'm starting to think he reserves for him. Not the one he dazzles everyone else with. A real smile. Right to his eyes. And I'm staring at him and I'm going to have to say something soon, because this will get awkward if I don't. Me and my brain. Why can't we ever find the right words at the right time? If this were a musical I'd sing now, wouldn't I? A song only I could hear about how I think I am falling for someone who isn't right for me at all. A song about being stupid and reckless and possibly, maybe, in love.

'OK,' I say. 'I'll do the damn scene.'

It's reckless. All of it. Choosing to audition with a scene over a monologue. Choosing to fall this hard for Noah. But I've never been reckless before and you know what? It feels kinda good.

FIFTEEN

I'm in the passenger seat of Noah's car, trying to hide how awkward and nervous I feel. He invited me over, after school, to work on this audition scene. Makayla thinks this is another sign that he likes me, and won't we just hurry up and start dating already? Yazi doesn't think I have a chance in hell with someone like Noah. So, yeah, I'm confused. And nervous. And awkward. It's quite a combination.

'You OK?' Noah asks as he stops at a red light.

'Yeah,' I say. 'You?'

He smiles and nods, and I find myself smiling and nodding back at him until a car beeps its horn, snapping us out of it. The light has turned green. Noah's focus returns to the road. We drive in silence.

'Does this feel weird?' he asks suddenly.

'Weird?'

'I dunno. I think I'm nervous. Sorry.' He runs his hand through his hair. I can't imagine Noah Winters being nervous because of me, but he is. Right now. 'Music might help. Can I put on some music?'

The smooth voice of The Weeknd fills the car. I love his voice. The way he can span from bass to the high notes of a head voice so effortlessly. I'm about to tell Noah about my undying adoration for this guy when, suddenly, he starts singing himself. And Noah is no Abel Tesfaye. Not even close. But he doesn't care. He is absolutely destroying the song, his voice nowhere near the key it's meant to be in, but he looks so happy. And cute. Extremely cute. And not even a little embarrassed.

'Sing with me!' he says.

'You know you're a terrible singer, right?' I tell him.

'Yep!' he shouts happily over the music.

And we sing all the way to his house.

*

The elevator opens straight into their penthouse apartment and it takes a lot of effort not to turn around, get back into the elevator and leave. Their place is like a palace. My brain keeps telling me, *You don't belong here*. Noah slips off his shoes and I follow his lead, trying to look calm and unfazed by the dizzying views from the huge windows, the baby grand piano, the chandelier, the lush, perfectly white carpet. *You don't belong here, Edie*.

But, as breathtaking as his home looks, it doesn't feel like a home. It feels like a movie set. Empty. Lonely. There is no-one here – in fact, it looks like no-one has ever been here. To look around, you'd never believe actual, real people live here.

I follow Noah into the kitchen, where I am surprised to see someone preparing food. A chef, I assume. She's wearing a white apron and looks like she's deep in concentration making these intricate-looking chocolates. Noah doesn't even speak to her as he grabs some bottles of sparkling water from the refrigerator.

'Who's that?' I whisper to him.

Noah shrugs. 'I dunno. Dad's hosting some dinner party or something tonight. Must be for that.'

'Hello,' I say to the unknown chef.

'Hi?' she says.

Noah ushers me out of the kitchen and up a winding staircase to his room. The nerves I thought I'd gotten rid of in the car suddenly come streaming back, and my heart is thumping so fast I am sure Noah will notice my whole body shaking with every boom.

He hands me a bottle of water, takes off his tie, undoes the top buttons of his shirt and flops onto the bed.

There are many, many places for me to sit. The reading chair by the floor-to-ceiling bookshelf, at his desk, on the beanbags in front the big-screen television that fills the opposite wall, on the expensive-looking rug that covers the floor ... or the bed. Next to Noah. I can't decide so I just end up standing there, trying to open the bottle of water because my mouth has gone completely dry.

'You need a hand?' Noah asks.

'No, no, I got it,' I lie. I use the bottom of my skirt to help grip the lid and it finally loosens, but not without fizzing up everywhere first. I can't believe this is happening. It won't stop. The water is spitting everywhere and the more I try to make it stop, the worse it is. 'Shit, sorry, oh my god, sorry,' I say. My skirt is soaked. So is the expensive-looking rug. Shit.

'Don't worry about it.' Noah laughs and disappears for a second.

I seriously think about leaving. Just putting down the bottle and walking out before I embarrass myself even more. But Noah is back with towels, and a huge smile on his face. 'My bathroom is through there, if you need it. You wanna borrow something to wear?'

'What is it with us and water?' I laugh, too, because what else am I going to do? 'It's like being pushed into the pool all over again.'

'That was an accident, and I am sorry. You know I'm sorry about that, right?'

Noah finds me a pair of tracksuit pants and a T-shirt, which are going to be too big on me, but at least they're dry. There is something about wearing his clothes that makes me grin in spite of myself. I feel giddy and stupid. Like I'm on a rollercoaster, but just that part that's dropping out from under you.

I try to concentrate on practising the scene with him. But the whole scene is about Romeo and Juliet literally falling in love at first sight. They touch, whisper to each other, kiss.

'Let's just focus on the lines,' I say. 'Work out the moves a little later.'

'You're the expert,' Noah says.

We sit on his bedroom floor, our copies of the play in front of us. We read through the scene together a couple of times. But Noah sounds like he is reading the lines or reciting a poem. His voice makes me want to fall asleep, not fall in love.

'Try to loosen up,' I say. 'Just say it the way you'd say it, the way Noah would say it.'

'But I wouldn't say this.'

'Yeah, but you are massive flirt, and Romeo is totally flirting right now. He's seen someone he thinks is hot and wants to make out with her. That's all. So just be yourself, trying to hook up with someone, but using those words.'

Noah laughs. 'I'm not a flirt.'

'Yes, you are.'

'Am I?' He looks genuinely confused. What an actor. Why can't he bring that to this scene?

'Sure, Noah. Sure.'

'You have this idea of me, Edie Emerson, and it's just not true,' he sighs. 'Didn't think you'd be so judgemental.'

'I am not judgemental!'

'Sure, Edie. Sure.'

We try the scene again only this time, as we go through it, we turn all the Shakespearian lines into contemporary lines. Like, what we would actually say if we were actually in that situation. It takes time, but he starts to loosen up, to get it, and when we go back to Shakespeare it sounds a lot better. Less like a robot reciting a poem, badly. He is working really hard. Making notes on his script. Listening. Trying. I didn't think someone like Noah ever really tried. I thought someone like Noah would be so used to getting what they want that they never attempted to work for it. But here he is. Putting in effort. Maybe Noah is right. I am judgemental.

'Let's get up, add the moves, I think I need to move,' he says, and pulls me to my feet.

We work out where we should stand, when he should take my hand, if I should walk away or turn my back, if we should stand face to face or back to back. And then we get to the first kiss. We stop.

'Can I kiss you?' Noah says.

I feel my face turn hot, hot, hot. 'Um,' I say.

'Just for the scene …'

'Oh, yeah, I know. OK.'

He says the line: *Thus from my lips, by yours, my sin is purged*. I feel a little wobbly. And he takes my face – Juliet's face – in his hands, and gently kisses her. Their first kiss. I feel sparks, like fireworks, going off inside of me. Exactly the way Juliet would have felt right then.

He pulls away, but his hands still cup my face. He looks into my eyes. Quietly, he asks, 'Can I kiss you, not for the scene?'

'Yes,' I say. And we do. And we do. And we do.

I mean, our scene is Romeo and Juliet's first kiss, so we need to get that right, don't we? They say practise makes perfect.

And I think he is the perfect Romeo.

SIXTEEN

'We can skip the kiss part, obviously – I just want to hear this scene, out loud, with you, if that's OK, cos something isn't working.'

Will and I have snuck into the upstairs rehearsal room during lunchbreak. The first read-through with the cast he and Aubrey have put together is happening next week, so, of course, now Will is doubting everything he has written, thinks it is a load of crap and wants to just forget the whole thing. I suggested we look at the scenes that are worrying him, which is why we're here. I wanted Aubrey to be here, too, but she had plans with Lexie that she couldn't change at late notice. They have started going off campus for lunch, because once you're in Year Twelve you're allowed to do that sort of thing. I don't see what the big deal is. When I mentioned that to Aubrey, she rolled her eyes and said, *Of course you don't*. I said, *What does that mean?* She said, *You never want to do anything*. I think she might have flung her hair, which is the most un-Aubrey thing I have ever seen, and then she was gone. Off campus. For lunch. When she should be here, with me, helping Will.

We sit on the floor. Legs stretched out in front of us. Scripts open.

'You highlighted your lines?' Will says, noticing my script.

'Um, yeah,' I say. I don't know why he looks so happy about some fluorescent pink lines across the page. I mean, that's just standard. Everyone does that. 'You OK?'

'It's just cool,' he says. 'That you did that. With the script I wrote.'

He is so weird sometimes. I start reading. The scene is the moment Lily (the dream-girl) realises Jack is an actual, living, breathing, superhero. The big secret he has tried to keep hidden from her is revealed, and they can finally announce their love for each other. The scene is awkward – not just because I have to be this total wimp of a girl, but because Will has written it like something from a bad soap opera. Also, his idea isn't all that original. I mean, we've seen this story a hundred times. Clark Kent, anybody? Only I'd never, ever say that to Will. He has worked so hard on this thing.

'Hold up, hold up,' Will interjects. 'I think we're sort of rushing it, but maybe if we slow it down a bit, take our time and really listen, really *see* each other, then maybe it will work a bit better?'

I raise an eyebrow. I am not used to get acting notes from Will. I don't know how I feel about it.

'Is that OK? With you? I mean, you know more about this stuff than me, but I'm just thinking, maybe –'

'It's fine,' I tell him. 'But we should both be standing then, so get up.'

I pull him to his feet. We stand facing each other and restart the scene.

As Lily, who has just awoken (because she is a girl and of course she has been knocked out during the climactic moment with the supervillain), I say, 'I can't believe it's you …'

'Surprise,' Will deadpans as Jack. The superhero with the very dry sense of humour.

We continue the scene, pausing between lines and taking a moment to let the gravity of this realisation set in. I don't think there's much gravity to it – it's all pretty light and fluffy to me – but I try it out, for Will's sake.

LILY: It's been you all along, hasn't it?

JACK: I wanted to tell you, so badly, but I couldn't – I couldn't risk losing you.

LILY: You'll never lose me.

JACK: Never?

LILY: It's always been you, Jack.

JACK: But –

LILY: I don't care about your superpowers. I fell in love with the man. Not the superhero.

JACK: Did you say … love?

LILY: I think I did … Are you going to say it too, or leave me hanging –

JACK: I love you.

LILY: I love you.

They kiss

SONG #8

We get to those final lines, and something happens. A tiny little nudge, right there in my stomach. I look at Will. He looks at me. I feel my face turning hot, a blush creeping up my neck to my cheeks.

'Right, and then a kiss. Done. And the song,' I say quickly.

'Yeah ...' Will says slowly.

'Did you still hate it? The scene? I find it quite sweet, really, and tender.' Tender? Why am I saying *tender*? Who says that? But I can't stop talking. 'And a vulnerability, which I like, and yeah, it is clichéd but that's OK, isn't it? I mean, it's about love so it's bound to get a bit mushy.'

'Mushy?' Will looks hurt.

'I meant it in a good way.'

'There's good mushy?'

'Like mashed potatoes?'

'Geez, Edie, this isn't getting any better. Can we read it again? I'm gonna record it this time, on my phone.'

I'm nervous to read it again. I can't stand the way my heart is thumping extra loudly, or this jumpy feeling in my stomach. It is not normal. This is not how I have ever been with Will. Ever. We're friends. Best friends. That's the way it has always been. But as we start the scene again, this feeling that maybe there's something *more* starts whispering at me.

I shake it off. Concentrate on the script. What is wrong with me? Who is this person? Kissing Noah Winters one day, and now what? Dreaming about kissing Will. Will!

I stare into Will's eyes ... dark and bright and those eyelashes that just ... ugh ... always with the damn eyes. I'm the mushy cliché, not Will's script.

'You all right?' Will breaks out of character. I realise I have been staring at him.

'Um, I, sorry, lost my place ...'

The door opens with a bang and I think, *Thank god, Aubrey's here,* but it's not Aubrey who enters the room. It's Noah. I feel my heart drop and my face start to burn. I'm red hot. I haven't done anything wrong, so why does it feel as if I have?

'What's he doing here?' Will whispers.

'Hey, Noah,' I say. 'Have I shown you this room? I don't think I have. It's my favourite rehearsal room. You see that view? It's breathtaking, isn't it?' Why am I speaking like this? I can't stop. I'm just rambling on and on about the view. Why would Noah give a shit about the view? He clearly doesn't. He just sort of stares at me, with this half smiling, half questioning look on his face. I stop talking.

'I thought we were gonna run the scene during lunch?' he says.

'We were?' I don't remember making those plans. I am sure I would have remembered. We also don't need to rehearse any more. We are so ready for this audition. But then Noah winks at me and I realise he didn't want to run through the scene at all. He wanted to hang out.

Will notices the wink. I see him look at me, then look at Noah, and start to put it together. Whatever *it* is. I don't know. I don't know if Noah is my boyfriend or just my scene partner, the potential Romeo to my potential Juliet.

I've never had a boyfriend. I've had crushes before. Plenty of crushes. And I've kissed people. Not just as part of a musical or play, but in real life, too. Not a lot of people. But some.

And by 'some', I mean two. One of those was in Grade Six, so it doesn't really count because we just put our lips together in the most G-rated version of a 'kiss' imaginable. And the other time was in Year Nine. That one was with Diego and he made me promise never to tell anyone, which is not really the sort of thing anyone wants to hear after making out with someone. I've only ever told Aubrey.

Diego and I had been waiting backstage, alone in the dark during a tech rehearsal, when it happened. I started it. Which was not like me. But he was being so sweet (which was not like him), complimenting me on my solo, and something sort of hit me, hard, in the stomach, and I thought I was in love, because I was fourteen and feeling all the feelings very strongly. It was like I was in some sort of trance and, without being fully aware of what I was doing, I found myself leaning in close to his face and closing my eyes and suddenly we were kissing. I kissed Diego, and he kissed me back. Then he said, *Never speak of this*, like he was some sort of super-villain from a Marvel film. Never speak of this? What an idiot. And me, being fourteen and also an idiot, did what he said. Except for telling Aubrey. I remember also telling Aubrey that maybe I'd ask him to be my boyfriend anyway, to which she sadly shook her head and said, *Not a good idea, Eds.* Which makes me wonder about this whole Noah situation, and what Aubrey would say about it. Would she shake her head and tell me it's not a good idea? I wish I'd had a chance to talk to her about it. Because there's no way I can talk to Will about it. Not if the face he is pulling right now is anything to go by. He looks like he's eaten something bad. Really bad.

'Are you kidding me, Edie?' he says.

'What?' I say.

'This guy? *This* freaking guy?'

Will picks up his bag, swings it over his shoulder, says he'll see me later and walks out. Just like that. A heavy silence falls over the room. I should go after him, but Noah is just standing there, looking so deflated and confused. I feel ripped in two – half of me wanting to go after Will, the other half wanting to stay here with Noah. I don't know what to do.

Noah runs his hand through his hair. 'Did I do something wrong?'

'No,' I say, 'he's just stressed about his musical.'

'He hates me.'

'He doesn't hate you,' I lie.

'Kinda sucks. I think it's important to be friends with my girlfriend's friends,' he says.

I stop. Dead. Girlfriend? Did he actually just say that?

'Who said I was your girlfriend?' I return his stare, steady and serious and trying really hard to keep the butterflies that are swirling inside me under control.

He moves a little closer to me, but before he can say anything, I pull him towards me and we kiss, softly and deeply. It's the love song in the musical, when their voices meld and the orchestra swells and the confetti falls from the rafters. Only it's better, because this is real life.

SEVENTEEN

There is an announcement that anyone interested in auditioning for the play needs to be in the Drama studio. Right now. NO EXCEPTIONS. So that's where we are, during the last period on a Friday. I should be in Biology. Dr Lee was not very impressed. Yelled out instructions for extra homework as half of us rushed out of the classroom.

Mrs B would never throw a surprise audition at us, but Toby Swan might. And I think I'm ready – *we're* ready. I spy Noah sitting up the back with Ari and Cody. He winks at me. I feel like the floor drops from under my chair.

'What on earth do you think this is all about?' Imogen sighs dramatically and sinks into the seat next to mine. Now I wish the floor had dropped from under me and saved me from this.

'I have no idea, Imogen,' I say, disappointed that I can't just stare at Noah in peace.

'Is it the audition?'

'I don't think so ...'

'I'm not concerned if it is. I am always performance-ready. You have to be when you have an agent, you just never know when an opportunity might arise,' she says. 'Are you prepared?'

'Absolutely,' I tell her.

She stares at me for a moment. Not blinking. Not saying anything. It's a little disconcerting. Finally, she says, 'I have been working with my vocal coach on Juliet's monologue in Act 3, Scene 2. Are you familiar?' I nod, but Imogen ignores me. '*Gallop apace, you fiery-footed steeds* ... There is a real skill with the Shakespearian language, lots of technique and training required to really do it justice.'

'OK,' I say.

'They probably won't mind taking on someone less polished for one of the supporting roles. The Nurse is a lot of fun. I could really see you making that role your own. Won't that be fun?' She adjusts her ponytail.

Imogen doesn't know I'm her competition, because I haven't told her I'm auditioning for Juliet. Because I'm a coward. I think about explaining it all right now but Toby Swan appears and the room erupts into applause. Unlike Mrs B, Toby doesn't seem to mind the attention. He bows, solemnly.

'I'm not here to waste your time,' Toby says, 'and you're not here to waste my time. So, let's get started right now. Show me what you've got.'

The excitement that filled the room fades into panic.

'You want us to audition now?' Imogen sounds a little nervous. So much for being performance-ready.

'Imogen, Imogen, you have nothing to worry about. Let's think of it as a teaser, a taster – an introduction rather than an audition. You know how I hate that word. You've got this.' Toby smiles at Imogen. Imogen glows. She looks around to see if anyone else has noticed how he used her name.

'Did I forget to mention we know each other?' she whispers to me proudly. 'I've taken a couple of his masterclasses.'

Of course she has.

Toby asks us to all sit in a circle on the floor, to create a sharing space into which people can give a 'taster' of a scene from *Romeo and Juliet*. He repeats that there is no pressure, and we only have to share if we want to share. I don't want to share. Nor does the rest of the group. We just want to do the audition the way we usually do it. Entering the room one at a time, or with your scene partner. Being warmly welcomed by Mrs B. Presenting your monologue. Taking on the direction she offers – *Why not try it like this? Could you show me how it might look if you do this?* – and then trying the scene again. Mrs B saying *Thank you*, kindly, like she means it. And then exiting the space. Done. That's it. Simple.

We all just sit there, in silence, as Toby nods and says, 'Good, this is good, I'm feeling a vibe.' The vibe is we're FREAKING THE HELL OUT because this isn't how auditions work. This isn't what we've trained for. But Toby doesn't seem to get it or care.

Suddenly he says, 'Noah Winters!' He says it like he's just noticed the cutest guy in the room when, in reality, Noah would be the first person anyone notices in a room. You can't help it. Believe me. I've tried.

160

Noah looks a little sheepish as Toby pulls him in for one of those bro-hugs, all fist-bumping and back-slapping. I know Noah said he had an 'in' with Toby, but I didn't expect them to be actual friends.

'Good to see you, man,' Toby says, and I'm taken right back to that drama class when Noah met Will and picked on him for using the exact same word. This time, Noah says nothing.

'Why don't you get us started?' Toby says. 'You up for that?'

'Sure. I'll need my scene partner, though,' Noah says and looks at me.

Imogen's hand shoots up. 'Oh no, Noah. Didn't anyone tell you? We don't audition with scenes. We audition with *monologues*,' she says as if she is speaking to a three-year-old.

'That's bullshit,' Toby says. 'Who told you that?'

Imogen shrugs, looks at the floor. I have never seen her lost for words before. It makes me feel a little bad for her.

'Can I do a scene?' Noah says, sounding a little nervous.

'You do you, man,' Toby says as he steps out of the circle.

Noah offers me his hand and pulls me up to join him in the middle of the circle. He whispers, *Good luck*, in my ear, the heat from his breath leaving goosebumps on my neck, and we take our positions. Back to back. Romeo takes Juliet's hand; it surprises her. Me. I am Juliet. And I am not expecting to fall in love tonight, but I do. Right here. Right now. In this fleeting, tiny, flirty, dangerous moment. His hand stroking my hand. We turn to face each other, our eyes locked in a gaze that we never want to end. We throw playful taunts at each other. We kiss. We break apart. We kiss again

161

and then … it's over. I tear myself away from him … walk away … out of the circle. End scene.

It's a bit of a daze, but we do it. And I think we do it well. It feels good. The sparks might not have been as bright as they were when we rehearsed it, but they were there. I could feel them in Noah's touch. See them in Noah's eyes. Hear it in the huskiness of his voice when he went in for the first kiss.

'Wow,' Toby says, breaking the silence of the room, 'just wow.'

I can't help but smile as Noah puts his arm around my shoulder. We're like contestants on *The Voice* or something, waiting for Rita or Jess to choose us.

'That was terrible. Just not sexy at all. And *Romeo and Juliet* is all about sex. You two. Wow. Sorry to say it. There's no – no chemistry, but it looks like you had a lot of fun preparing for it. Noah, man, you've got plenty for me to work with. You're a natural. Got that edginess I like for Romeo. But, um … sorry … what's your name?'

I can't remember my name. In that second, everything is blank. I can only concentrate on not crying. Not crying.

Noah answers for me. Squeezes my shoulder as he says, 'This is Edie.'

I can't look at him right now. Can't look at anyone.

'Edie? Cool. Look at me, sweetheart,' Toby says. I don't want to look at him and I definitely don't want him calling me *sweetheart*. 'That was kinda blargh. Boring. Didn't capture me at all. I know it's difficult but, hey, thank you. Thank you for trying. It was so brave of you to try in front of all of us. I know that's tough, so good on you.' He leads the group in a round of applause.

I want to leave, but I can't. I know how bad that would look. Instead, I sit in the circle with everyone else, and avoid making eye contact with any of them.

Noah sits next to me and puts his hand on my knee. I can't bring myself to take his hand, but I appreciate that he's still there. At least I haven't scared him off with my terrible performance.

Imogen leans over. I can't deal with her shit right now. I ignore her, but she whispers anyway, 'For what it's worth, I thought that was really great.' I pull my eyes up to meet hers. She isn't smirking or laughing at me. She gives me a little shrug. Things must be bad when Imogen takes pity on you.

The sharing circle continues. People perform what they can remember from the script – short scenes or monologues – or improvise something completely new and cringey. It doesn't matter how good or how terrible they are, Toby Swan doesn't have anything nice to say about anyone. He is particularly harsh on the girls. He calls us all *sweetheart* or *honey* in this super-patronising voice and gives us these sad-puppy-dog eyes like he feels so sorry for us and our complete lack of talent. It makes me feel slightly better, the fact that everyone is getting notes like that. Well, almost everyone. Noah is the only one to get anything positive out of Toby.

It's Imogen's turn.

She moves gracefully to the centre of the circle. Takes a moment before she begins. Even without speaking, she has our full attention. She just has this aura when she's in performance mode, and you're drawn in by her very presence. As much as I sometimes hate to admit it, Imogen is remarkable. And as I watch her there, in the middle of the circle, giving her all to that monologue, I start to doubt myself. A lot. What was I even thinking? Going up against Imogen for this role. She is perfect.

Although, not according to Toby. 'Oh honey,' he says, 'I don't know what to say. That wasn't it. I think you feel that, don't you?'

Imogen nods.

'Derivative. A bit of a yawn-fest. And far too polished. You've been working with your voice coach on this, haven't you?'

'Yes,' she says in her best Cate Blanchett voice.

'You need to stop that. It's not exciting. It's not ... sexy.' What the hell is with this guy?

Imogen blushes, murmurs, 'Thank you for the feedback,' before sitting down next to me again. I can't believe she *thanked* him. I can't believe she considers that *feedback*. It's my turn to tell her I thought she was great, not only because she complimented me but because it is true. She was. I tap her shoulder.

'Got something to share with the group, Edie?' Toby interrupts me mid-whisper.

'No,' I say quickly.

'You sure?' He looks so smug. And maybe it's his face, or the fact that he is so freaking rude, or that him demanding we be here means I now have a heap of extra Biology homework I wasn't expecting – I don't know what it is, exactly, but I decide, right then, to say something.

'Well, actually ...' I stand up so I'm no longer looking up at him. I need to be on the same level as this guy. I can see that takes him by surprise. Good. 'I adored Imogen's performance.

I thought it was … riveting. And exciting. And I really enjoyed her interpretation.' There I go, gushing like I do. And saying words like *riveting*. But for once, I don't care.

'That's very sweet,' he says.

'No, it's not *sweet*, it's true,' I counter.

The sound of a snort escapes his nose. 'I'm not here to argue.' He waves his hand in my direction like I'm a pesky blow-fly. 'I'm here to help you make the best show possible. To make something important. To create *Art*. We will start on Sunday. No auditions. I don't believe in them. So, this Sunday we will do what I like to call a workshop. If you want to be in the show, I will see you at the workshop. Now go. Leave. I have nothing more to say to any of you.'

'Sunday?' I blurt it out before I can stop myself. 'I work on Sundays. I can't –'

'Not my problem.' And with that he turns his back on us, takes his phone out of his back pocket and starts scrolling. End of conversation.

We all gather our things and walk out of the Drama studio in shocked silence. The place I once considered the safest, most special space in the entire school has just been turned into something unrecognisable. A place where you feel belittled and stupid and voiceless. The bell rings. The day is over. All I want to do is get home and forget it ever happened.

'What the hell was that?' I ask Noah.

'That's just Toby Swan,' he says.

'He's awful.'

'He's a genius, Edie, seriously. It's gonna be great for us, working with someone like him …'

'I can't,' I say. 'I have work on Sundays, Noah. I can't do it.'

'Just get out of it. It's only work. This is your future, Edie.'

There's so much he doesn't know about me and will probably never understand. Noah doesn't have to work. He doesn't have to worry about anything. There are so many things I need to tell him, so many questions I need to ask.

'So, you wanna lift home, we could hang out or –'

I panic. There is no way in the world Noah is seeing my house. 'I've got plans,' I say. 'Sorry.'

'All good,' he says. 'See you Sunday?'

'Sure, yeah,' I stammer.

And then he's gone. He catches up with Dom, who is carrying a basketball down the corridor. I watch him steal the ball from him and dribble it down the corridor, Dom chasing after him and out the exit.

I see Imogen heading my way. A determined look on her face. Shit. I don't really feel like having this out now, but Imogen looks ready for an argument.

'You are a piece of work, Edie,' Imogen says.

'Me? Why?' I say innocently.

'Tell me you're not auditioning for Juliet. That you're not reneging on our agreement. That you're not dishonest and disloyal and –'

'OK, OK, I get it and I'm sorry, but come on, you can't seriously think I'll get the role over you?'

'Of course not,' she says, 'but it's the principle of the matter. Maybe I would have liked to have auditioned

166

for Charity. But I didn't. Out of respect for you and our agreement.'

'You can't sing, Imogen,' I say. I am so over this. 'You can't audition for a lead in musical theatre when you can't actually sing.'

'Fine. Be that way,' she snaps and storms down the hallway.

I stand there, dazed, for a second. It was not the way I wanted that conversation to go but at least it happened. It probably should have happened years ago.

'You missed a very exciting Biology class,' Will says, bringing me back to earth.

'You missed a very awful audition,' I tell him. 'And a peak Imogen moment.'

'Wanna talk about it?'

We haven't really spoken since the whole Noah thing, and we definitely haven't spoken *about* the Noah thing. And I won't. Will doesn't like him. And he doesn't have to. I mean, I'd like it if he did, but that's not going to happen, and that's OK. Right? Aubrey didn't really care if we liked Lexie or not. They just started dating, and now she seems to have dumped us for Lexie's friends. I hope Will doesn't think I'd do that. I'd never do that.

Will holds out his arm and I loop my arm through. We wander out of the schoolgrounds together and I tell him all about the horror show I just endured.

EIGHTEEN

I feel like I am the only person at Arcadia who doesn't get the whole Toby Swan thing. Everyone has crossed paths with him; at his shows (I have never seen any of them, but Imogen calls them *very avant-garde* and *life-changing*, which sounds like an over-exaggeration to me) or in his masterclasses and workshops (which Imogen also described as *life-changing*). I can't afford theatre tickets, or a spot in an exclusive acting masterclass. Even if they are life-changing. I really can't even afford to be here, in this *Romeo and Juliet* 'workshop' on a Sunday. But I'm here. Nan found someone to cover my shift and told me not to worry about it. I am worried, though. Very worried. She told me to stop being ridiculous.

In preparation for today, I spent all of Saturday doing research on Toby Swan. Watched some YouTube, read some interviews, tried to get an idea of what he might be looking for in a Juliet. I texted Noah for some tips, and his replies included the always unhelpful *relax, just be yourself.* Easy for him to say. I discovered the Winters and the Swans are old family friends. *We sometimes see them at Aspen,* Noah said as if that's a totally normal, usual thing for people to do. Then I remembered it *is* normal for the people I go to school with. I'm the abnormal one.

This thing that Toby calls a workshop isn't really feeling like a workshop.

I always thought workshops were judgement-free places, where we were allowed to try out some new acting techniques or ideas and not feel like we were on display. That's how they've always felt to me, anyway. But then, I have only ever done workshops here at Arcadia, under the guidance of Mrs B. Maybe they're different out in the real world. Everyone else seems completely fine with the way Toby has set this thing up, which is basically him telling us to do something and then yelling at us for doing it badly. Well, not all of us.

I'm sitting in the front row of the auditorium with everyone else who wanted to audition for Juliet. There's thirty of us. That includes Imogen, of course, who seems to be dealing with the fact we're competing for the same role in typical Imogen style. She told me I'd be a better actor once I'd felt what it was like not to land a lead role. *You need to experience failure,* she said. And it seems like I already have. According to Toby, we've all failed miserably. He told us to sit down, and then he called up all those who want to be Romeo or Mercutio or Benvolio or Tybalt. There are so many more interesting male characters in this play. It's always like that. In *Romeo and Juliet* they get to fight and behave badly. What do the female characters get? A lot of crying and hand-wringing. If I get this part I am going to try to make Juliet as feisty as Mercutio. Not that it looks likely I'll get the role. Not if this workshop is any indicator. Actually, it doesn't look like any of us will get the role. We all messed up the exercise Toby got us to do. Badly. We can't even look at each other, it was so humiliating.

Toby had instructed us to run. 'Run!' he screamed. 'Like your life depends on it. Like you have to run to survive.' But it is difficult to run on a stage. You can fall into the orchestra pit or slam into a wall pretty easily. I still remember that poor Year Seven kid who broke their toe during *Sweet Charity*. Anyway, Toby didn't seem to care. He just wanted us to run, run, run. 'Stop thinking! Stop getting in your own way!'

We ran for what seemed like forever before he screamed, 'DROP!' and we had to drop to the floor. Imogen did a good job of that. She just fell. Floated to the floor like she was piece of tissue paper. I sort of collapsed, too hard and with zero grace, onto my knees. Tara did a slide into her fall, which looked pretty spectacular but made Toby say, 'Stop showing off!' Some of the others freaked out entirely and just stood there, unsure of what to do, until they lowered themselves carefully to the ground.

Once we were all on the floor, he made us repeat the whole thing again. Run, drop, run, drop, run, drop. It was enough to make me wish I was working with Marshall in the deli section. And I hate Marshall.

Just when I thought it couldn't get any worse, or any more painful, Toby told us to pause. We all stopped, mid-stride, like kids playing musical statues at a birthday party. Then he said, 'Turn to the audience and tell them about a romantic encounter. A kiss, holding hands, sex – I don't care what it is, but it needs to be true. Shout your story from your whole body. Your toes, your ribs, the back of your neck, the top of your head. GO!'

But we didn't GO. We all just looked at each like, *Is this guy for real?* I mean, firstly, who says 'romantic encounter'? And who the hell does Toby Swan think he is that we'd share that sort of personal stuff with him? With everyone in this room?

There was a very awkward silence that was only broken when Toby lost it at us.

'Bad actors. Look at them!' He turned to the rest of the group in the auditorium, who shifted uncomfortably in their seats. 'A good actor is vulnerable and open. They are connected to their bodies, their instincts. They display humour and playfulness, and a sense of gravitas and determination. Bad actors are those lacking in any one of these areas. What I see is a group of people lacking in all of the above. You are bad actors. And I cannot work with bad actors. It isn't fair on you or me.'

Imogen stepped forward then and I wanted, desperately, to pull her back and save her from what she was about to do. But she was too quick. She held her head high, arms back, feet grounded, and proclaimed, 'Last summer, at our beach house, I had sex for the first time with –'

We never found out who it was because Toby shouted for us all to sit down, and invited those who wanted to try out for the male roles to get up.

So that's where we are now. Deflated, embarrassed Juliet-wannabes. Bad actors watching a group of mainly young men running around the stage.

I try to get Imogen's attention, to check that she's OK, but she keeps her eyes straight ahead, focused on the action in front of us. Imogen has never dated anyone from Arcadia. Not as far as I know. She has always seemed too mature and sophisticated to waste her time with the boys from this school. Like she's above all that stuff somehow. But she must have a boyfriend, or had a boyfriend. Or girlfriend. It's weird that I can spend almost six years with someone and know so little about them.

I take Imogen's lead and focus on what's happening on the stage. Or, mostly, what Noah is doing. He makes the running look effortless, and the way he drops to the ground is a lot like Tara's move – like a goalkeeper in a soccer match – except Toby doesn't shout at him about it. I can imagine how Will would have interpreted this exercise. He would be doing some big, physical comedy routine on every fall. Running like he was in slow motion or stuck in a wind tunnel or something. In Year Eight drama class we had to do clowning and mime, and everyone was pretty terrible at it – except Will. He just had this way of making everything hilarious. I sort of wish he was here now.

Finally, Toby tells the group onstage to pause. They all look pretty pleased with themselves. As if this run-and-drop exercise was a competition they just beat us at. Noah runs his hand through his hair. I wonder if he is going to talk about us when Toby asks the question about a 'romantic encounter'.

But Toby doesn't ask that question. 'Turn to the audience and, from the depths of your souls, from your fingernails, your kneecaps, tells us of a time you were … enraged!'

Enraged? What? I can talk about that. I'm feeling that right now. Why don't they have to talk about something as personal as we did? I know Toby said I am a bad actor because I lack ... what was it ... a connection to my instincts? Well, right now, my instincts are telling me this is wrong. So wrong. And I'm saying something about it. But Imogen grabs my arm, just as I'm standing up, and shakes her head at me.

'What?' I whisper.

'It's his process, Edie, just let it go,' she pleads in my ear. 'Please.'

So I do. As much as I don't want to, I let it go.

*

Toby has a new humiliation for us after lunch.

He makes us walk across the stage, one by one, and he barks out all the things that are, supposedly, wrong with us. The thing is, what he's saying isn't true. He tells Makayla she has *disgusting posture*. That's not even close to the truth. Makayla has done gymnastics for years. She doesn't know how to slouch. I don't how she does it but, after his ridiculous 'note', she manages to straighten her spine even more and hold her head high and continue to glide across the stage. Toby tells her she is trying too hard, so she relaxes, and then he tells her she looks like a giraffe. She runs off the stage, crying.

It's Imogen's turn.

'Heavy! Too heavy!' he shouts from the auditorium. 'How much do you weigh?'

'None of your business, Toby,' Imogen says softly.

'If you want to make it in this business, you need to learn that it is everyone's business. You look OK now, but I doubt you're gonna keep that shape for long. I suggest you stop eating so much bread. OK. Next!'

Everyone looks at her sadly, as if Toby's given her twenty-four hours to live. They feel sorry for her. I hate that. I hate that words like *heavy* or *fat* or *overweight* are still thrown at us like insults. I hate that Toby thinks he can say something like that because he thinks it will hurt Imogen. Hurt us. I hate that it does hurt. I hate that I buy into this bullshit about my body and that I obsess over how I look and that now, no matter what happens, Imogen is going to freak out over eating bread. I hate that. I love bread. We should all love bread. Toby is a piece of shit. I notice the more masculine types in the group don't receive the same sort of notes as the others. It seems as if the more feminine-looking the body, the more it allows for judgement and criticism and insults. I hate that, too.

I'm nervous as hell as I step onstage. I get halfway and Toby still hasn't said anything. Maybe I'll be safe. Maybe he'll have nothing for me.

'Trailer trash!' he shouts.

'What?' I spin around to face him.

'No class, no sophistication, you don't command the space – the space commands you. Pathetic.' He says it very matter-of-factly.

Tears prickle at the edges of my vision. I blink hard. I will not cry in front of this man. And I will not cry over this. I take a deep breath, focus on filling my diaphragm the way I do before belting out a song. 'What does that mean?'

He stares me down. 'It means you don't belong here. OK. Next!'

I stand in the wings, feeling more alone, more out of place, than I have ever felt during my time at Arcadia.

Noah is the final person to cross the stage. Toby tells him to *stop looking so arrogant.* It's true. Noah can look like that. He has that good-looking-guy swagger going on. But it's hiding something more. I know it. You can't just judge people like that. You never know what's happening behind the masks we all wear.

When he reaches me at the other side, I throw my arms around him and whisper in his ear, 'You're not arrogant.'

He grins. 'And you're very commanding,' he whispers right back to me.

'All right! Everyone onstage, please, and sit down, sit down!' Darcy shouts from the seats.

We do what they say. Begrudgingly. No-one is feeling particularly good about themselves right now. Except maybe Darcy, who is letting their first stage manager gig, having been assistant stage manager for years, go to their head.

Toby Swan stands there, downstage, eyes closed, hands together like he's deep in prayer. I wonder what part of his 'process' we're going to be dragged through now. I look at Imogen for a clue – does she look terrified or eager? – but she is preoccupied with her fingernails. Probably to hide the fact that she feels as crap as the rest of us.

'Let's take a moment.' Toby speaks slowly, like he's delivering a sermon to his faithful followers. Like he's a cult leader and we're all being brainwashed. 'How did that activity make you feel?'

He pauses long enough for us to think he wants an answer. Cody goes to speak but Toby shushes him.

'Uncomfortable? Anyone feel uncomfortable?'

That's one word for it, I suppose. We nod in solemn agreement.

'Good!' he shouts excitedly. 'I wanted you to feel discomfort. Acting is all about getting out of those comfort zones, people. You understand?'

We nod again. There's a shift, though. Some people are starting to smile now, like they've just been let in on the joke. I still don't get it.

'What I told you wasn't true. What I told you are the lies you tell *yourself*, you see? I pinpointed the stuff you're most scared of. Your deepest, darkest fears. I brought them all out into the light, and you faced them. There's nothing to be afraid of now. I have cleared the path so you can be better actors. You're welcome.'

Someone starts a round of applause, and soon everyone is clapping for Toby. I hear Makayla laugh and say, 'He is amazing!' Imogen looks slightly impressed and relieved, like this somehow undoes all those awful things Toby has done and said today.

'See? Genius. I told you,' Noah says, but I can't see what he sees.

I feel like I'm losing my mind. Perhaps I have landed in a cult after all.

NINETEEN

I try listening to music on the long bus-train-bus ride home. Try to get my mind off the fact I'm not getting this part. Not getting this chance. This big opportunity. It's over before it even really started. No way will Toby cast me as Juliet.

I can't find the right kind of playlist. The right album. It's all too sad or too happy or too angry or too repetitive or stuff I've heard way too much or stuff I don't know and can't be bothered getting to know right now. I leave my headphones on even though there's nothing playing through them. They're there to stop any random strangers feeling like it's OK to start talking to me. The only person I want to talk to is Aubrey. But I've already tried calling her and it went straight to voicemail after one ring, which means she saw my call and chose not to speak to me. I sent her a text, too, which I shouldn't have done because it's just so desperate. I watched the three dots as she wrote a response, but then they disappeared, and the response never arrived. I don't think we're fighting – I can't remember an argument or anything bad happening between us – but it feels like we are. I wish I knew what I'd done wrong so I could fix it.

My phone rings through my headphones and I answer, without looking at the screen, 'Aubrey!'

'Excuse me?' a perfectly modulated voice says. I have to look at the screen to prove who it is because I cannot believe who is calling.

'Imogen?'

'Have I got you at an inconvenient moment?'

I tell her she has not and ask her what's wrong, because there must be something very, *very* wrong for Imogen to be calling me. There's silence on the other end and for a moment I think she must have hung up, but then I hear her sigh.

'I found the workshop quite destabilising and wondered if you might be available for a quick debrief?' she says.

'Of course.' I still can't quite believe this is happening. That Imogen is not only calling me, but wanting to confide in me.

'I think Toby Swan is behaving like a complete buffoon. A misogynist, narcissistic buffoon.'

'Buffoon?' I smile.

'Don't tease me, Edie, I've had an awful day.'

And she spends the next ten minutes outlining exactly how this day has been particularly awful for her. Because, after all, it is Imogen I am speaking to. And it is always all about Imogen.

'And then,' she's saying, 'I'm the only one, the *only* one, who actually does the exercise properly and speaks with truth and vulnerability about a romantic encounter.'

178

'Are you OK?' I whisper into the phone. 'I mean, everyone knows …'

'I don't care about their gossip. I care that no-one else did the exercise the way it was supposed to be done.'

'What?'

'Explain this to me, Edie, why does everyone have to get so excited and gossipy when a girl has sex? A boy gets to wear it like a badge of honour. But girls? It has to be this big deal. We still get whispered about, gossiped about, labelled sluts and shamed for something that is natural and normal. It doesn't have to be such a big deal.'

'It's a big deal to me.'

'And that's fine. You can make it a big deal. I mean, you're Edie. You make everything a big deal.'

'What does that mean?'

'You're a perfectionist. You like to have everything planned and prepared. It's like that with your performances, too. You're never quite … in the moment. Spontaneous. You understand?'

'Oh,' I say, feeling myself turn red.

'Have to run. Thanks for the chat!' And just like that, she's gone.

I stare out the window – keeping my headphones on, but listening to nothing other than my own thoughts. I wonder if I should quit. I've never done that before. It would be spontaneous of me, wouldn't it? Or am I even planning that out? Like Imogen said – there's nothing exciting or unexpected about anything I do. I learn my lines, I know my moves, I hit my mark every single time. Perhaps that's why Toby Swan despises me. I am just too boring for his avant-garde show. Maybe I'm too boring to be an actor at all.

The bus stops and the driver hops out to help a woman with a pram. The toddler in the pram is super cute. Smiling and giggling at the driver. The woman wheels the pram into the empty space at the front of the bus. She takes the toddler out of the pram and holds her on her lap, but so that they are facing each other. I watch as the toddler's chubby little hands reach out to touch the woman's face. I listen as the woman sings softly to the child.

It reminds me of my mum. She was always teaching me songs. Singing with me. To me. She was always so proud when she watched me sing. When she saw me onstage. I so wanted her to see me, just once, on the Arcadia stage. I know how much it would have meant to her to see me play Juliet. How much it would have meant to me.

*

Here's what happened with Mum. The thing I can never tell my friends. The reason they all think she's a struggling actor trying to make her way in LA via NYC. The truth.

The issues started long before I arrived, but I didn't know that then. Back then it was just me and Mum against the world. She was funny and had a very loud laugh and gave these massive, tight hugs that took all the wind out of you. She hated crying and never let either of us do it. It wasn't allowed, she said. If I fell over or something and started to cry, she'd use this really silly voice and say, *Suck it up, bucko*, which would usually make me laugh.

Sometimes our house was very, very quiet. I hated those days. When Mum stayed in bed and wouldn't get up even when I begged her. *Suck it up, bucko*. In those moments she

180

wouldn't use such a funny voice, but I always knew I wasn't to cry. I had to get on with it. Even if I was hungry or didn't have a clean uniform for school.

Mum hated the dark and always had all the lights turned on, even in the daytime. At night she'd light lots of candles and turn on the fairy lights. She put them up for Christmas one year and never took them down. I loved it. Which is why it was so strange to get home from school one day and find the house so dark.

And, look, I'm probably remembering what happened all wrong but, in my defence, I was only young – I wasn't even six years old yet – so things can get a little mixed up. In my memory it was winter and one of those rainy days when it's so dark it feels like the middle of the night but it's really only three o'clock or something. I had walked home from school with our neighbours like I did almost every day. We'd gotten pretty wet because we'd jumped in puddles, and I remember feeling uneasy about Mum seeing me like that. I never knew what Mum I was coming home to. I hoped for the one who found everything funny and would laugh and perhaps run outside with me to jump in more puddles. But I could have got the one who smacked me and yelled at me for being selfish.

I had to let myself in with my own key, which was weird because Mum usually stood at the door waiting for me. I shouted, *MUM,* but there was no answer. And I was relieved. I took off my shoes because they were really, really wet, all the way through to my socks, and I dripped across the hallway to the kitchen. Mum wasn't there. And I felt even better. Which I feel horrible about now, but at the time not getting into trouble was my number one priority. I called her name a few times, just to make sure, but the house was so quiet and still, as if no-one had been in there for a long, long time.

I poured myself an extra-big glass of orange juice because Mum wasn't there to ration it out the way she normally did. I remember overfilling the glass and the juice splashing onto the bench and me freaking out about leaving a mess because Mum was a neat-freak and hated sticky counter-tops or dirty floors or untidiness. Or she used to. Things were changing in the house.

About a month before, Louisa – who lived next door and, because of that, was my best friend – told me our house smelled funny. I was so upset. When I told Mum she made me help her clean the whole house even though it was late and I had school the next day. I did it without complaining because I liked the house better when it was clean, too. And from then on, I always tried to make it nice so Mum would be happy. Most of the things I did back then were to make Mum happy.

I remember I carried that glass of juice into the lounge room so carefully and drank it in front of the TV. I can't remember what I watched. I don't know why I can't remember that, but for some reason I can remember the orange juice. The taste of it, the smell of it, the care I took not to spill any of it on the rug. I can't drink orange juice anymore. Just the smell of it makes me gag.

I was probably only home for twenty minutes or so, but at the time it felt so much longer. I had that uneasy feeling I used to get when I was younger. Like something bad was about to happen. It could turn from good to bad, or bad to good, very quickly in our house.

I don't know what made me go to Mum's bedroom. The door was closed and I was scared to open it because she didn't like me going in there on my own; I'd done it once and she'd called me a *snoop* and I was so upset I never went in there without her permission again. But this time, something made me open the door. Even though it was dark, I could see her. Mum. Sort of half-sitting, half-lying on her bed. I knocked on the door the way she liked me to and said, *May I come in,* but my voice barely came out. I turned on the light, because the dark was scaring me, but she didn't move. It was as if she didn't realise the light had been turned on. Like she didn't even know I was there. I moved closer to her. She was dressed exactly as she was when I'd left for school that morning, still in her jeans and bright white sneakers and the pink sweater that reminded me of fairy-floss. Her eyes were half-closed, half-open, and she kept rolling her head forwards and backwards like she was sitting on a boat in the middle of the ocean. Then suddenly she opened her eyes real wide and said, *Hello honey,* in this voice that didn't sound like her. And then she closed her eyes again.

I shook her, but she didn't even feel it. I said, *MUM?* And she didn't answer. It looked like her head was too heavy for her body and she was trying so hard to keep it up. It made the orange juice curdle in my stomach. *MUM?* I said again, louder that time, and she smiled and said, *Good girl,* but I don't know why she said that or what it meant. I tried to get on the bed with her but she started swatting me with her hands. Not hard. Gentle swats, like I was bit of smoke she needed to get out of her face. And then she said she was *too hot, too hot,* and so I went to the kitchen to get her some water but I dropped the glass and it shattered all over the tiles. That's when I started to cry, really cry.

When I went back to Mum's room she had this funny smile on her face and tiny eyes and she was saying something but her voice was all mumbly and I couldn't understand her. She tried to drink the glass of water. She held the glass loosely and took a sip but then seemed to forget she was holding anything at all and almost tipped it all over herself. I took the glass and held it to her lips so she could take a sip. She pushed it away and as she did her face turned back to normal. For a second. A moment. She looked at me, she really saw me, and she said, *Call your Nan. Sorry. Sorry.* Then her eyes started closing again.

I called Nan from Mum's mobile. When she answered she said, *What's wrong?* in a very angry voice, but when she heard it was me her voice went all soft and wavering and she kept saying, *Oh god, oh god,* and that she would be there soon. *Just hold on*, she said, *hold on*. As if I had any other choice. Now that I'm older I realise Nan was telling Mum to hold on, not me.

I curled up next to Mum on her bed. I'd taken her shoes off because I knew she would hate that shoes had been on the bed. It seemed to matter at the time. I put my head on her lap and wrapped one leg around her leg. She used to call me her baby koala when I did that. This time, she said nothing. Just murmured words I didn't understand. She was hot and sweaty, but I didn't care. I clung on to her. Because I loved her.

I must have fallen asleep because the next thing I remember was Pops picking me up from the bed. He was strong then. He was my BFG. Scooping me up and carrying me away from the mess and confusion of that place.

Mum had to stay at the hospital for what felt like forever. I stayed with Nan and Pops. Finally, Mum moved in, too, but she wasn't herself. She stayed in her room and rarely came out, not even for dinner, and she was always asleep when I tried to sneak in there to speak with her. Which I did a lot. Mostly because I wanted to tell her about the Christmas play we were doing at school. I thought she'd be happy to know I was being an actor like her, but she didn't say anything about it. Still, I practised and practised my part because I knew I had to be perfect for Mum. I was Merry the Elf who'd lost her Christmas Spirit. Pops helped me learn my lines and Nan made me a costume and Mum started to smile, just a little, when I practised the dance in front of her.

And when the big night came, my whole family was there: Nan, Pops and Mum. All in the front row. I did everything the way I was supposed to. Every line, every step, every note. When we took our bows, Mum stood up and clapped and cheered. She got her voice back. I had my mum back.

That night, we had fish and chips for dinner, and Mum talked and talked and talked. She was so excited and happy. She said I had saved her. Saved her! Me? My performance had made her better. And because I was six, I believed her. I thought I'd cured her with my performance. Like magic. Somehow.

It worked for a while. She was better for almost four years. But we never moved back to that house; we stayed with Nan and Pops. It was crowded and sometimes Mum and Nan would snap at each other, but I still thought it was better that way. I never had to worry about what was waiting for me when I came home from school.

Mum went to auditions again and when she didn't get the part, she was calm about it and said, *Oh well, next time*. And she taught me how to sing and said, *Damn, I think you're better than me*, and would help me learn monologues from movies and promised to send me to real classes one day and get me an agent and head-shots and make me famous.

'You have a gift, Edie,' she said, 'you have to promise not to waste it like I did.'

I really believed that if I kept learning songs from her favourite Disney films with her and reciting lines from movies she loved, she would keep on getting better. Because my performances saved her. Didn't they?

I'm older now, of course, so I know that's not true. I know she got better because she went to doctors and therapists and because Nan and Pops supported her. But there's always something inside me, like a superstition, that doesn't want to jinx it. I almost lost her once and the thing that kept her going, the thing that brought my mum back, was that stupid Christmas performance. I never want to risk losing her again. Even if she chose to lose me. To walk away and leave me behind. I can't do that to her. She's my mum. It's not her fault she's unwell, that she has this disease that eats away at her, that she never had the chance to be all she could have been. And I think my mum could have been everything.

She was a triple threat.

TWENTY

We have somehow convinced Will's parents to let us use their house for rehearsals. We still don't know where we're going to put on the actual show but this, at least, is a start. Aubrey, Will and I came straight here from school. Everyone else is meeting here in an hour. And by 'everyone else' I mean the cast that Aubrey has pulled together. There's Lexie, of course, and Tara. (She didn't want to be in the school play. *I can't be Juliet if my cousin might be Romeo. Ew. No way,* she said. When I mentioned there were other roles – like the Nurse or Lady Capulet – she just said, *Ew, musical theatre is so much better than those boring old plays*). There's Yazi (who never auditions for the mainstage productions because, she says, *they're too mainstream*, but I wish she would because she's really good), Martha and Samrah (I think they're a package deal, serious dancers from Lexie's dance world), CJ (who should be getting a lot more roles than they do and is an amazing alto and great actor), Kellen (who can't sing or dance but is a good actor so that makes up for a lot) and Caleb (a bigger musical theatre nerd than me, which is saying something), me and Will. It's a small cast by Arcadia Grammar standards, but some of the best people have agreed to be a part of this. Which shows how much people love Will and his work.

Will heads upstairs to get his keyboard, leaving Aubrey and I alone for the first time in ages.

'I called you on Sunday. And sent you a message. You never responded.' I try to make it sound like it's nothing, no big deal, but I can hear my voice wavering a little.

'I've been busy,' she says.

'Doing what?'

'Look, Edie, no offence but I just don't have time to fix your problems right now. I'm directing this show, I've got exams to prepare for and stuff going on at home and I just don't have the time to be sorting out your shit anymore.'

I don't know what to say, so I say nothing at all. My eyes feel hot and there's a knot, tightening, in my throat. I tell myself, *Don't cry, don't cry,* and close my eyes to try to force the tears back to wherever they sprung from.

'It feels like I'm always the one helping you, encouraging you, and I'm just tired of it. You're so naïve, Edie. You have to grow up.'

Naïve? I hate it when she says that, and she says it a lot. Usually when I don't want to go to a club with her. *Why won't you come?* she'll say, and I'll say, *Because I'm underage and it's illegal,* and she'll say, *Ugh, stop being so naïve.* I don't even think she's using the word in the correct context but if

I say anything it will only annoy her more. The Aubrey now is not the Aubrey I met and became best friends with in Year Seven, bonding over our laminated and decorated timetables and that outsider feeling. The Aubrey back then would never have even considered buying a fake ID or going to a club. She was serious and sensible, and she was never annoyed or angry with me. Even when, at times, she probably should have been.

'I don't know why you auditioned for *Romeo and Juliet*. We promised Will we'd do this. Years ago. And I don't know about you, but I keep my promises,' she says.

'What does that mean?'

'If you're gonna break your promise to Will just hurry up and do it so we can move on.'

Aubrey has this big issue with liars. It's because of her dad. Everything with Aubrey is about her dad. He had affairs and she was the one who found out and it was a lot. I get it. But I am not her dad. I'm not cheating on anyone.

'A little help!' Will shouts from the top of the stairs, and Aubrey rushes off.

I want to walk out, right now, and go home, but I busy myself with setting up the chairs instead. I can't let Will down. I won't do that. Despite what Aubrey seems to think of me.

*

The difference between Aubrey's rehearsal and Toby Swan's 'workshop' is huge. In this rehearsal, people laugh and look happy and relaxed and not one insult has been thrown at anybody. Even though Aubrey lost it at me earlier, she is a calm and kind voice throughout our first rehearsal. Gently asking people to try reading a line in a different way. Experimenting with different ways of interpreting lyrics in the songs. *When you sing 'I'm in love' maybe it could be more of a question, like you're not too sure, what do you think?* She suggested in this very sweet ballad Will wrote, and it brought a whole new element to the song.

Will is pretty tough on himself, which is to be expected, I suppose. He's been using a red pen all over his script while we read – crossing out whole chunks of dialogue, underlining words aggressively and then drawing a line through entire scenes. I don't know if he noticed how often people laughed in the right places. Or the nice things they said at the end of the rehearsal. He seemed to be in some parallel universe where his musical was the worst thing ever written and he has zero talent.

'It's really great,' I tell him once everyone else has left. Aubrey left with Lexie and never said a word to me outside of her direction. I don't know if anyone else noticed how weird it was between us. Will obviously didn't.

'I just want to make it worth everyone's while, you know? I don't want to waste your time –'

'You're not!'

'I know the Toby Swan thing is a big opportunity for you and this is just … kinda dumb.'

'It isn't dumb. I love it.'

'OK,' he smiles, finally. 'Good.'

'And, look, I don't even think I'm gonna get the part. So you don't need to worry. I'm all yours,' I laugh.

TWENTY-ONE

The cast list for *Romeo and Juliet* has gone up. It's not the way any of us were expecting to hear the news. I'd assumed Toby would turn it into some mind-game disguised as an acting exercise. Like he'd make someone cry and then shoot a confetti gun and scream *YOU GOT THE ROLE* but then make them run a couple of laps of the theatre before they could formally accept, because that would make them a better actor or something. Instead, there is just a piece of paper stuck to the Drama studio door. The way Mrs B usually does it. I wonder if she's had something to do with this.

I hear the news before I see it. I get a couple of texts. Makayla shouts it out to me across the hallway. Cody gives me a high five. But I need to see it to know it really is true.

When I get there, no-one is around. It's not like those movies where the school gathers around the casting notice, pushing and shoving and screaming over who got what. I'm not going to lie – it can be like that. Especially when we're doing a huge musical. Perhaps us musical theatre kids are just more dramatic that way. 'Real' actors are too dignified to squeal over a cast list. Anyway. It's a bit of an anti-climax, really, after everything, for it to come to this. Me standing in front of a piece of paper sticky-taped to a door. Wow.

If this were a musical, the cast list would be in a spotlight and my character would be edging ever closer to it as she sang about her destiny. But this is definitely not a musical theatre moment. There is no spotlight, no singing, and whoever typed up this cast list didn't even bother to format it correctly.

I read the list. And there it is. My name. Next to Juliet's.

I'm shaking. I don't know why. I should be excited and happy – happy? Thrilled. I should be thrilled. This is what I wanted. Wasn't it?

I read the rest of the list. Noah is Romeo. Noah. Is. Romeo. He did it. I mean, there was never any doubt, but still, he turned up and did the work and now his name is there. Next to mine. I imagine how excited his mum will be for him. How excited Noah will be. Because we'll be doing this together. Romeo and Juliet. Noah and Edie. It will be fun – and much easier to do all those romantic scenes with someone I'm actually into, and who is into me. Not just some dumb show crush, but a real one.

I read the rest of the list. Imogen is Lady Capulet, which doesn't sit right with me at all. Makayla is the Nurse even though she begged for the chance to try out for Mercutio and would have been incredible in that role. Not that she won't kill it as the Nurse. I know she will. Mei is playing

Lady Montague, which is such a small role; she deserves more, but what else is there? There are only four speaking roles for women in the entire play, which means heaps of people who auditioned for a female role are now listed at the bottom of the page as an 'extra'. What a waste. They could have played any of those male roles. So much for Toby messing shit up. His casting is just as traditional as every other Arcadia show. This is not a groundbreaking cast list at all. Cody is Benvolio and Dom is Mercutio, which will make Noah happy. There is nothing unexpected about anything on this list.

I take a photo of it on my phone and send it to Mum. I wait for her emoji-filled response, but there isn't one, which makes sense – it's the middle of the day. She's probably at work. I assume she works. I don't really know. I send the same message to Nan and Pops. They won't see it either. I know for a fact what they'll be doing. Nan will be working, Pops will be asleep. I send the photo to Noah, too. I hesitate over adding it to the group text; Aubrey hardly ever responds to anything on there anymore. I send it anyway. I want her and Will to know the news. If anything, it may affect some of our rehearsals for the musical. My phone buzzes almost right away. I expect it to be Noah sending me some stupid gif – I always end up over-analysing them, then spending a long time trying to find the perfect response gif, which I never seem to be able to do. Why can't he just text like a normal person? But it isn't Noah. It's Will.

I KNEW IT! ABSOLUTE SUPERSTAR!

He always knows the right thing to say. I feel myself smiling.

'Looks like I will be playing your mother.' Imogen appears beside me. 'There is a sophistication and underlying sadness to Lady Capulet. She is a much more nuanced role. Very challenging. I can see why he cast me. You will be a very ... *sweet* Juliet.'

'Thank you, Imogen,' I say, even though I know she did not mean any of that as a compliment. She never does.

I watch as she makes a show of carefully examining the cast list and copying it down into a notebook.

'I took a photo of it, I can send it to you,' I offer.

'This is part of my process, Edie. I don't expect you to understand,' she smiles.

I want to like Imogen. I really do. I have tried. It's the whole reason I agreed to her stupid deal in the first place. And lately I thought we were getting somewhere. She called me completely unexpectedly. She seemed to share my dislike for Toby. What's going on with her?

'I'm sorry,' I say. She looks at me, confused. 'I know I broke the deal, and this part, Juliet, it should have been yours, and –'

'I don't care about a stupid high school play. You need this far more than I do, Edie.' She snaps her notebook shut and takes off down the hall.

*

Everyone in the cafe starts clapping when Noah and I enter, hand in hand, at lunchtime. It's ridiculous, but also kind of nice. I think Noah is actually blushing. Dom stands on the table and declares Noah the next Leonardo DiCaprio and

194

Phoebe says, *Watch out, Hollywood*. And I can see that it means a lot to Noah right now.

Will is sitting on the other side of the cafe, his head in the pages of his script. As usual. I should go over to him, check in and make sure he isn't making himself crazy with unnecessary edits, encourage him to leave the script be for a little while and just let us try it out. My heart twists to see him sitting there, all by himself. I wonder if Aubrey feels like that when she looks over from where she sits with Lexie and the dancers. Does she feel bad? Does she miss those days when it was three of us hanging out all the time?

I sit down next to him.

'Hey, Juliet,' he says.

'I am also Lily,' I say. 'This doesn't change that.'

'You know why I called her Lily, right?' he says.

'It's my nan's name?' I already told her that Will named the character after her, so she better not find out otherwise. She was super chuffed.

'It's your middle name.'

'Oh, yeah, but I thought –'

'I wrote the musical for you, you know.'

'You what?'

Noah calls me from the other side of the room. 'We're going off campus. Come with us!'

I look at Noah. I look at Will.

'Go,' Will says. 'You should celebrate. It's a big deal.'

'You know I'm going to do both shows. I can do both. Your show is just as important.'

'I know,' he smiles.

This is going to be fine. Better than fine. It can work. Easy. The musical will mainly be lunchtime rehearsals and maybe a couple of after-school sessions. And the play will take up my weekends. Too easy. I can manage. Especially if it means I can help my best friend with his musical *and* be the lead in my final Arcadia show alongside my boyfriend. My *boyfriend*. Doing this show with him is going to open up a heap of opportunities for me. It will be so worth it.

TWENTY-TWO

I want this first *Romeo and Juliet* rehearsal to go perfectly. And not because, as Aubrey used to tell me all the time, I'm a perfectionist. I'm not. Not really. I just like to be prepared. Ready for anything. Especially in rehearsal. Especially for Toby Swan. The more prepared I am, the more confident I can feel for whatever that man might throw at me. So I have already learned most of my lines; it will make things easier not just for me, but for everyone. I also feel like I need to prove I am the right person for this part. That I deserve to be here. I imagine everyone thinking, *She was so perfect in rehearsal! She knew all her lines! She commanded the stage! She belongs here! No wonder she got the part!* I want them to forget what Toby said in our final workshop. I need to forget it, too.

Toby, however, is not impressed with me.

'I'm going to have to undo all the preparation you've done,' he cries.

'I thought it would be easier, without the script, you know, getting in the way? I thought –'

'Overpreparing is as bad as underpreparing. Everyone!' He claps three times to get the whole cast's attention. 'Write that down!'

Toby makes us write a lot of things down. In this first rehearsal he has already made us write down gems like *great acting is not acting* and *act from your soul, not your brain* and *don't think, DO* and *PROJECTION IS KEY* and *stop moving your eyebrows.* A lot of what he says contradicts stuff Mrs B has taught us. And a lot of what he says contradicts his own advice. It's very confusing. But no-one argues. We've all learned it's better not to. Instead, we quietly copy his meaningless mantras into our notebooks and scripts.

Toby does not believe in working in a linear way. That means, we haven't started at Act 1 Scene 1 but are beginning with what he calls the more challenging scenes. It's not a bad idea. I sort of like diving into the more difficult stuff early on. It feels strange to agree with Toby's process for once. Maybe I was too quick to judge him.

Noah is nervous. I can tell because he is being stupid with Dom and Cody and behaving a bit more like that guy I met in Tara's swimming pool than the guy I now call my boyfriend. Or try to. The word never sounds right coming from me.

'You OK?' I drag him away from the boys.

'Relax. I'm just warming up … it's my process, Edie.'

'You do not have a process.'

'Maybe I'm working on one. The Noah Winters method,' he grins. 'It's all about calming down, going with the flow, just letting it happen ...'

It's so easy for Noah. He hasn't prepared because he doesn't feel like he needs to prove himself to anyone. At all. He knows he belongs here. He thinks he deserves this. No-one would ever tell him otherwise.

We are doing Act 3 Scene 5. This is a massive scene for Juliet. An emotional rollercoaster. I need to take her on a journey from the joy of being madly in love with Romeo, to dread and doom when her parents tell her she will be marrying Paris, to the feeling of utter betrayal when the Nurse tells her to forget Romeo, to the strength and conviction of dying for her one true love if Friar Lawrence can't offer her a solution. It is a lot. When Toby said we would start with the most challenging scenes, he wasn't kidding.

The problems start from the very beginning.

This scene is set in Juliet's bedroom. In Juliet's bed. Me and Noah. In bed. Together. We lay there, awkwardly, side by side, pretending to be asleep – but I am very aware of his body next to mine. To make it more natural (remember, *great acting is not acting*), Toby has asked Noah to take off his shirt. Noah has no problem with that because Noah is one of those people who works out and so likes to show off the results.

'And you, please, Edie,' Toby says.

I sit bolt upright. No, no, no. This is not ... I look at Noah for help. He grins, then notices my I'm-freaking-out-here

199

face and tries to look more serious. 'Yeah, Toby, I dunno. Maybe we can work up to that?' he says.

'She can keep her bra on,' Toby says dismissively. 'I told you all from the get-go this is going to be a dark, dirty, contemporary production. I mess shit up. If you can't deal with it, then go.'

'Aw, come on, Toby –'

'Has your girlfriend lost her voice or something?'

We learned about the flight or fight or freeze response years ago, in Biology. I feel like I am going through every single one of those responses right now, sitting on this pretend bed with my real, half-naked boyfriend. 'No, he was just – I'm just ...' I feel like everyone is watching me to see how this is going to play out. I take a moment to find the words I need. 'I will not be doing that.'

'You what?'

'I will wear a singlet or something like that, but I'm not –'

'Good actors say yes,' Toby speaks over me. 'Everyone, please write that down.'

Noah shrugs like, *Oh well, I tried, what you gonna do?* 'Pretend you're wearing a bikini or something,' he whispers. 'You're hot, so don't stress.'

He has so completely missed the point, it isn't even funny. I get up. Move downstage so I can see Toby properly. He is sitting at this little desk Darcy has set up for him in the middle of the auditorium. A blue lamp lights up his script. Coffee cups litter the table. He sits back in his chair, folds his arms. 'Toby' – I try to sound as polite and reasonable as possible – 'I respect your process and your choices, but –'

200

'Right,' he interrupts, 'move on. We can discuss costumes later. Let's get on with it.'

I go back to my starting position. Noah gives me a little thumbs up, as if I've just won something. But I feel like the fight is on hold, not yet won.

As Juliet, I am desperate to keep Romeo with me, to hold onto him and this moment as long as I can. I want him to stay but I also know he has to go. Toby tells me to pull him closer, tempt him back into the bed, into my arms. I try, but Noah seems cold and distant. I try again, this time taking Toby's note to kiss him. I move close but don't realise Noah is also moving close, and we bang our foreheads together. I hear someone laugh in the wings. Toby screams *QUIET* and tells us to start again, from the top. I do. I try to think of the way Juliet would be thinking right now – absolutely out-of-her-mind in love with Romeo and just wanting him to be as close to her as possible. I pull him back to the bed but he loses his footing and falls right on top of me, but Toby shouts *KEEP GOING* so I think it must be OK. I move in for the kiss and we smash our teeth together and Noah recoils, holding his mouth, and for a moment I think he might be bleeding. The whole theatre bursts into laughter. Noah is laughing, too. Toby is having a full-on meltdown and demanding *SILENCE! SILENCE!* I lie on the bed and wait for everyone to calm down, as I slowly, painfully die inside.

'I knew this was an issue,' he says. 'Didn't I tell you? In that first workshop? No chemistry. You two have no chemistry!'

He keeps saying it as if that's somehow going to fix it. I don't move. I lie on the bed and stare up at the lighting grid and wish one of those heavy lights would drop, bang, right on top of me. Right now.

Toby gets up on the stage and kneels next to me. Looks at me with concern. 'I need this scene to be hot. Do you think you can manage that?'

I sit up again. 'I suppose I just see it a little differently – like there's a real fear, isn't there? A fear that she's going to lose him forever –'

'IMOGEN!' He stands. 'I need Imogen to show Edie what I mean.'

'No, you don't need to do that, I get it, I can do it.' I am panicking. The last thing I need is an acting class from Imogen.

Toby ignores my pleas and ushers me into the auditorium, where I am told to sit, front row and centre. He huddles with Noah and Imogen in the wings. There is a lot of whispering and nodding before the two actors take their positions. Imogen in my place. Noah in his. They both have their scripts in hand, but it doesn't matter. They work well together, the intensity of the scene and the moment building between them. Imogen kisses Noah. No. Juliet kisses Romeo. They don't hit heads or teeth. Romeo decides he will stay after all; who cares if he is found and killed. And after that kiss, I believe him. I believe he'd put it all on the line for one more second with Juliet. But Juliet won't let him, and now Imogen moves effortlessly from sensual and playful to this sense of growing fear and sadness as she makes Romeo leave. She is good. They are good. Together.

'Right,' Toby shouts. 'Edie. Get up there. And do it just like that.'

I avoid Imogen's eyes as we swap places.

*

We take a break at lunchtime. Toby disappears and everyone relaxes.

'You wanna get out of here?' Noah whispers to me, so close that it feels like I might burst into flames at any moment.

'We have rehearsal …'

'So?' He kisses me. Just like that. In front of everyone. I can feel them watching us.

'We have to stay, Noah,' I say, pushing him away.

'Nah, I'm gonna go. Last chance to come with me …' He waves his car keys in front of my face.

'Are you serious? First of all, you don't have my back in there. At all. And now you just want to leave? That's shitty, Noah. Really shitty.'

'I spoke to Toby and told him to lay off you a bit. OK? So I *do* have your back,' he snaps.

'Well, stay then. If you have my back, you'll stay at rehearsal.'

He jingles his car keys again.

I'd like to get out of here. I can't deal with Toby Swan and his 'process'. Can't deal with Imogen showing me what to do. But I can't just leave. I've made a commitment. Not only to the show, but to Nan. She's covering my shifts at the supermarket so I can go to these rehearsals, not so I can hang out with Noah.

'Please, let's get out of here,' he says again, more insistent this time.

'I can't,' I say, 'it isn't right. If everyone else is here until five then you should be here til five.'

His jaw flexes a little. I can see he is thinking, weighing up how big a douche he will look like for leaving against spending another three hours in the theatre.

Darcy shouts that it's time to head back in; break is over. I don't want to go back in. I really don't. This is the worst rehearsal of my life. But I do go. Reluctantly. I think, *Noah will follow me in*. He'll take his time, wait a moment so he gets the full effect, and then burst through the doors like, *Surprise! I'm a good guy. Of course I'm doing the right thing! How could you ever doubt me?* But he doesn't. I turn to find him, but he's gone.

TWENTY-THREE

I'm probably avoiding Noah, or maybe he's avoiding me. It might be a little of both. Either way, it's kind of immature. I should just talk to him about it: the way he walked out of rehearsal, the way it made me feel. But I don't know how. Or, rather, I do know how but I'm scared. Scared he's going to reject me. Break up with me. I know how that sounds. Pathetic. Sad. Weak. I hate thinking like that. And I hate how this is making me feel. I've started writing bad, tragic love songs. I even got out my old ukulele and went full Taylor Swift in my bedroom. That is never, ever a good sign. Only Taylor can Taylor.

Our next rehearsal will be this Sunday, so I'll speak to him then at least. I don't know whether I'll be speaking to him as Edie to Noah or as Juliet to Romeo, though. I also don't know if he'll actually show up for it. I think about it while working at the checkout. I'm covering a Thursday night shift because someone called in sick, and even though I have a heap of homework I should be doing, I felt I couldn't turn it down. Since Nan is looking after all my Sundays, I need to take on any shifts I can to help with the bills.

Luckily, it's not too busy, so I pull out a long piece of blank docket paper and start writing another verse for my awful wannabe Taylor song. I should stop. It's a terrible song. I've even rhymed 'Romeo' with 'don't you know'. Yikes.

'Do you take cash?' A familiar voice interrupts my poetry. My heart stops. No, no, no, it can't be. I don't want to look up. I don't want this to be happening. 'Hello? Edie?'

I look up from my scribble. It is him. Noah. Here. Standing at my checkout. Seeing me under these fluorescent lights, in this maroon polo shirt, working in this crappy store in this shitty suburb. I think I'm going to throw up, or faint, or both.

'What are you doing here?' I manage to say as I screw up the docket and shove it into my pocket.

Marshall is staring at me from the service counter. Watching. Waiting to tell me off.

'I wanted to see you,' he says. 'And get this gum.'

'I have a break in ten minutes. Meet me in the carpark, OK?' I scan the gum and take the money and hand him his receipt and change in silence. This. Is. Not. Happening.

*

In fifteen minutes, because Marshall wouldn't let me out on time, I'm in the carpark. The carpark. I see it through Noah's eyes, in all its asphalt awfulness. The broken, abandoned trolleys, the flickering streetlights, the graffiti and tagging, the rundown cars. Noah is leaning against his car. He waves when he sees me and my stomach flip-flops at the sight of him.

'Did you wanna go for a drive or something?' he asks.

I shake my head. I don't have time. And I also want him to see as little of this place as he possibly can. 'We can sit in your car, though? It'll be more comfortable than out here,' I say. I want to hide him from all of this.

We sit in silence for a moment. I can hear the frogs in the creek that runs just behind the carpark, sirens in the distance, my heart thumping loudly in my ears. I'm not going to speak first. He is the one who turned up, unannounced and uninvited. He can talk. Not me.

'I owe you an explanation. It's not an excuse, but it's why I sometimes ... I sometimes act super confident,' he says. 'It's a cover. I'm faking it. You know what I mean?'

I do know. I know it very, very well, but I don't say anything. I just nod.

'I'm not used to all the school stuff. The noise, the crowds, all those people in your face all day, and the rules. There's so many rules, right? And I'm trying, Edie, I am, but sometimes it just gets ... it gets a lot. And I hate telling you this, but ...' his voices trails off and he looks me, his eyes all watery. He blinks hard a few times.

'You don't have to tell me any of this,' I say.

'No, no, I want to.' He takes a breath. 'I couldn't go to school because I was nervous about leaving Mum. I know how that sounds, but she was sick. Breast cancer. I was in primary school and I thought, like I honestly believed, that if I left her side she would die. So, when Dad found this incredible doctor in Washington, I couldn't not go there with them. I had to be there. With her. Just in case. You know?'

I think about my mum and how I would have followed her anywhere if I'd had the chance. I get it.

'So, I went with them to the States for her treatment. And Mum – she liked having me around too, I think, and we sort of got used to it. She said life is too short to be apart. I travelled with them everywhere, and that meant I never did the school thing. Dad hired tutors so I could keep up with my schoolwork, but I knew he was upset I didn't go to the boarding school he went to. It was where all the men from his family went. All the way back to, like, my great, great grandfather or something. But there's no way Mum could have dealt with that. Or me, to be honest.

'Then we moved back here, and it hit me. I had no friends. Like, zero. But I was so nervous, I had no idea how to … And so I started small. Like playing sport – not water polo …'

'Sorry.'

'Don't be. It's funny.' There's a tinge of sadness in his smile, though. 'And then this doctor suggested that I try acting classes, just to help with my confidence and stuff. Weird, right? I mean, you think it wouldn't make it worse, but it really helped. And I loved it and so when I mentioned I might like to try the acting thing for real, Dad got excited. He always wanted me to experience high school – he really thought I was missing out on something. And Arcadia Grammar has this reputation. And Tara goes there, so it seemed like a no-brainer. Mum sorted it all out. That's why I'm there. Or trying to be there. The last couple of days have been a bit … difficult. It's a bit overwhelming, with all these new people and then Toby's workshops, and rehearsals are – they're just a lot more full-on than I expected, and … yeah … I'm just not used to it. The whole school thing, I suppose.'

He pauses, and I think I should say something; maybe apologise for any part I had in making it difficult. I feel bad. Maybe if I'd known all this, I wouldn't have been so hard on him about leaving the rehearsal, and if I hadn't been so hard on him about the rehearsal then maybe he would be in a better headspace right now.

'Yeah, so,' he continues, 'I'm trying to apologise to you. I shouldn't have left rehearsal. Or you. It was a shitty move.'

I want to say *you're forgiven* or *it's OK* or something like that, but I still feel so hurt. 'And then you ignored me all week. All week, Noah!'

'I thought you were ignoring me!' He turns to face me. 'I'm so sorry, Edie. That's no way to treat my girlfriend. I'm sorry.'

And he looks and sounds so sad and so sorry that I lean across the handbrake and kiss him and he kisses me back, and I feel that fizz like a sparkler lighting up inside of me.

I pull back. 'Hang on. How did you know where I work?'

'Aubrey told me.'

I try not to think about how she could do that to me, so I can concentrate on making up with my boyfriend. I only have five minutes left on this break, and I don't want to waste a second.

*

I call Aubrey when I get home. She ignores my call. I text her and tell her not to ignore my call. She texts back that she is busy. I text back that I don't care, and call her again. This time, she answers.

'What the hell, Aubrey?'

'What?'

'You told Noah where I worked and he turned up and now he's seen me in that shirt, in that place, and I don't know what you were thinking.'

'I was thinking that if he's your boyfriend, he won't care. And if you're his girlfriend, you'd want him to know the real you, right?'

I hate it when Aubrey has a point. I hate it when she's right. And I hate that I haven't been able to speak to her about any of this. I always talk with Aubrey about this stuff. My stuff. And she's always been able to talk to me about her stuff. Or she used to.

I sigh. 'Sorry.'

'Yeah, me too,' she says. 'I should have at least warned you. I know you hate surprises.'

'No, I don't hate them – it was just that one time.'

She starts laughing then, and so do I, at the memory of my doomed Year Eight surprise party. She'd tried so hard and it just went so incredibly wrong.

She clears her throat. 'So, it's almost my birthday soon …'

'I know, I know,' I say. As if I'd ever forget.

'I was thinking about going to karaoke, in the city. What do you think? Karaoke? Would you come?'

'You want me to come?'

'Of course,' she says.

I feel so relieved I could cry.

'And you'll come clubbing, too. After?'

I want to say no. I have a list of excuses ready for this. Pops. Work. No money. A strict curfew. Those are my standard responses when this comes up. I hesitate for a moment, trying to figure out which one will be the least annoying to Aubrey right now. But I can't ruin this, this moment, this little opening she has given me back to what we used to have. Her friendship means too much to me. So I say, 'You'll have to get me an ID.'

And then, just like that, we start talking. And talking. And talking. And I can't remember why or how we ever stopped.

TWENTY-FOUR

Lexie has managed to book one of the dance studios for an after-school rehearsal, on the premise that she's working on a choreography task with Martha and Samrah. Which isn't completely untrue. She just chose to leave out some other important details. But the dance department don't need to know that. And Old Man Healy definitely doesn't need to know. He was very clear that no Arcadia resources were to be used in the making of this 'unsanctioned' production.

I ask Noah if he wants to come along to see what we're doing, because I'm proud of it. I just wish we could have a stage and a set and a full orchestra, although even without all that stuff I think people will fall in love with Will's show. It's funny and sweet. There's this whole moment where one of the characters dreams about living on their *Animal Crossing* island because life would be so much better there, fishing and building wooden cabins and shaking trees for gold coins. I try to explain this moment to Noah, and sing a couple of bars of the song Will wrote for it. Noah stares at me blankly.

'I hate musicals,' he says.

'That's not true,' I say.

'I hate this one.'

He doesn't come to the rehearsal. Says he should focus on preparing for our next rehearsal, which I know he won't do. I don't think he's even read *Romeo and Juliet* all the way through.

*

It feels good to be dancing again. I'm not the best, I know that. I never will be. Lexie has been dancing since she was two or something, so it's not like I could ever catch up to her. Plus, I think it's one of those things you've either got, or you haven't. I can be taught and I can learn and I've even picked up a bit of tap and ballet along the way. But for people like Lexie, Martha and Samrah, it's just effortless. At primary school, they'd have been the kids who could do backflips on the oval like it was no big deal, while you were proud of your basic cartwheel or handstand.

Part of the rehearsal today is the choreography for what Will has titled 'Song 8' because, surprise, it is the eighth song in the musical. It's the love song – just after the big kiss. *Never said it before / But I'll say it again / And I'll say it forever / To you.*

He has laid down a really nice track for it, which Lexie is using for some simple choreography. Or what she calls simple. She is trying to be patient as she steps through the routine. *Face each other. Hold hands. Both hands. Release one, spin out, hold one-two, spin in, back against his chest Edie, arms around her waist Will, now sway, left, right, left, right.*

We are so close. It feels like Will is shaking, just a little, as he takes hold of my hand. Is he nervous? I can feel his heart thumping against my back as I lean up against him. Or maybe that's my heart. And every time he touches me it feels like I'm on fire and my stomach flips and what the hell is this?

'Great chemistry, guys,' Aubrey says from the sidelines.

I pull a stupid face at Will and he laughs.

'No! Now, you've lost it!' Lexie sighs. 'From the top …' And we start again.

*

The rest of the cast are working on their ensemble number. Yazi is losing her temper at Martha and Samrah because they are way too advanced and making everyone look bad. Lexie is trying to get her to calm down. Will and I watch from the other side of the room. We're not getting involved.

There's something I've wanted to broach with Will ever since that awful *Romeo and Juliet* rehearsal. Something about the way Toby was reducing Juliet's character, objectifying her – literally wanting me to be naked and vulnerable – that just made me think … *Why?* Juliet is just as strong as Romeo. Stronger, even. Noah said I shouldn't take it so personally. But it was personal. Really personal. And I hated the way it made me feel. I want to be stronger than this. I have to be.

'I know what's wrong with the musical,' I say.

'There's something wrong with it?' Will says.

'No. I mean, not really, but hear me out. This might be weird or whatever, but I think … I think Lily should be a superhero.'

Will almost chokes. 'Jack's the superhero.'

I'm ready for this, I've planned exactly what to say. 'It makes it more empowering for the female lead. I think we've seen more than enough of disempowered women in the media. It's time to give female characters the autonomy they deserve.'

'OK …'

'Why is it that the male and masculine characters are always the superheroes, and the girls are weak victims or ditzy love interests? Why can't the women have superpowers?'

'Um, I think you'll find they do,' Will says. 'There's Supergirl, and Black Widow and –'

'OK. There are *some* but not that many, not really, and I think you could do something really interesting with this piece if, stay with me here, if Jack and Lily are equals. What if they *both* have superpowers, and they're hiding their true selves from each other?'

'So, neither knows the other is a superhero?' It sounds like Will might be warming up to the idea. I keep going.

'Yeah. They've both been hiding their true self from the other. Never knowing the other shares the same secret. Don't you think that would be way more interesting?' I say hopefully.

'It could be …'

'Maybe their powers work together or something and, I don't know, they can save the world. Together. Rather than

Jack just going it alone, you know?' I take out my script. 'I've highlighted some parts where I think it might work ...'

Will has gone very quiet. I think I may have crossed the line. I should have been gentler about it, especially knowing how sensitive he gets about his writing. Plus, this is Will's script, not mine. I'm worried I've just done a Toby Swan on him – making him doubt himself, undermining his confidence ...

'I love it, Edie,' Will says seriously. 'I think it will really work. Show me what you've got ...'

We move to the floor, lay our scripts out next to each other, and I show him the places where I think we can incorporate this new idea. We start filling the margins with new lines, new ideas for scenes and moments. We're on a roll, talking over each other, scribbling all over the other's notes. It's not quite the same as being onstage but it's not entirely different; there's a buzz from creating something, a character, a moment, a feeling, only this time it's not through singing or dancing or acting but with my own words. Our own words.

*

Everyone has gone, leaving me and Will to pack up the room. I'm hoping he hasn't forgotten about his offer to give me a lift home. I don't want to mention it, but I also really, really don't want to catch the bus. I hate it. It takes forever. I just want to get home and chill out in front of a bad action film with my grandparents, the way all teenagers want to spend their Friday nights. Right?

'What are you two doing in here?' Miss Sharma pokes her head into the studio. Her arms are full of tutus.

'Lexie asked us for feedback on her choreography. It was brilliant,' I say.

Miss Sharma raises an eyebrow. Tells us she doesn't believe us for a second and to get out of here, but she's laughing. Even so, we get out of there.

The passenger side of Will's car is full of Macca's hash-brown wrappers.

'What the hell is all this, William?' I laugh as I slide into the passenger seat.

He desperately tries to get them out from under my feet. 'Sorry, it's an addiction. I can't help it. Please don't tell my mums.'

'This car is a disgrace.'

'You wanna take the bus?'

'No thank you.'

We laugh and it feels easy. But when he reaches over and touches my hair, I feel that nudge, a jolt, in my stomach. 'You got some fluff on your hair,' he says, pulling it off. 'It's from these car seat covers. They're the worst. Sorry.'

I know what's happening. This always happens. I just hadn't expected it to happen with Will. But it makes sense. It may even be a part of my process, or whatever. It's the show-crush thing. It happens every time I do a show. I had a massive crush on Lexie when she had to help me one-on-one with some choreography. It was way before her and Aubrey were a thing, but I'd still never tell Aubrey about it because it's too weird. It happened with Caleb when he played the Beast to my Belle, and with Phoebe when were both screaming about a bird in *The Crucible*. What happened in my rehearsal with Will is just like all those other times. It's fake. Pretend. The lines, the song, the choreography are all tricking me into thinking I'm in love. I'm not. And nor is Will. He totally would have cleaned out his car if he was into me. No-one would want someone they liked to see that kind of mess.

'You going out with your boyfriend tonight?' Will never uses Noah's name. Before we became 'official' he'd refer to him as 'that Winters jerk' and now it's always 'your boyfriend'.

'I have a date with my grandparents and John Wick,' I say.

'Exciting Friday night.'

'Have you seen those films? They're very exciting.'

'Is that an invitation?'

'Yeah, sure,' I say. Will is my best friend. This is normal, usual, best friend stuff. And what happened in the rehearsal was the normal, usual, show-crush stuff. Nothing more.

And still … I'm hyperaware of Will the whole night. I notice how pleased he looks when Nan calls him the guest of honour, his almost-genuine laugh at Pops's cringey jokes, the way he covers his eyes in the violent parts of the film (*You have to stop that*, I tell him, *or you're seriously gonna miss the entire movie*), the way our hands brush against each other fighting for the last good pieces of popcorn. I pull back quickly. Shove the rest of the bowl at him. Say, *All yours. No*, he insists, *you take it*. We've never been so polite to each other.

I stand in the driveway long after Will has left.

Something feels different. It's not quite that spark that I get when I'm close to Noah, but almost … but I can't feel like that, can I? I like Noah. And Will is my friend. It's just this stupid musical.

'I've been calling you,' Nan says, coming up beside me and wrapping an arm around me. 'All OK?'

'Yeah,' I smile. I rest my head on her shoulder, which is getting harder to do now that I'm taller than her.

'Will is a lovely boy,' Nan says, stroking my hair away from my face.

'I have a boyfriend,' I say abruptly. 'I've been meaning to tell you but it just … it hasn't …'

'It's not Will?'

'No! Nan!' I move away. 'Will is my friend.'

'So? He could be both, couldn't he?'

'Well, he's not. My boyfriend's name is Noah. Noah Winters.'

'OK,' Nan says, but she doesn't sound convinced. 'I look forward to meeting him.'

We drink tea in front of the late-night news. I'm not really watching. I'm looking at Nan and Pops' rundown armchairs, noticing the worn carpet, the old television, the fact we only have one bathroom in this tiny house, Pops's tracksuit, the flyscreen door we've never fixed, the cracks in the ceiling … There's no way I will ever bring Noah here. No way he can meet my grandparents. I know what Aubrey said, but I just can't. There are some things about me, about my life, that I have to keep to myself.

TWENTY-FIVE

I don't think I have ever been so busy. Between rehearsing twice a week after school plus all-day Sunday for *Romeo and Juliet* and twice-weekly musical rehearsals *and* doing actual schoolwork, there hasn't been much time for a life. It's just rehearse, study, eat, sleep, repeat. And repeat. Noah keeps talking about taking me on a real date. I keep saying, *I have no time!* Noah seems to have all the time in the world. I don't get how he can be so relaxed about everything when I feel like I'm drowning, like at any moment my head is going to slip under the next wave and I'll be pulled under and never get to the surface again.

But on Saturday night he insists we go on a date. It isn't really a date because it's just at his house, but it's important to him that I'm there. At the soiree, he calls it. I don't know why they can't just call it a party but supposedly it's more than that. And when I arrive (I won't let him pick me up) I realise he is right. It's a lot more than that.

I'm wearing a black dress because that's the dress code. It's the one I wore to our Year Eleven dance. Aubrey helped me choose it and always used to say I should wear it more. She'd be impressed. Nan helped me add some curls to my hair and lent me her diamond earrings – tiny little studs that Pops bought her years and years ago, which she only ever wears for special occasions. I was nervous about wearing them, but she insisted.

Noah greets me in the foyer downstairs in a very expensive-looking suit. I feel underdressed but he says I look great, and there's no turning back now so I'll just have to fake it until I make it, or however that saying goes. He puts out his arm and I link my arm through and he guides me to the elevator and it feels old-fashioned and special.

Their penthouse is full of people. A woman in an elegant red dress plays the piano; soft, classical music that wafts under the sound of people talking and laughing. Waiters wander around, gracefully carrying trays of champagne flutes and canapes. The guests nod at Noah, say hello, smile at me and then whisper things they think I can't hear. *How cute*, one says. *What does his mother make of that*, another comments.

Mr Winters is commanding a corner of the room. A small group has gathered around him as he speaks animatedly about some disgusting red wine he was fooled into buying, or something like that. It sounds very boring to me but everyone else seems to find the story hilarious.

And then he sees us. Or me. 'Ah, good! The entertainment has arrived!' I look over my shoulder, expecting to see someone else standing behind me – a clown or a magician, perhaps. But there's no-one there. 'Everyone! This talented young lady is my son's friend, Edie – she's going to sing for us. Isn't that right, Edie?'

Is this some sort of joke? I look at Noah to see if he's laughing, but he's not. He pulls me away from his father – who is telling everyone, *Don't worry! She does have a voice! I can assure you!*

Noah pulls me into the hallway. There's no-one around. Only black-and-white family photos staring down at us from the walls.

'What the hell is going on?' I demand.

'Don't be mad,' he says.

'I'll be mad if I want to be mad.' The moment anyone tells me not to be mad, I feel mad, even if I wasn't mad in the first place. When someone says *don't be mad* they are just deflecting the fact that they shouldn't be saying or doing the thing they are about to say or do. I cross my arms. Raise an eyebrow. I am mad. And I'm going to stay that way.

'OK. Look, I just – I thought you might like to sing a couple of songs. Because you're so great. You're amazing. And I wanted other people to hear how amazing you are. There are some really important people here. It could be great exposure for you.'

Being an actor means always saying yes. That's something Toby Swan said. *Being an actor means taking every opportunity available.* Mrs B told me that. And Noah looks so genuinely excited by the idea of me singing here tonight that I am finding it difficult to hold onto that mad feeling. Instead, I feel like bursting into tears.

'Dad's going to pay you, too. Don't worry about that.' He gives me a little half smile.

'What? No. I don't want him to pay me!'

'OK. OK. No payment. But please, do this. They should all hear you sing. You're amazing, Edie …'

The pianist is just as shocked as I am about this impromptu performance. We spend five minutes huddled together in the kitchen discussing a set list. She knows every single song I throw at her. She's pretty incredible and kind, despite this interruption to her carefully curated repertoire.

'This is very rude, don't you think, springing this on us?' she whispers to me as we make our way to the piano.

I sing three songs. No-one listens. Not even Noah. People keep having their conversations and drinking champagne and eating canapes. Noah was right: it was great exposure. Exposure to how shallow and self-absorbed these people are. Including him.

*

I sneak upstairs to Noah's room as soon as it's over. I need a moment alone. A moment to breathe. I feel so stupid. So stupid. I call Nan. She insisted that I call her when I was ready to come home. *Doesn't matter how late it is*, she'd said, *I'll wait up*. I think she just wanted a chance to see where Noah lived. I suppose I've been a little secretive about the whole thing. She sounds surprised by my call.

'It's only eight-thirty. Is everything OK?' she says.

I tell her I'm fine and she tells me she is on her way. This is going to be the longest fifty minutes of my life. I sit on the edge of Noah's bed and tell myself not to cry. I'm so stupid.

Naïve, that's what Aubrey calls me, and she's right. I thought I was invited to a party, as Noah's girlfriend. But I'm just the help. The entertainment. That's what he called me. Who did I think I was? Wearing this dress, these earrings, curling my hair. What an idiot. It's so humiliating.

'Hey.' Noah is standing at the door. Shit. I should have hidden somewhere else. I should have started walking home. 'People are asking for you. They loved you out there!'

'Bullshit,' I say. My tears are dissolving into anger. Good. I'd rather be angry than sad. 'That was an awful thing to do to me, Noah.'

'What? Why?'

'You are so entitled and privileged you can't even see it, can you?'

'I have no idea what you're talking about.'

'Of course you don't.' I can't have this conversation. Not here. Not now. I need to get out of here.

'Are you breaking up with me?' he says quietly.

His question stops me. I haven't brought it up, haven't even thought about it. This is just an argument, right? People have arguments all the time.

'We're just very different people …' I say.

'That's what I love about you, Edie.'

I tell him I have to go because Nan wants me home and there's a taxi waiting. He looks confused, but I ignore him and rush out of there as quickly as possible.

*

Nan pulls into the driveway, and I don't wait for the car to stop before I open the door.

'Careful, Edie, careful,' Nan says.

'You can keep going.'

'I want to get a look at the place. It's very impressive, isn't it? What's it like inside?' I don't say anything. 'Maybe you can take me up. I put on my face and got changed, just in case. I won't embarrass you.'

I look over at her. She's wearing her favourite silk blouse. Her hair is pulled back in a low bun. Red lipstick on. She's made an effort to dress up and she looks lovely; it breaks my heart to think she thinks I'd ever be embarrassed of her.

'I can't go back in there,' I say softly. 'Can we just go? Please?'

TWENTY-SIX

I don't think rehearsals are meant to be so anxiety-inducing. I feel like I spend most of the *Romeo and Juliet* rehearsal period worried about the next hurtful thing Toby will tell me, all in the name of making me a *better actor*. If feeling crap about yourself makes you a good actor, I should be Meryl Streep by now.

The physical pain I feel before each rehearsal starts in the morning, even when the rehearsals are in the afternoon. My stomach aches and cramps. Food tastes like cardboard mush, and my arms and legs feel heavy. My eyes blur. It's like my whole body is shutting down, going on strike, refusing to work with that man – all while my brain says, *This is your chance, Edie!* My brain also tells me I'm useless; a worthless, talentless actor. It says, *Imogen should be Juliet, and why did Toby cast you?* It says, *You should accept Noah's apology for what happened at the soiree, and move on, get over it; you can't be Juliet if you're fighting with your Romeo. And stop being so mean to him,* my brain says, *he loves you, he said it, he loves you and why would anyone love you? Poor Noah, he was only trying to help you. Only trying to open some doors, the way working with Toby Swan will open some doors.* My brain says a lot of things, even when my heart says something else. It's confused. I'm confused.

I drag myself to every rehearsal. I get there twenty minutes early, as always. Not just to warm up and focus, like I've done for every other production, but to calm those voices and my stomach as best I can before we begin.

I lie on my back in the middle of the dressing room. It's empty at the moment. Cleaned and clear of all the costumes and racks and make-up and hair supplies. Soon, it will be overflowing with disorder and mess, but right now, in between seasons, it is quiet and still. And the perfect place to get some calm and focus before hell begins. I place my hands on my diaphragm and breathe in and out. Slowly. Deeply. Count in for five, count out for five. Imagine myself sinking into the floor.

I don't know how long he's been there, but I feel his presence before I open my eyes. At first I think I must be imagining it. That it's my brain being unhelpful. But for once, it's not that. And I sort of wish it were. I see him. Toby. Sitting on one of the dressing room tables. Watching me. Was he here when I came in? Did I somehow not notice him? He waves his hand as if to say, *Go on,* but I can't go on. Any sense of calm I'd managed to find has been shattered.

I get up quickly. Too quickly. My head spins. He's up and at my side and helping me into a chair. I sit. He kneels on

227

the floor beside me. His hand still on my arm. I pull my arm away. A wave of unease rolls over me.

'Just take it easy,' he says softly.

'What the hell are you doing in here?'

'You almost fainted. It was good that I found you. Imagine what could have happened.'

'You shouldn't be in here.' I am louder this time.

He reaches out and touches my chin, lifting my head up with his fingers. 'You have a good profile,' he says. 'But you always look so defeated. Keep your gaze lifted. It will help.'

And then he is gone.

I am shaken, but what am I going to say? And who am I going to say it to?

*

Toby declares to the cast he's going to spend some time working on my monologue from Act 3, Scene 2. *Gallop apace, you fiery-footed steeds* ... It's Imogen's favourite monologue. In *West Side Story*, the musical version of this moment is Maria singing *Tonight*. The excitement, anticipation and nervousness as she waits for Tony, for their first night together, builds in that song. I've listened to it a lot. Those emotions, which are captured by the swell of the orchestra and voice, are in the monologue, too. There's a musicality to this. In the words, the alliteration, the repetition, the commas, the quick lines and the long, flowing sentences. It's just a little harder to find. But reading it over and over in my bedroom, I started to hear the music. And it's helped me. Helped me get here, to this moment: onstage, alone with Toby Swan, rehearsing the monologue.

He tells me to show him what I've got.

Which I find confusing, considering he has been so angry about all the preparation I've done. I don't know whether to pretend I don't know my lines and hold onto the script, or leave the script in the wings. I carry the script onstage.

'You don't know your lines yet?'

'Yeah, yes, I do.'

I put the script on Juliet's bed.

'Did I tell you to abandon the text?'

I hesitate.

'The words are sacred. They are to be respected. Every. Single. Word. You think you've got that? Every single word of this monologue?'

Toby has one scene take place in a boxing ring. The boys throw punches, dance on their toes, jump from the ropes. Toby has made a lot of edits to the words in that scene. Whole lines have been cut. Some are pre-recorded as a voiceover that will play over the fight while techno music blasts from the speakers. But now, here, with me, he wants to ensure every single word is respected? I feel like he's directing me for an entirely different production. Or maybe I just don't get it. I don't have much experience with Shakespeare. Or Toby Swan. Perhaps this is just what it's like.

'What did I say about your gaze?' he says, and I automatically lift my chin.

I pick up the script and flip to the page I need. I don't think I know every single word. I doubt I know any of it anymore. All the preparation I've done for this moment is starting to fade away. The voices come back, saying, *You're shit, worthless, why is Toby wasting his time with you?*

I close my eyes, take a deep breath; try to steady myself. And start the monologue. In this moment, I am Juliet. Excited and nervous to see Romeo again. Desperately in love and longing for Romeo's touch, his kiss, his arms wrapped around my body …

I don't get far.

Toby is on the stage, standing directly in front of me, hands on my shoulders, staring into my eyes. He says nothing. Just stares at me. Unblinking. I don't know where to look.

'At me, at me,' he whispers. Can he read my mind?

I look at him. Stare into his eyes until they turn into one blurry image. A blob of colour all mashed together.

'I want you to speak the lines to me. Just to me. No-one else is here. Just by yourself. Be Edie. And say the words to me. Don't act. Just speak.'

Does he have to stand so close? Does he have to stare at me like that. Does he have to keep his hands on my shoulders, his breath on my face, his body so near?

I close my eyes. He tells me to open them. I take a deep breath. He tells me to stop overthinking. I open my mouth. He tells me to start again.

Toby moves closer.

The words are stuck in my throat. They escape as a whisper. A hushed, stilted sound. There is none of the longing, none of the excitement that I'd rehearsed. That's been ripped away from these words now; they're empty, bare words, reduced to nothing.

As I talk, he strokes the side of my face.

I turn away from him.

'Just go with it,' he says. 'Speak into it.'

I keep going. My eyes full of hot tears. My heart full of sick.

'Better!' he says when I finally, painfully, reach the end of the monologue. He lets me go. Storms from the stage. 'Again! From the top!'

I stand alone on the stage, which feels somehow both bigger and smaller than when I started. I start the monologue again. Staring straight ahead. Eyes up. Voice little more than a whisper.

*

Toby schedules extra rehearsals. Just for me. On my own. To really focus on the monologues. He says I am very weak with the monologues and if I don't work on them I will let down not only myself, but the entire show. He says he's doubting why he cast me as Juliet when Imogen would have been so much better. He says I have to meet him every Wednesday, at lunchtime. I don't want to go alone, so I ask Noah. We've sort of worked it out. He said *sorry* – he does that a lot – and I forgave him, which I seem to do a lot. It was all a misunderstanding, really, and we're fine, really fine, but he says he can't come to Toby's monologue sessions with me because he plays basketball on Wednesdays and the team needs him but, *You're lucky, Edie*, he says, *sounds like you've got an in with Toby*. And so I ask Mrs B. She tells me she can't, and she's sorry, but aren't I lucky? To be getting this sort of one on one coaching from Toby Swan! She says it is wonderful. She can't wait to see what I do. I want to scream or cry or both, but nothing comes out. Nothing.

I go to the extra rehearsals.

Alone.

Because I don't want to let anyone down.

Because I am lucky.

Toby Swan stands close. He follows me across the stage. He shouts. He tells me I am useless. He touches my hair. He cups my face. He leans into my body. Pushes me. Shoves me. Brushes against me.

And I speak the lines. I speak the lines. I speak the lines.

TWENTY-SEVEN

Monologues are haunting me. In Drama with Mrs B we are working on the ones that will be used to determine our final grade; they will be presented as part of our exams and performed in the end-of-year showcase. Even though it would make sense to use one of the many monologues I'm learning for the show, that is against the rules. We can only choose from a preselected list. None of them are very appealing to me. But that doesn't matter, it just has to be done.

I have tried to work on it. To find a connection. Learn the lines. Develop a character. Discover the beats and objectives and blah, blah, blah. I just haven't had the energy. Or the motivation. It feels a little pointless right now.

But today, we are meant to show Mrs B where we're at with it. In the safe and welcoming space that is the Drama studio, we are to share our performances with the class. No props or costumes. Scripts can still be used – it's early in the process, but Mrs B likes to check in and says deadlines like this help us meet the important milestones.

I have not met any milestone.

I haven't even chosen the monologue.

It's the first time, in twelve years of schooling, that I haven't done the homework. That I'm not prepared. I keep looking at the clock, hoping that, somehow, time will run out before Mrs B calls on me. Or that the fire alarm will go off. Or that a sink hole will open up right under my chair.

Mrs B is taking her time with everyone. Asking them about their choices. Giving them ideas for changes. It's burning me up inside, watching her being so nice. So kind. It's a load of bullshit. Mrs B doesn't care about us. She didn't care when she stepped away from *Romeo and Juliet*. Didn't fight for us. Didn't turn up to offer support. Where has she been? How could she just leave us with someone like Toby Swan? Because if she hadn't, if she'd been directing the show like she was supposed to, things would be different. Better. But instead …

She calls on me. Of course she calls on me. I get up. The monologue I've never read from a play I've never heard of is in my hand. I'll just read it. Out loud. I can do this.

I open my mouth but there are no words there.

I try again but there's something in the way. It's like I'm in a fog. Thick, grey fog clouding over everything. It's stuck in my throat, my eyes, my lungs. I can't speak or see or hear properly. I'm underwater and I'm drowning.

Mrs B's face comes into focus. She's standing in front of me. She's asking me what's wrong and I'm shaking my head because I don't know how to say it, and I can't say it, not here, not to her, not in front of everyone. This is all her fault.

'Edie?'

'I haven't done it, OK? I don't have anything.'

'That's all right …'

'No, it's not. It's not all right.'

'Edie?'

Why does she keep saying my name like that? Why is she still standing there? But she won't stop. She won't leave me alone. I drop the script and cover my face with my hands. I feel her move closer and then she puts her hands on my shoulders. Hands. Holding. My shoulders.

'Stop it,' I shout and push her off me. It shocks her. Shocks me. But it's out now. I'm angry and violent and I can't stop. I won't stop. 'You pretend you care but you don't give a shit. You just left us with him. You're a fucking fake.'

'What?'

'You have no idea what those rehearsals are like, no idea how hard I'm working.'

'Edie …' But I don't hear what else she says, if she says anything at all, because I run. Run from her and them and Arcadia, and keep running and running until I'm as far away as possible. Until I'm on a bus. Until I'm home.

*

Pops is waiting for me.

'You're early,' he says as soon as I open the front door.

He's been expecting me. He's sitting at the kitchen table, not sleeping in his armchair, and he's made a pot of tea. Pots of tea are for serious talks. We rarely do it because it takes too long and we're all very impatient when it comes to tea.

I already cried it all out during the bus ride home. Now

I'm just exhausted. And embarrassed. I want to curl up under my doona and sleep for a million years and wake up in a future where no-one remembers my outburst. I definitely don't want to talk about it with Pops, but it looks like I don't have a choice.

I join him at the table, where he has already made a start on his cup (like I said, we're impatient) and pours one for me. His hand trembles as he lifts the pot. My heart aches when I see him shake like that, and I reach to help him but he mutters, *I've got it.* Hand wobbling as he slowly pours tea into my old Little Miss Sunshine mug. A little milk. A little stir.

'Your teacher called today,' Pops says.

Pops doesn't get angry. It isn't his style. I have never heard him shout or raise his voice. Instead, he gets disappointed and sad. I think that's even worse. At least if he shouts I can shout back and we can get it over with. Nan and I fight. We shout. We're both a bit dramatic like that, and there's something cathartic about it. A good rant. A vent. A slammed door. And then we cry and apologise and we're better. Pops will just sigh quietly and give you these sad stares. Which is what he is doing now.

'I'm sorry, Pops.'

'I don't think it's me you have to say sorry to.'

If I think about Mrs B's reaction, her face, the concern in her voice, I am just going to start crying again. I grab a biscuit from the tin Pops has left out on the table and start breaking it up into tiny, crumbly pieces.

'We think you might be stressed. Taking on too much,' he says.

I don't say anything.

'I've spoken with your nan and we've decided that you won't be working at the shop anymore. Not until exams are over, at least,' he says.

'What? No. That's not happening. I have to work. I know it's not a heap of money, but it's important.'

'Edie,' Pops says, 'you need to study and focus on your future. Let us worry about the things grandparents are meant to worry about for a change. We'll be fine. Don't worry.'

The thing is, I don't think grandparents are meant to worry about this kind of stuff. I want my grandparents to worry about what cruise to take next, like Aubrey's grandparents do, or where they should retire to, like Will's grandma, or what matinee movie they want go see or which new hobby they want to take up. Instead, they have me.

'But is it something more than that?' he says.

'No,' I lie. 'I mean, I'm not really enjoying the play. That's all.'

'Don't know why you agreed to do it in the first place.'

'I have to do the play,' I explain. Again. 'I've told you this. It's a good opportunity. It might lead to something.'

He scoffs and takes a long sip of his tea.

'And Mum said she's going to actually see this one, Pops. And you know how long I've waited for that to happen. Plus I'm the lead now. So I can't let everyone down like that. I've got a responsibility to the rest of the cast. I have to do it.'

'But do you *want* to do it?'

I don't say anything. I'm pretty focused on pulverising this biscuit into nothing right now. What do I want? I want this conversation to be over.

'I just wish everyone would leave me alone.'

'Edie.' Pops stops me with his serious voice. I look up from the pile of crumbs I've created. He is watching me and is about to say something, but I see him change his mind. Like he's thought better of it. His eyes get a little glassy.

'You OK, Pops?'

'You have some soul searching to do, I think,' he says.

'Pops?'

'I have to have a little rest now.' And with that, he pushes himself up from the table, takes his walker and slowly leaves the room.

I brush the crumbs into the bin, collect the mugs and the tea pot, wash everything up, dry it, put it away. Try not to think about anything. But all the time there is a nagging, creeping sadness that I can't shake.

*

When Nan gets home that night she says she is too angry to speak to me. And, *You're bloody lucky you weren't suspended.* And, *I'm so ashamed of you.* And, *Don't you dare turn into your mother.* For someone who is too angry to speak she sure manages to say a hell of a lot.

I hide in my room and try to write Mrs B a letter. Apologising for my unforgivable behaviour. Blaming it on exhaustion and stress. But I know that's not true. The truth is Toby Swan. It's the way his words eat away at the corners of the bits of myself I used to actually like. It's the smell of his breath and the closeness of his body and the touch of his hand on my back, my shoulder, my face, my chin.

I have messages from everyone, checking in to see if I'm OK. Noah and Yazi and Makayla and Kellen and Will. I've told them all I'm really sorry and that I'm fine, just tired and emotional. What else am I going to say?

I know how these things are supposed to work, when a man treats someone like this. Like what Toby is doing to me. I'm not stupid. I've read articles and listened to talks and watched TV shows and movies and read Twitter threads and I *know*. Logically. Practically. I know. I know I should tell someone what's happening. I should ask for help. But what does that mean, what does that actually look like, in the real world? I don't have any idea. It feels like I'm standing right at the edge of a huge cliff and the rocks are crumbling at my feet and falling into the darkness below, and I'm going to go over, into that darkness, at any moment.

My phone starts buzzing and it's Imogen. Calling me. Again. I think about ignoring it but, this time, I don't.

'I know what's going on,' she says before I even say hello. 'It's Toby Swan, isn't it?'

*

She knows it will be difficult to face school today, so she's agreed to meet me. Before school. So we can walk in together.

Imogen waits in the small park opposite our school, and waves at me as I head her way. As if I wouldn't notice her sitting there. Perfect posture. Black-blue hair shimmering in the sunlight. Imogen will be famous one day. You can just tell. And she'll be one of those combos my mum thinks is rare. Famous *and* talented.

Last night we spoke for hours. I said, *You told me he was a genius.* She said, *He is, but ...* And then she went quiet and I said, *Don't do that. Don't go quiet, because I feel like*

239

I'm going crazy here, like there's something wrong with me. And she said, *There is absolutely nothing wrong with you, Edie.* Then she explained the rumours she'd heard and how she thought they were just rumours because the girl who had made the accusations was someone no-one really trusted, but now she could see it happening with her own eyes and maybe they should have trusted that girl after all. And so, I explained it all. The way he made me feel from day one. The creeping sense of unease. And then all the rest. The dressing room. The stage. The extra rehearsal session. His hands. His breath. She cried. And I cried. And we agreed to meet here. This morning.

She's speaking before I even sit down. 'Are you OK? Oh my god, Edie, I'm so sorry you're dealing with this. It's so shit. So shit.' Her voice is different. Less polished and careful, and more … real. It's nice hearing her speak like that. But then she says, 'Look, I think we do need to keep doing the show.'

I feel like throwing up. 'Not with Toby –'

'Yes. With Toby. I hate to say it, but his name on your résumé is going to open so many doors, Edie. I think we just have to get on with it and get what we can out of it. But, from now on, we stick together. You and me. He can't hurt you if I'm there. Or vice versa.'

It feels like that tiny spark of hope I've been holding onto all morning – the one that got me out of bed, the one I carried with me on the long commute to school – has suddenly gone out. Bam. Shrivelled up into nothing. What she's saying makes sense. And if she's with me, I'm sure nothing bad will happen again. So why do I feel so incredibly sad?

TWENTY-EIGHT

I'm trying really, really hard, but I feel like I'm drowning. Drowning so slowly that no-one seems to notice how I'm slipping under right in front of them. My alarm goes off at a quarter to six. At ten past six I'm on my first bus on the journey to school. It's still dark out. I sit in one of the front seats, close to the driver. Headphones in. I listen to Will's music and run the lyrics under my breath, the choreography in my head. I read the script and learn my lines. The lines for Lily. The lines for Juliet. The lines for the pointless Drama monologue. So many lines. I'm usually good at learning lines, but at the moment nothing seems to stick.

I change buses, take the train, then get on one more bus that eventually pulls up at school at eight-fifteen. I'm at Aubrey's locker seven minutes later, decorating it for her birthday the way I always do. I hope it's OK to do that this year. I didn't check with Lexie and now I'm worried that she has plans and I'm stepping on her toes. But it's too late. I have balloons and streamers and I'm going to use them.

Will asks me to meet him in the cafe because he wants to talk about the script, so I wait for him there. Catch up on some biology homework. I think about buying a coffee but can't decide if I really want one. But when Will sits down in front of me, he's bought me one anyway.

'I don't know if I want that,' I say.

'Don't drink it, then,' he shrugs.

'Why didn't you ask me first?'

He looks at me like I've slapped him. Maybe I'm speaking too sharply. I apologise. Take a sip of the coffee even though I know now I really don't want it.

'I heard the play is getting a bit … you know … full on,' Will says casually.

'What are you talking about?' I snap. I can hear it. I try to soften it. Smile. Laugh it off. But it's not working.

'People are talking about the sex scene,' he says.

'There's no sex scene. What the hell is wrong with everyone? It's a high school play. They can't do that. They wouldn't do that. Fuck.'

'OK. I just wanted to check that you're OK.'

I don't like the way he's looking at me. I shove his script at him. 'You're the writer, not me. You can fix this shit yourself.'

I storm out of the cafe and almost walk straight into Noah, who says, 'Woah, babe, slow down.' I hate being called 'babe'. What a stupid word. I tell him not to call me that and he laughs like it's a joke and ignores me completely and starts talking about some show he was watching on Netflix last night.

'People are saying there's a sex scene in the play,' I interrupt him.

'Um, OK,' he says. 'Who cares?'

'I care.'

'Toby says you're too uptight, Eds. You gotta let this shit go.'

'Toby is an arsehole.'

'No, he's not. Not really. He just tough cos he knows you can handle it.'

I can't handle it. I'm not handling it. I want to scream, but I don't. I tell Noah I have to find Aubrey.

But Lexie finds me first.

'What the hell, Edie?' she stands, hands on hips, blocking my path. 'I had plans and then you go and do that to her locker? You could have asked me. Geez.'

'Sorry.'

'Yeah, right, whatever. Here. You can have all this back.' And she hands me a plastic bag full of all the streamers and signs and balloons I'd put on Aubrey's locker. 'I had to make room for my own stuff. You understand, right?'

I don't understand, but Lexie disappears before I get a chance to tell her. Not that she'd care. I stuff the plastic bag into the nearest bin.

*

At lunchbreak I watch Lexie present a cake to Aubrey as everyone sings her 'Happy Birthday'. Will won't look at me. Noah is playing basketball. I head to the Drama studio because I don't know where else to go.

'Edie?' Mrs B sounds surprised to see me. Which makes

sense. After my outburst, we've not really spoken, not the way we used to.

'Can I just hang out in here for a bit?'

'I'm in the middle of marking –'

'You won't even know I'm here,' I tell her, relieved that we won't have to talk. Because I don't know what to say to her. I don't know if I have the right words. Or any words at all.

'Of course,' she says and heads back into her office, closing the door behind her.

*

Will is waiting for me at the bus stop. I didn't even know he knew where the bus stop was, to be honest.

'Thought you might like some company,' he says.

'Oh.'

'Sorry about this morning. I was only checking in. I didn't mean to upset you.'

'I'm not upset.'

He sighs. Stares at his shoes. We stand there, in silence. I don't know why he is here. I don't know what he wants from me. 'Still coming to Aubrey's party tomorrow?' he says.

'Yes. Why wouldn't I?'

'Just checking.'

'Maybe you can stop with all the checking all the time. Just leave me alone.'

He looks up at the sky, squints into the sun. Says nothing.

The bus is two minutes late. As usual. I get on without saying goodbye. Put my headphones in. Listen to the music from his musical and try not to think about how wrong everything feels right now.

TWENTY-NINE

Okey Dokey Karaoke is one of those places that is so bad it's good. The place is lit up in neon lights and has this really old-school anime theme – there's Dragon Ball Z and Sailor Moon everywhere – which Aubrey absolutely loves. The building is a maze of private rooms, full of groups of people singing their hearts out really badly. There are monitors in the entrance that live-stream from the rooms in silent, fuzzy black-and-white. I think it's so the staff can keep an eye on things and make sure nothing dodgy is going on, but it is also hilarious to watch. Will and I stand there, transfixed by the live feed of a middle-aged man in a suit dancing on a tabletop like some sort of demented robot, until we are ushered into a private room. A sign reading 'HAPPY 18th BIRTHDAY AUBREY' is stuck to the door.

There's a big group of us. Normally it would just be me, Will and, as of last year, Lexie at Aubrey's birthday celebrations. Tonight, there are twenty of us and we've all crammed into the private room. I wonder if I held Aubrey back and if, for the past five birthdays we've celebrated, she would have preferred a big group like this? But this year is extra special because it's her eighteenth. There was champagne at her house before everyone loaded into a stretch limo to bring us into the city. It's all a bit cheesy but Aubrey seems happy. That's the main thing. She's wearing a sparkly silver tiara that says BIRTHDAY GIRL and matches her silver dress. She looks amazing. As usual I'm feeling a little less than amazing next to her. I misinterpreted the dress code and turned up to Aubrey's house in jeans. She promptly pulled me into her bedroom and started shoving clothes at me. Now I am very uncomfortable in a red dress that is a bit too small. At least I convinced her to let me keep wearing my sneakers.

Aubrey said I could invite Noah, and I did, but he had plans. Something with his parents. I didn't push it. I know it makes me sound like a horrible girlfriend, but I was secretly relieved when he said he couldn't come. Since I snapped at him it feels like all we do is argue. And he made it very, very clear that he despises karaoke (*It should be outlawed*, he said). But it's not just that; Noah not being here makes things a little easier. There will be none of that awkwardness I always sense when Noah and Will are in the same room, and it means I can focus on my friends. My best friends. Because it doesn't feel like we're in such a great place right now.

'Are we OK?' Will asks as we head inside.

'Yeah, of course, sorry, it was a shitty day and I was shitty and I shouldn't have taken it out on you. I'm sorry.' I'm trying to convince myself as much as Will right now. Because it doesn't feel like it was just one shitty day – it feels like everything is wrong all the time. But Aubrey's birthday party is not the time or place to talk about it. So I put my arm around Will and he puts his arm around me and I know we'll be OK. We always are.

A purple velvet couch borders the walls of the room, and everyone piles on it. In the centre of the room is a long, low table full of drinks: bottles of beer and bright blue cocktails that smell like cough syrup. Will finds me a Diet Coke. He never makes a big deal over the fact I don't want to drink. One day I might, but not right now. It might have something to do with Mum. Or the fact it tastes gross. It's probably a little of both.

There's a screen at the front of the room, a small stage and two mics on stands. A disco ball hangs from the ceiling and spins slowly. Lexie drags Aubrey to the stage.

'Attention, attention!' Lexie shouts into the mic. 'How hot does the birthday girl look tonight?'

Everyone whoops and cheers. Aubrey beams.

'Happy birthday Aubrey. You're fucking amazing! I love you.'

They kiss and everyone cheers some more. It isn't much of a speech. I would have spoken about how kind Aubrey is, how she makes everyone feel like they're her friend the moment they meet her, how she takes care of stuff and is so organised it can be annoying but also comforting, how much her little sisters look up to her, what a rock she's been for her mum through all that stuff with her dad and how she is my best friend and I hope she always will be. I wrote it all in her card, so she'll read it, but part of me would have liked everyone to hear it. To know that she's more than Lexie's girlfriend, more than just 'hot', more than 'amazing'. They feel like such empty, meaningless words. But Aubrey is pretty much glowing right now, staring at Lexie like she's some kind of goddess. I feel that stupid twinge. That little twist in my heart that makes me want to snatch Aubrey away from Lexie, to pull her out of here and have her all to myself again. I wish we could jump into a time machine and go back to her thirteenth birthday – a sleepover that we spent hanging out in our PJs watching scary movies and eating pizza and talking and laughing into the early hours of the morning. Life was so much simpler then.

The singing begins and it gets pretty rowdy with everyone trying to outdo each other. That's what happens when all your school friends are extroverts with performing arts backgrounds. Diego has already cornered me and demanded we perform our usual number. Thankfully 'You're the Top' isn't on the Okey Dokey Karaoke list. I suggest we do a different song but he just rolls his eyes like I've said something stupid. So, I assume that means I'm not singing with Diego tonight. I am, however, singing with Will. He is going through the folder of songs, trying to choose the perfect duet for us to perform. He's been staring at it for ages, flipping the pages back and forth.

'Just choose something,' I laugh and go to take the book from him, but he holds on tight.

'It's a very important decision, Eds. We have to get this just right,' he says as he tries to prise the book from my grip.

'I know you, William Yoon, you are going to choose something embarrassing.' I won't let go of the book.

'I am taking this decision very seriously.' He pulls the book closer and I move with it, almost falling into him.

'You two all right there?'

It's Noah. Noah? Here? He's standing right in front of us. I didn't even notice him come in. I drop the book and jump up from the couch and hug him. He lifts me in the air and kisses me sweetly.

'What are you doing here?' I say.

'Change of plans.' He sits next to Will, forcing him to shove down a little. 'But I am not singing. I'm just here, waiting it out for the afterparty.'

I've been trying to forget about the afterparty because if I thought about it too much I'd have got too anxious and not shown up at all. Lexie has got our names on the door of some exclusive club; most of us are all legally allowed to go. Those of us who aren't have fake IDs or connections that mean they can do whatever they want regardless.

'I don't have time to make you feel better about this,' Aubrey says. I have managed to get a moment with her. We're in the bathroom, which is such a cliché, but there you go. She's reapplying her lipstick as she speaks. 'How many times do I have to say it: little steps, Edie, little steps.'

'This is kind of a big deal for me, Aubrey.'

'For you? It's my eighteenth birthday. This isn't about you.'

'But –'

'I'm not going to beg you. Here.' She hands me the fake ID. 'Use, don't use it. I don't care.'

'Please don't be angry at me.' I realise how babyish it sounds as soon as I say it. But Aubrey doesn't comment. She just kisses my cheek, leaving a bright red lipstick mark, and drags me back into the karaoke room. And I let her. It's her birthday party and I'm not going to ruin it.

Noah refuses to perform. It hasn't stopped him from adding his own hilarious commentary to every performance, though. A small group of admirers surround him and laugh along. Every time I've got up to sing I have shot him a look, daring him to make a smart comment. Which he hasn't. He wouldn't want to. I give him the same look when I get up with Will for our duet. I still have no idea what song he has chosen for us but, judging by the smirk on his face, it's going to be very embarrassing. For me. Not Will.

'OK buddy, what hell are you putting me through?' I ask Will as we take our places in front of the microphones.

He smiles, then holds out his hand to me and says, 'Do you trust me?'

And I know exactly what he has chosen. Of course. I whack his arm. 'Oh my god, Will!'

Everyone laughs and cheers as the opening bars of 'A Whole New World' from *Aladdin* begin.

As we sing, I remember how fun it is to be onstage with Will. One night the flying carpet stopped working and Will ad-libbed his way through it so well that the audience gave him a standing ovation, thus cementing his position as 'class clown'. Our voices still sound pretty good together even though it's been a while since we did a Disney number. I look around the room; everyone is singing along. I'm grinning so hard my face hurts, but there are tears in my eyes. Can you be so happy you feel sad? Is this what nostalgia feels like? Is that what I'm feeling? Because, I realise as our voices swell, there won't be many more moments like this with these people. Will will be too busy studying medicine to be the Aladdin to my Jasmine anymore – soon, there will be no more musical productions, no more karaoke nights.

We remember some of the moves, and Will stands behind me and wraps an arm around me like he did in the show.

'Watch it, Yoon!' Noah shouts from the couch.

Will quickly moves away from me, but I grab his hand before he can go too far and force him to stay by my side. I shake my head at Noah, who just shrugs at me like, *What did I do?* Will shouts into the mic, 'Come on, birthday girl, get up here!' and Aubrey runs onto the little stage and stands between us and helps us belt out the rest of the song. The three of us. Best friends. I hope we never lose this.

*

Noah pulls me onto his lap and I let him. I usually feel totally awkward with the whole PDA thing. Seeing anyone kissing in public makes me really uncomfortable. I don't know where to look or how to react. So being on the other side of it – being the person who could be making others feel uncomfortable – is something I just can't do. Not that I really had the chance to before I started dating Noah. But still. Tonight, though, things feel different. I feel freer or something, like anything is allowed. It might just be the aftereffect of the nostalgic group sing-along, which has given me the kind of buzz I usually only feel after a really great performance. Or maybe it's being in this room, which is full of so much love for Aubrey right now. Or the fact that it is dark in here and people are starting to pair off.

Noah gives me one of those blue cocktails. The glass feels sticky and it smells so sweet. I scrunch up my nose and he says, *Cute*, and kisses me – right on the nose. Which is very sweet and lovely and makes me feel all warm inside. I look at the drink and think, *Why the hell not?* It's as terrible and sugary as I'd imagined, but surprisingly easy to drink.

'Your lips are blue,' Noah says.

'Are they?' I laugh and lean in to kiss him. I don't even care that people are right there, next to us. I just do it.

Lexie is singing that romantic Rihanna song, 'Love on the Brain', which she has dedicated to Aubrey. She sounds so good. The singing lessons she's started with some big-shot teacher are paying off. Aubrey is swaying at the front of the stage, looking up at her and totally in love. It is very sweet.

'You should sing me a song,' I whisper to Noah.

'Not gonna happen. I hate that crap,' he says.

'What do you hate?' Will plonks down next to us and I suddenly feel very self-conscious about sitting on Noah's lap. I go to move but Noah wraps his arms around me.

'Singing,' he says to Will. 'Don't like it. Won't do it.'

'You won't even sing a duet with your girlfriend?' Will is stirring. He loves this. 'That sucks for you, Edie.'

'I can sing solo, Will. Not all of us need the support of another voice to get through a number,' I tease him back.

'So, how long have you had a crush on my girlfriend?' Noah says out of absolutely nowhere. I feel the blue cocktail swirling in my stomach and for a second I think it's going to come back up. I can't believe Noah said that.

Will just sits there, looking confused. 'What are you talking about?' he says quietly.

'It's a bit sad, bro,' Noah says.

I twist around to look at Noah's face. To see if he's making one of his stupid jokes. I whack him, playfully, on the chest and tell him he's an idiot. He laughs. He was kidding. Messing around. I turn to Will. 'Ignore him. He's being an idiot. Like me. A big idiot!'

'You're not an idiot, Edie,' Will says.

Phoebe has started singing that song from *Frozen* and everyone is screaming at her to STOP! Will jumps up to join in the protest. I look at Noah, who is smiling at me. It is so stupid, but when he smiles like that he really does get out of trouble.

*

People are over the karaoke now and are desperate to get to the club. Some are already starting to leave. Noah wants to know when we're getting out of here.

'I think I'm going to skip it,' I say.

'What?' Noah says. 'No, you have to come. It's your best friend's birthday.'

'It's not really my thing ...'

'You've been to a club before?'

'No.'

'So, how do you know it's not your thing?' I can't answer that and he looks pretty happy with himself. 'Ha! I gotcha. Now you have to come. It will be fun. I promise.'

'I don't know ...'

'You're allowed to have fun, Edie.'

We get a spot in the limo and Aubrey squeals when she sees I'm there. I don't think I have ever heard Aubrey squeal before. 'Finally! My girl's come through for me!' she announces to everyone in the limo.

I think I've come through for her in the past. Just in different, non-club-related ways. But I'm not going to argue. Not now. Not when she looks so happy.

'Is this gonna work?' I fling the fake ID around in front of Aubrey's face.

'It's all sorted. Don't stress,' Lexie says.

Noah hands me a plastic cup of warm champagne. I think, *Why the hell not*, and drink it. Or try to. I don't really like it. But perhaps that's not the point.

'You're drinking?' Will slides into the seat across from us.

'And you're clubbing?' I laugh. I did not expect Will to be here. He hates this sort of thing even more than I do. I take another sip of the horrible drink and notice Will watching me. 'What?' I ask him in a voice that probably comes out a little meaner than I'd expected. He shakes his head. Turns to Holly and starts telling her some stupid joke, which she seems to find absolutely hilarious. I finish the champagne and Noah finds me another.

*

Lexie doesn't have it sorted. Not at all. She definitely knows people; she takes us to the front of the queue and says something, maybe some kind of secret code, that makes the scary bouncers smile and open the doors. But they still want to see IDs. And my fake one isn't cutting it. The bouncer is apologetic, which is nice considering I am the one trying to break the law. I wonder if he'd be like this if I wasn't a part of Lexie's group.

I don't really mind. The champagne has made me feel a little sick and wobbly and I just want to lie down. I sit on the kerb while my friends crowd around me and fight over what to do.

'We can't just leave her!' Aubrey is shouting at Lexie.

'Oh my god! It's your birthday, Aubrey! You can't go home already!'

I try to get up to stop them fighting, because they are in love and a perfect couple and they shouldn't be arguing today of all days, but the words won't come out and I can't really stand up and maybe this is what being drunk feels like. Oh my god. Am I drunk?

'Uber!' I yell. 'I'll get Uber!'

'I'll take her home,' Noah says and he goes to lift me up, but I push him away.

'No,' I say.

'What the hell, Edie?' he says. I look up and see his face. He looks sad. I hate that I have made him sad, but I really don't want him to see my house. It's old and ugly and embarrassing and I don't want him to see it. Right now I don't even want him to see me like this, some stupid, drunk girl who can't get into a club. I try to explain this to him but nothing comes out right and, just like that, I am watching him storm away, going into the club without me. It feels like I'm watching a movie and not a moment from my real, actual life.

Aubrey sits next to me. 'You had too much champagne.' She speaks to me like I'm a little kid who has skinned their knee or something. 'Will is going to take you home, OK? You need to promise me to drink a lot of water, eat some toast and take two Panadol. Got it?' I nod. Or I think I nod. 'I'll check in on you tomorrow.'

I stick my head out of the car window and let the cool night air hit my face. It makes my eyes water. Or maybe I am crying. I can't really tell. My hair is whipping around like crazy. Will taps me on the shoulder.

'You OK?' he says.

I am starting to feel a lot better. The Uber driver's complimentary water and the fresh air are definitely helping. I sigh and rest my head on Will's shoulder.

'What are you doing?' he says softly.

'Thinking.'

'You can't do that.'

'Think?'

'No.' He gently lifts my head from his shoulder, pushes me back into my seat. 'You can't do that. Lean on me like that.'

'Why not?'

'You know why not.'

I'm about to ask *why not* again but I catch a look at his face. His serious face. There's that little furrow he gets in his brow when he's deeply considering something. And I suddenly understand why not. Actually … no. That's a lie. I've understood for ages, but I've ignored it. Will likes me. I think I've known that for a while. I think I knew it before he even knew. And I like him too. I've liked him for a long time. Since Year Seven at the ice-skating rink, if I am honest with myself. Will as Aladdin was perhaps my first ever show-crush.

But that show-crush became a best friend, and I decided long ago I was not going to ruin that for anything. I don't think it was a conscious decision. Just something that happened. Like our friendship.

And now I have a boyfriend. So, Will is right. I should definitely not be leaning my head on his shoulder. Even if he is my best friend.

'Sorry,' I finally mutter. 'I should have taken myself home. I'm sorry. I don't know why I did that.'

I feel like crying. I've stuffed everything up. Badly. I need to text Noah and apologise. I didn't mean to hurt him. I hunt through my bag for my phone.

'You're not gonna be sick, are you?' Will whispers.

'No,' I say. 'I'm going to text Noah.'

'You're different around him, you know.'

I put my bag down. 'No, I'm not.'

'Right. Because getting drunk and trying to get into clubs is such an Edie thing to do.'

'People change, Will.'

'They sure do.'

'What the hell does that mean?'

He ignores me, takes out his phone and starts scrolling. I watch him, waiting for his answer, until my eyes feel heavy and my head rocks forward and I'm drifting off to sleep.

THIRTY

Noah doesn't respond to any of my texts or my rambling, apologetic voicemails. And he doesn't bother to tell me he's not coming to today's rehearsal. I only find that out when Darcy announces it as they go through a list of scenes we're meant to concentrate on. We were supposed to be doing the balcony scene, but that won't be happening now. Obviously.

There's about four weeks to go until opening night, which sounds like a lot but really isn't. The crew is all in, building and painting the sets, and the costume department keeps whisking us away to the dressing rooms for measurements and fittings. It's always exciting when all the pieces start coming together. It makes me remember that I'm just one small part of something so much bigger. I like that. I'll try to remember it through these last four weeks, push aside all the other crap and focus on the bigger picture. It helps, I think. What also helps is the simple fact there are more people around. I feel a little better, safer, with all these extra bodies here. Imogen has kept her word and is always hovering, always there, even for the one on one rehearsals every Wednesday lunchtime. *We're a team*, she said. And then also proceeded to give me some of her notes on my delivery. I don't mind. Her notes are actually way more useful than anything Toby Swan offers.

I'm being pinned into Juliet's wedding dress when Imogen comes in to get measured up for another Lady Capulet outfit. She has a lot of costume changes – a different dress for every single scene she appears in. She's very proud of that. All of our costumes are white. Everything. That was part of Toby's vision. He said it is to symbolise how these warring families have more in common than they think, but I think it looks like we're all at one of those old-fashioned debutant balls. Not that I'd say that. The only exception is Juliet's wedding dress, which is red. Riz, our costume designer, told me that brides in Pakistan often wear red because it is good luck. It was all his idea. I remember him arguing with Toby over it. It got pretty heated at times. Once, Riz even walked out. But as soon as Toby saw how it looked, he changed his mind. Now, he'll tell anyone who will listen that he always wanted a red wedding dress because red represents passion and death. Riz rolled his eyes when he heard that and whispered to me, *We know the truth.*

Toby likes to say his vision is edgy and contemporary. The set is covered in graffiti and there's a lot of scaffolding and neon lights, and Romeo and his friends spend a lot of time in a boxing ring. I find it confusing but everyone else seems super excited so I'm probably just missing something.

'Imogen, this is getting ridiculous. You don't need another dress!' Riz sighs.

'Maybe we could go for a pant suit this time?' Imogen says. 'I was thinking something a little Kamala, a little Hillary ...'

Riz claps his hands. He is a sucker for a good pant suit. 'Let me see what I have in the wardrobe,' he says as he rushes into the extensive collection.

Imogen stares at my dress. She reaches out and touches the fabric. It's like she has forgotten I am there, wearing it, and is transfixed by the dress itself. It is pretty spectacular. It's a little sad I only wear it for one tiny moment in the show. It's also sad that I don't get to keep it. I am a bit in love with it, I think. 'You look beautiful,' Imogen says.

'Oh,' I say. I didn't expect her to compliment me. The dress, yes. But me?

'Red is not my colour. I couldn't make that work,' she says wistfully.

'I don't think that's true ...'

'Condola's coming. My agent. To opening night. She's really busy so I wouldn't usually bother her about seeing a high school show. But I told her about you and she's going to come. To see you. I thought you should know,' she says.

I scream.

'Edie! Don't scream.'

'You? You spoke to your agent about me?'

'Oh my god, do you have to act so surprised? I can be generous. And supportive. Can't I?'

I've never, ever seen this side of Imogen. If someone stands in her place during curtain call she will physically push them out of her way. She went off at the lighting guy once because the lights weren't capturing the spirit of her performance. And she reduced her romantic lead in *The Importance of Being Earnest* to tears when he forgot a line. So, yes, I am very surprised by this.

'Thank you, Imogen,' I say, beaming.

'I don't want to be like Farah. She was so awful and sometimes I think – I worry that maybe, when I leave here, that's what people will think of me, too.'

People adore Farah. I don't have the heart to tell her that. So instead I reach out to hug her.

'There's pins in there,' she says as she pulls back from me. 'Don't get your hopes up. It may lead to nothing. Condola is in high demand. But … you are doing a really great job, and I think you deserve to be seen.'

I wait for the next 'but', for the advice or tip she wants to give me that will improve my performance. It doesn't happen, though. I can't believe Imogen has just given me a compliment *and* a connection to her agent. It's a lot.

'I know it's been difficult,' she says. 'This experience has been … challenging. And I may not always show it, but I am grateful that you stayed. And that you're here.'

'I'm grateful you're here, too, Imogen,' I say. And I mean it.

*

We're going through that scene where Lord and Lady Capulet tell Juliet she has no choice, she has to marry Paris. It's a pretty emotional scene. At least, that's how Toby wants me to play it. A lot of crying and throwing myself around. It's not how I think it should be done, but I remember Toby saying *sometimes a director will have a vision that doesn't fit yours* and I know there's no point arguing. If Mrs B were directing, I'd be able to show her how I think the scene should go, but Toby's style is more dictator than collaborator.

We are attempting the scene for the third time. I fall to my knees, stare up at Imogen as Lady Capulet and am just about to get a good cry going when Toby shouts, *Stop!* Imogen helps me up and whispers, *You were doing fine.* I wipe away the tears that were starting, not because of Toby but because of the scene. I don't want him to think those tears are for him.

'Loosen up, for god's sake!' Toby stalks on to the stage.

'I'm trying,' I say softly.

Suddenly, he takes me by the shoulders and starts shaking me, back and forth, side to side, like I'm a ragdoll. 'Loosen the hell up. Relax. Relax.'

I try to move with him, let my body go floppy and loose, but I have never felt less relaxed in my life. My heart is beating too fast, too fast, and I'm looking around for Imogen because she's meant to be here right now, she's meant to stop this from happening.

'Relax, just relax …'

'Get your hands off me!' I shout. Louder than I have shouted before.

He drops his hands from my shoulders as if they've just burned him. 'That was unnecessarily aggressive,' he says.

'Leave me alone.' I stare him down and for a second I think I've done it. I've won. He's backing down. That's what bullies do, isn't it? You just have to stand up to them.

'Obviously Noah was unable to fix this little issue, either,' he says. A smirk plays at his lips.

'Excuse me?' I have no idea what he is talking about.

'I told him he had to get you to loosen up. Show you some fun. I sent him on an excursion last night, which clearly didn't work. You're still very … boring.' He turns to address the entire cast, as if they hadn't all been eavesdropping anyway. 'Write this one down, people: Boring people make bad actors. It's a life lesson for you all. You're welcome.'

'I'm not boring.' I feel my face starting to get hot. 'You know nothing about me.'

'I don't need to,' he says. 'OK. That scene, again, from the top.'

In my first dance classes at Arcadia I often felt like this. I was really behind in dance. Everyone else had been going to dance classes since forever, so they knew all the terminology and the moves and could jump into the positions the teacher told them to get into without even thinking about it. Me? I was learning everything from scratch. And sometimes I'd go left instead of right, or face the wrong the way, or forget the routine and just stand there, stranded, while they all danced around me. I hated feeling like I couldn't keep up, like I didn't belong. And that is exactly how I feel now. Stranded out on this stage. The weak link in the rehearsal process. At least with dancing I knew how to fix it. I just had to work harder, spend extra hours in the studio. But I don't know how to fix this. In these rehearsals I am utterly lost.

'I don't know what you want from me.'

My words stop Toby in his tracks. He takes off his baseball cap and scratches at his bald head for a moment. 'I didn't want you at all,' he says flatly. 'You can thank your boyfriend for getting you the part.'

It feels like the stage has just disappeared from under me and I am falling, falling through this big, black hole of nothing. I can't believe this.

'Imogen,' Toby shouts, 'can you please help me out here? Show Edie what I need in this scene?'

I look in horror at Imogen. *Imogen. Of course. You're an idiot, Edie. How could you ever trust her? Imogen, who just stood by and let it happen after she promised you, promised you, she would be there. Imogen, who should be Juliet. Not you. Who are you kidding? You're not good enough and you don't deserve it – you only got the part because of Noah. You're a fraud. And now Imogen and everyone knows it. You are useless, pathetic, and you don't belong here …*

'No,' Imogen says.

It takes me a second to realise what she's said. No? Imogen actually said no?

'No, I will not be doing that,' she says again and now she puts her arm around my shoulder and I'm not going to cry, I refuse to cry, and I put a shaking arm around her waist and we stand together. United. A team.

Toby looks like he is about to lose it. 'Fine. Take a break, everyone. Get out of my sight. I don't want to see or hear any of you for fifteen minutes. Go.'

I slam the door behind me as I leave.

*

The last person I expect to see is Noah. But there he is. Sitting outside the theatre, head in his script. Any regret or sadness I felt about pushing him away last night has definitely disappeared. I want to tear the script from his hands and rip it into tiny pieces. I don't care that the whole cast is out here and would see me do it. Let them see it.

'What the hell are you doing here?' I stand right in front of him.

He looks up slowly. Raises his eyebrows. But doesn't say a word.

'Toby told me everything.'

He shrugs and keeps reading like I'm not even there. I take a deep breath. 'Toby told me about your little mission. That's why you turned up last night, right? That's why you gave me drinks and wanted me to go to that stupid club.'

'Hey' – he finally speaks – 'nobody *made* you do anything. I didn't force you to drink that shit.'

'But you did force Toby to give me this part.'

He puts the script down. I want him to tell me it's a lie. That Toby is being a dick or trying to psych me out and this is all part of his genius process. But when I see the way he is looking at me, I know the truth.

Toby isn't lying. I have never been so humiliated.

I start walking away from Noah, from the theatre, from Toby, as fast as I can. I hear someone, maybe Imogen, calling out after me, but I don't stop. I just walk and walk. It's not until I reach the rose garden that I realise Noah is following me.

'Remember when you showed me this place? I really wanted to kiss you. That first day. We were sitting right here,' he says.

'I'm surprised you didn't. You always do whatever the hell you want.' I am angry and embarrassed, and no cute smiles or sweet stories can change that. Not now. 'I know why you wanted me, Noah. I'm not an idiot. If you'd let him cast Imogen you would have been overshadowed – no-one would notice you against an actor like her. But an actor like me? You knew you'd take the spotlight because I'm shit. I can't do it. I can't do the part.' I feel sick.

'You can do the part – you *are* doing it. You're better than all of us,' he says.

'You're a liar.'

He rubs his hands over his face. 'I fell for you the moment I saw you, Edie. And I wanted you to fall for me, too. That's why I made Toby give you the part. Because I wanted to be with you.'

'That's pathetic,' I say.

'I know. But also kinda sweet, right?' he says with a grin. Like he thinks that's going to get him out of all this. I shake my head at him and the grin disappears. 'The truth is, Edie, you make me a better actor. You make me work harder and focus and just – you just make me want to be better. I can't do this without you. I don't know how.'

'It doesn't matter what you want,' I say, fists clenched, teeth gritted. 'I don't deserve the part. I didn't earn it. I didn't get it fairly.'

'Nor did I. Nor did Toby. Dad's paying him for this gig,' he says.

'What?'

'Come on, Edie, like you didn't know. Dad got Toby in – he needed the work, so Dad made it happen. Toby owed me. So, I told him to give you the part. It's just how things work.' He says it so matter-of-factly. Like it's no big deal. Like I should just get over it.

'What about needing my help for the audition? That was

266

a lie. You lied to me. You already had the part. You didn't need me. You didn't even need to audition.'

'I wanted to work with you on it. I thought we had fun.'

'Fun?' I almost spit the word at him. 'You should have told me.'

'Why? It doesn't change anything.'

'It changes everything.'

'Don't be so naïve, Edie. This is just how the world works.'

Darcy bursts into the rose garden and the middle of our argument, out of breath and looking really pissed off about it, waving a phone in front of their face like it's on fire. 'This. Has. Been. Going. Off,' they huff, and shove the phone at me. It's mine. I must have left it in the theatre. And left it turned on, even though I know the rules. Phones off and in bags. Darcy is very strict about it.

'Sorry, Darcy.'

'Toby is not happy. It has been very distracting,' they say before marching back towards the theatre. 'You have five minutes!'

Darcy was right, my phone has been going off. There is a screen full of notifications. Missed calls and text messages. They're all from Nan.

I feel like I am watching myself from above. Like this is happening to someone else. On TV or in a movie or maybe a nightmare. This is not really happening. My fingers feel heavy as I try to open the messages, and my vison goes blurry. Noah's voice sounds far away: *Are you OK?* Echoing in my ears. I am not OK.

Pops has been taken to hospital.

THIRTY-ONE

I'm desperately trying to move, move, move, but every step I take feels like I'm moving backwards and every time the nurse tells me something it sounds muffled and distant, and I can't quite make out the words but keep nodding anyway. And then someone gently pushes me towards yet another corridor and keeps their hand on my back, helping me move forward, forward, forward, and I realise it's Noah. He is here. Beside me. Guiding me through the hospital. Directing me through the fog.

He drove me here. I don't remember asking him. I don't know if I even had to. I do remember him telling Toby to go to hell when Toby said I couldn't leave rehearsal.

I didn't expect him to come in with me. But here he is.

We are at a door. Room 402. I wonder if that means something? Is it a lucky number? Significant in some way? Or is it just a room like any of the other rooms in this hospital?

Don't they realise how special Pops is, how he deserves something better than what everyone else has? I want to ask the nurse about it. I should check, shouldn't I? Make sure Pops is in the best room they have. I turn away from the door to find someone, anyone, who can help me out.

'You have to go in,' Noah says.

I know he's right. But I don't want to. 'I should get some flowers or one of those *Get Well Soon* balloons. Did you see a gift shop? There must be a gift shop.' It feels very, very important to not walk in there without something nice for Pops. He will say, *Edie! You shouldn't have!* And I will say, *Of course I should!* And we will laugh because he will be getting ready to leave this awful place, he won't even be staying overnight, because surely it was all a misunderstanding, because he is fine. Absolutely fine. And we will sing a duet as I wheel him out of here, something bright and silly, with all the doctors and nurses popping their heads out of the rooms that line the corridors to harmonise with us, and patients dancing with their IV drips and crutches ...

'I'll wait out here,' Noah says as he opens the door, like he's the concierge at his fancy apartment building and not in some sad hospital ward.

I step into Room 402 and immediately want to leave, but Noah has closed the door behind me and I know there's no turning back.

There are other people in this room. A frail old man lies in the bed nearest the door, hooked up to all these machines that beep and whine, his mouth hanging open as he stares, blank-eyed, at the TV screen above his bed. I try not to look at him. The other beds are encased by blue curtains that don't quite close properly. I can hear people whispering behind them. Coughing. Scraping their chairs against the floor. I listen for the familiar sound of my grandparents' voices, not wanting to walk in on the wrong person, not wanting to draw back the curtain on someone else's pain. I wait in the middle of the room, and want to click my heels together like Dorothy and be whisked back home. Home to Pops in his chair and Nan in hers and a cup of tea and an action film. The smell of disinfectant and cheap soap is overwhelming, the flicker of the fluorescent lighting hurts my eyes, and I'm about to give up when I hear Nan's sigh from the curtained-off bed right at the back of the room. I pull back the curtain. And burst into tears.

Pops's eyelids are fluttering. It looks like he's trying to escape some bad dream, and I want to shake him, tell him to wake up, tell him it's OK, we're here. But I can't touch him. There are too many wires and cords attached to him. Oxygen under his nose. A drip in the back of his hand. He looks even smaller than usual, propped up on the pillows, lying under the hospital sheet, like everything has been sucked out of him.

Nan wraps her arms around me.

*

The doctor has no answers. She says we need to be patient and that they're running tests and that he is in the best possible place and they have their best people on it.

Pops had a seizure. Nan keeps calling it *just a little seizure* but I think she's trying to downplay it for me. A seizure sounds serious and frightening. The word *little* does nothing to make it sound any better. She found him in the garden. He was doing the weeding, which is the job I should have done weeks and weeks ago. Maybe if I had, then this wouldn't have happened. I feel sick with guilt. It was the one thing I could have done to have made his life a little easier, and I couldn't even manage that. After everything he's done for me. What kind of granddaughter am I?

Nan thinks it means the cancer is back, but the doctor tells her not to get ahead of herself. Since I've arrived, we've seen three different doctors. This one is the nicest. Even if she has nothing to tell us. She is at least taking time to listen to Nan and has a sympathetic face and writes a lot of notes. The doctor who came in before her was so dismissive of Nan's questions that I'm sure I even saw him roll his eyes at one point.

Pops has been awake. I held the hand that doesn't have the drip in it, and he squeezed it and said, *Don't cry, don't cry*, which of course made me cry even more. He's been sleeping for most of the time we've sat here. Which, according to the nice doctor, is a good thing.

'He needs rest,' she says. 'And so do you.'

It isn't a request. We have to leave. Nan has already asked if she could sleep in the chair by Pops's bed but the nurse was very clear that was not going to happen.

I have lost all sense of time, but I know it must be late. My stomach growls but I'm not hungry. Nan looks so tired. Her eyes look tiny, all dark and swollen underneath. She's been here all day. The seizure happened not long after I'd left for rehearsal. I wonder if the ambulance drove past my bus. Lights flashing, sirens blaring, while I sat there thinking about myself. I think about all the pointless things I was doing while Pops was being rushed to hospital. Trying on costumes, playing make-believe, arguing with Noah, while Pops was going through all of this. While Nan sat in the waiting room, alone and scared. I try not to be mad at her for not calling me from the ambulance. But I wish she had. I should have been here. With them.

Noah is in the waiting room. I don't see him at first, but he leaps from the seat and waves and jogs over to us. I can't believe he is still here. It must have been hours and hours of waiting.

'Who are you?' Nan says. She must be too tired to care about making a good impression. Which is so unlike my grandmother.

'Hello, Mrs Emerson,' Noah says and gives her one of those smiles that usually makes women like my nan melt. She is not melting today. She is done. Noah doesn't seem to notice, though. 'I'm Noah. Edie's friend. I'm going to drive you ladies home.' And with that he puts out an arm which, much to my surprise, my nan accepts, and he leads her out to his car as if it is a carriage taking her to the ball.

*

Nan sits in the front passenger seat and promptly falls asleep. Noah and I don't speak. The only sound is the voice from the GPS telling him when to turn left or to take the second exit at the roundabout or to keep going. Keep going.

I never wanted Noah to come back here. Once was enough. But here he is again, driving through our streets. I try to imagine how it looks to someone like Noah. The houses that have seen better days, the strip of fast-food restaurants, the flatness and sameness and blandness of it all. I know that's all someone like Noah will see. But there's more than that here. You just have to look a little deeper. There's fruit trees and nice gardens, and magpies that sing in the morning and cockatoos who run amok during the day. There's the mural at the skatepark, the oval that becomes a dog park on Saturday mornings, the fish-and-chip shop that is always very generous with its serves, and Nan and Pops, who have lived here forever. Their house is not as fancy as the Winters', but that doesn't make them any less important. Any less loved. But I still hate Noah seeing all this. Because this place is a part of me. And if he turns his nose up at it, if he sneers at it, or hates it, then he is saying I'm not good enough. He would be sneering at me.

Nan wakes up as we pull into the driveway and tries to act like she hasn't been sleeping. 'You want to come in for a cuppa, Noah?' she asks.

He swivels around in the seat to look at me. 'If Edie wants me to.'

What can I say? The guy has just sat in a hospital waiting room for four hours and driven us all the way home. 'Sure,' I shrug – there's no turning back now. 'Come on in.'

*

As soon as we got inside, Nan said she had to make herself presentable and rushed off to the bathroom. So, it's just the two of us. I'm trying to make tea and grilled cheese sandwiches because I know Nan hasn't eaten all day. Noah wants to help. Says he wants to be useful. He keeps bumping into me like he isn't used to sharing such a small space. It's infuriating.

'Where do you keep the cutting board?' he asks. I point vaguely at one of the cupboards. He opens and closes every door before I grab it for him and slam it onto the bench. He doesn't even flinch, just says, 'How about I make grilled cheese and you go chill?'

He says it so kindly I want to scream. But I don't. Instead I say, 'You know how to make grilled cheese? I thought your chef would do that for you.'

'Who do you think taught me?' he laughs. What the hell? I must be pulling a face because he quickly adds, 'That was a joke, Edie.'

I only sit down because I'm tired. And because I want to see if Noah actually can make grilled cheese.

Turns out he can. Which is also infuriating. The three of us sit at the dining table and devour them. Nan says it is the best toasted cheese sandwich she has ever had, even better than Ronny's, which is saying something.

'My dad is friends with some of the country's top doctors,' Noah says from nowhere. 'We could easily get Mr Emerson into a better hospital.'

Nan covers her mouth as she finishes chewing. I wait for her to say something. She is taking a long time to finish that sandwich.

'We don't need your help, Noah,' I say on Nan's behalf, because I know that's what she'd be thinking but would be too polite to say.

'No offence, Edie, but I think you do,' he says quietly.

'Thank you, Noah, that's very kind, but we know that hospital very well. Ed was there …' her voice wobbles when she says Pops's name and she trails off, wipes her eyes.

'Nan?'

'I think I might go to bed. Lovely to meet you, Noah,' she says and shuffles off to her bedroom. Alone. The last time Nan slept alone was when Pops was having treatment. They never spend a night apart or go to bed angry with each other. They told me that was their promise to each other when they got married.

'I didn't mean to upset her,' Noah says. 'But your grandfather doesn't even have his own room. Surely you want him to be comfortable?'

'We can't afford it, Noah.'

'We can. Let us help you. We've been through this, remember, with my mum. I know what you're going through. We can help.'

'You have no idea what we're going through.'

I start to pack up. Noah helps me carry the cups and plates to the kitchen. He looks a little shocked when I tell him there is no dishwasher, but recovers quickly and starts to fill the sink with hot water. 'Leave it, please,' I say. 'I'll do it in the morning.'

'I'm trying to help you, Edie.'

I see it then. Clearly. The pity in his eyes. He feels sorry for me. For us. I hate that. There's nothing about me, about my life, to feel sorry about. I have so much more than so many other people have.

'We don't need it.'

'Jesus, Edie, look around. You do.' He throws down the dishcloth.

'You have helped. Driving us. Making supper. That's helpful. Thank you.' I try to sound calm and reasonable, but

I don't think it's coming out like that. He goes to speak but I cut him off. 'You should probably go. I need to get some sleep,' I say.

*

I curl up into Pops's old armchair. The arms are worn, and the seat needs more padding. But I don't care. I take his blanket from the back of the chair and cuddle into it. I can hear the hum of the refrigerator. The streetlight shines through the gap in the curtains. Pops has left his crossword book open on the little coffee table beside his chair. I make a note to pack that for him tomorrow. I know I should go to my room, to my bed. I will sleep better there. But in this chair I can pretend Pops is here, with his arms around me, and that everything is OK.

THIRTY-TWO

Will turned up unannounced this morning because, he said, *You should not have to catch a bus today.* He brought Nan a bunch of flowers, fresh from the petrol station, and gave her a huge hug. It broke my heart watching her trying not to cry. I didn't have the heart to tell her she was wearing two different earrings, but I did, very gently, let her know she was wearing the glasses she'd spent five minutes searching for. Nan is not herself today. None of us are. But despite this, and despite my best efforts to convince her otherwise, she insisted I go to school.

Words feel hard at the moment. Putting them into sentences, making banter, laughing, that all seems beyond me. But Will is chatting away. And that helps.

'Are we OK?' I say suddenly. The karaoke night feels like a distant nightmare.

'Of course,' he says. 'Are *you* OK?'

'No …'

I've been thinking about this all night. I can't do Will's show. It was selfish to think I could do the musical and the play and exams *and* be there for my grandparents the way I'm supposed to be. Mum always told me to pull my weight. She was very adamant about that. *You can't be a burden.* She said that a lot when we first moved in with Nan and Pops. I think she was worried they wouldn't want us there if we were too messy or loud. That they'd ask us to leave if we ate too much of their food, as if we were boarders rather than family. It wasn't until Mum left that I could relax and start to feel like Nan and Pops' home was my home too. Our home. But Mum's lessons stayed with me, and I always made sure I did my share. Not because I thought they'd kick me out, but because I felt like it was my responsibility. And perhaps to make up for Mum leaving the way she did.

But lately, I haven't been doing my share. Not at all. If I had, Pops wouldn't have been in the garden, picking up my slack.

'I can't do the show, Will.'

He doesn't speak.

'It's just too much now. With Pops and just … everything … I can't.'

'You're not the only one dealing with stuff, Edie,' Will says coldly. It takes me by surprise – not just what he's saying, but the way he's saying it. 'We're all dealing with shit. It might not be as important as your shit, but it's still shit.'

'I'm sorry.'

'You know why I'm so obsessed with my musical?'

'Because you want to go to New York. But you know what? You can go with or without that musical. You can just go. You can do whatever the hell you want. Some of us don't have those options.'

'I wanted to show Arcadia what I could do,' he says.

'What are you talking about? They know what you can do.'

'When? In Year Seven as Aladdin? Cos that's it. That was the pinnacle of my acting career at Arcadia. There were never any lead roles for me,' he says. 'I had to write my own.'

'I know, you've told me this.'

'But I don't think you get it. You don't understand cos there's always a role for you, for people like you –'

'People like me?' I can feel the rage building, the anger in my voice. 'I had to fight to get into this school. I had to prove myself and work harder than anybody –'

'I'm not saying it wasn't hard for you, Edie. I'm saying … You always saw roles for yourself, didn't you? In the musicals and plays they chose, there was always a part for you. Someone you could kinda relate to, see something of yourself in. Even if you had to put on a New York accent or wear a wig or whatever. But I'd look at those cast lists and think, *Nope. There's no-one on here like me*. And if someone like me isn't there, then they clearly don't want me. Do you know what I mean?'

I think back to Year Nine, when we all did *Guys and Dolls*. Will auditioned for one of the leads but ended up with small, comedic part even though he out-sang and out-acted all the other boys who auditioned. He told us he preferred that role and it was what he'd really wanted – and, stupidly, we believed him. Perhaps because it was easier to go with that than question what was really going on. He never auditioned for a mainstage production again. I thought it was because he hated the old-fashioned shows. And I suppose, in one way, he did. But it was more than that. We made him feel like there wasn't a place for him. And we didn't even notice.

'You always go on about your mum and how this is your last chance to show her something at Arcadia, but you know what? This musical, my musical, is probably gonna be my last show for a long time. Maybe ever. It's my last chance to do something like this. I'm going into medicine, Edie. I want to – but I also have to. We all have things we have to do to keep our families happy. Not just you. But you can do musicals for the rest of your life if you choose to. Me? This is it, my musical is it, my last chance, and I need my mums to see it. To see *me*. To understand why I want to do this sort of stuff, and give me a chance. Your Nan and Pops support you no matter what. You're so lucky. You don't even realise it.'

'They might support my dreams, Will, but when you don't have the money to turn them into something real then they're only ever dreams.'

'Bullshit,' he sneers.

'I think it's *you* who doesn't understand,' I snap back at him. 'You can still do the musical. Tara will be an amazing Lily and the show will go on and your mums will love it and New York will love it and you'll go to New York and have a wonderful life.'

'Not without you I won't …'

I go to ask him what he means but he turns on the radio. Turns it up loud. It feels like the longest drive in the world to school.

*

There's a soft tap at my bedroom door and Nan's voice asking to come in. I sit up and turn on my lamp, and Nan sits next to me on the bed. I can smell her lavender moisturiser cream, the one she uses every night on her dry hands. I bought her a more expensive hand cream last year for Christmas, from David Jones. I don't think she's even taken it out of the box.

'Can't sleep?' I ask. She shakes her head. 'Me neither.'

We sit there for a moment, in silence. The soft glow of the lamp casts gentle shadows across Nan's face. She takes a deep breath. I get that from her – the readying of yourself when you need to say something you really don't want to say. I don't know how to ready myself to hear it, though. The urge to cover my ears is strong. I reach out and hold Nan's hand instead. To help her say it, and to help me hear it.

'Your pops is going to have to stay in the hospital a little longer,' she says.

'It's back?' I don't know why I'm asking. I already know the answer. It's in the curve of Nan's shoulders, the wrinkles on her brow.

'He's a fighter, Edie. You know that. He'll get through it.' She pats my hand. 'We all will.'

I've been so selfish. My problems are nothing compared to this. Teeny tiny blips of unimportance dotted onto a life. I need to quit both shows – not just the musical – and spend more time right here. With them. I owe it to them. How could I ever think being on a stage was more important than being with my grandparents?

I try explaining this to Nan. 'It just puts everything

into perspective,' I say. 'I can't keep performing if it means neglecting you and Pops. I'm not Mum.'

Nan squeezes my hand. 'You're right, you're not your mother,' she says. 'You've worked so hard and you're damn talented, my girl, and I refuse to let you give that up. Besides, your pops would never forgive himself if you threw it in because of him. You can't do that, Edie. It isn't fair on you or any of us.'

'So, should I keep performing for Pops?'

'Edie. No. You should do it because you love it. You should do it for yourself.'

'I don't know if I do love it. Not anymore.' And without much warning, I start to cry.

Nan hugs me, envelops me into her fleecy pink dressing gown, and tells me it's OK and that she loves me as I tell her everything that's happened. Everything. Even the parts I never thought I'd be able to tell anyone.

She listens. Her face twists with anger and sadness, but she doesn't say anything. Just lets me get it all out. And when I'm finished, she tells me about the Toby Swans in her life. The baker at her first job who grabbed her bottom, back when she was fourteen. The teacher who told the girls when they needed to start wearing bras; all the girls called him a creep, but nothing was done about it. The customers who commented on the size of her breasts. The manager who pinned her against a wall and kissed her and said it was a perk of being the boss.

'You can't let the bastards get away with it,' she says.

And I know she's right. Because she's Nan. And she's always right.

THIRTY-THREE

I'm on the cover of some glossy brochures for this school. I am the good news story for their fundraising appeals, and the lead in their big, shiny musicals. I think I've forgotten that as much as they help me, I help them, too. Or maybe I've just never realised that before. Either way, it's time to remind them, so I make an appointment to see Mr Healy and Mrs B.

'Is everything all right?' Mr Healy sounds nervous as he clutches his *Phantom* mug.

I start with Mrs B. Tell her I'm sorry and that I blamed her for things which were not her fault, and that it was really wrong she got pushed aside on *Romeo and Juliet*. With that, I shoot Mr Healy a look. He squirms in his chair, picks up his *Phantom of the Opera* stress ball and starts squeezing the life out of it.

'For what it's worth, Mrs B, I think you would have directed a much better version. And I wish you had. But that's not how it worked out and you can't keep ignoring the show, pretending it's not happening, because it is – and we really, really need you. It is not safe in that rehearsal room. You need to get over it and be there for us. Please.'

Old Man Healy really gives the stress ball a workout when I explain exactly what's been going on. I don't skip any details. Even the ones that make me feel awkward and embarrassed. Mrs B looks like she's about to burst into tears.

'I'm very sorry about all of this, Edie,' Healy says and offers me a mint. 'We'll sort it out.'

'I've got it,' I say. 'But I'll need you both as back-up.'

That makes them laugh, and they both seem to relax a little.

'I'm so, so sorry, darling girl,' Mrs B says while dabbing at her eyes with a scrunched-up tissue. Her mascara has slid all over her face.

'I'll be OK,' I tell her. And I know it's the truth. After talking with Nan, it felt like some of those clouds that had been hanging over me lifted. That there was some light breaking through. A way out of it. A way that started with me, and this meeting.

But mostly with me.

*

Toby Swan is out-Toby-Swanning himself today. He is in a rage. At everything. The costumes are wrong and the set is disgusting and we, his cast, are a bunch of useless, untalented little bitches who are going to ruin his career, his reputation. I feel like Toby is doing a good job of that last part all on his own.

We are fractured. We have not become that tight-knit, loveable but dysfunctional sit-com family like other casts I've been in. We even managed that backstage during *The Crucible*, and that play is dark. It is very volatile backstage, and front of stage, at *Romeo and Juliet*. People are fighting and arguing and crying a lot. Riz has threatened to sell all the costumes on eBay. Darcy has thrown their clipboard at the wall on three separate occasions. Someone painted PRICK in big letters on the back of the set. It's not just the Capulets and Montagues at war – it's everyone. All the time.

Noah and I are barely speaking. He says he's giving me some space while Pops recovers, but he says it too carefully, as if it's a line he's rehearsed. It makes those romantic Romeo and Juliet moments difficult, but I focus on the lines, the meaning, the character, and keep going. It's called acting for a reason, right? But still, it would be way too hard to attempt those scenes alongside an ex. No. We need to be together, boyfriend and girlfriend, if we're going to get through this show. Toby keeps telling us we're awful, so imagine how much worse we'd be if we weren't together. But his cruel words about us are nothing compared to what he said to Makayla.

Toby told Makayla he was going to cut all her lines if she didn't do something about her face. He never said what she needed to do about her face, or how she should do it. She has a lovely face, but now Makayla is staring at a mirror trying to work out how to fix something that clearly isn't broken. That's where Imogen and I find her.

'Let's talk,' I say. I have a plan, but I need to make sure everyone is with me.

Unsurprisingly, we are united in our hate for Toby Swan. Maybe we will get that tight-knit cast feeling after all.

*

'Maybe you should quit.' I give him a chance. He doesn't deserve it. And I don't offer it in front of everyone. I have learnt that Toby loves an audience, enjoys what he calls *teachable moments* that are really just a chance to humiliate us and feel powerful. Imogen hovers nearby. She's out of sight, but she's there. Keeping watch. Just in case. It makes me feel stronger, knowing she's there.

I found him outside during a break, by the back of the workshops, vaping this sickly sweet raspberry-smelling stuff that reminds me of cordial. He ignores me, so I say it again. 'Maybe you should quit.'

'I have. That's why I vape,' he grins weakly.

'The show. Quit the show.'

'I can't. I need the money.' Is he crying? I can't tell if it's the vape making his eyes water or if he is genuinely upset. Not that I should care if he is. Looking at him now, I don't know how I ever cared what he thought. He looks so … ordinary.

'We're probably more alike than you think, Edie,' he says. 'I grew up with nothing. Had to fight my way through. No scholarships, no handouts, just hard work and passion and talent. I suppose I get a bit pissed off when I see kids like you getting handed these opportunities and squandering them and getting lazy and complacent. So, yeah, I was tough, but only because I wanted to push you. A bit of tough love. To make you better.'

'That's such bullshit,' I say. 'I know you holiday in Aspen with Noah's family.'

I wait for him to respond. To tell me I'm wrong or stupid or a pathetic actor with no talent, or that I'm fired or all my lines have been cut, or that I'll never make it in this industry (that's one of his favourites). But he says nothing. Just pushes at some gravel with the toe of his boot.

'I can handle tough,' I go on. 'But you crossed a line.'

'It's the process. If you can't deal with it –'

'You crossed a line. More than once. And you know it.'

He sighs, rubs his eyes. 'The truth is … I'm scared. I'm just as scared as you. I don't know what the hell I'm doing.'

'OK …'

'I think I've lost it, I was so good, *so* good and now … I just don't know.'

I'm about to say, *That's not true, you're still so good!* Because that's the way I'd usually react. I'd want that person to feel better and to be OK. But this is not usual. This is Toby Swan. I don't want him to feel better. He doesn't deserve to feel better.

Instead, I say, 'Mrs B and Mr Healy will be at rehearsals today. And tomorrow. And all the rest. If you don't change, you won't even have a chance to quit. They will fire you.'

This time, I'm not waiting for a response, because I don't care. I don't need to hear it. And perhaps Toby needs a bit of tough love himself.

*

When I return to the theatre, I see that Mr Healy and Mrs B have arrived. It looks like they have tried to sneak in without anyone noticing. They're sitting at the back of the auditorium, like they're undercover cops on some sort of stakeout. But people have noticed them. Imogen is already up there, demanding Mrs B's attention, and Darcy is chatting away to Old Man Healy, looking the happiest I've seen them in ages.

We hear Toby shouting before he gets back inside. We can't hear exactly who he is shouting about, but he is clearly in a foul mood. I'm guessing that could be my fault. He is ranting and raving as he crosses the stage, all of us just watching, waiting for him to realise we have visitors – that my warning was not some empty threat – but he doesn't look up. He is mumbling something about *useless fucking kids* as he reaches his place in the auditorium.

'Darcy! Where the hell are you?'

'They're up here, with me, Toby,' Old Man Healy calls from the back row.

Toby pulls off his hat and scratches at his bald head, as if figuring out what his best move is. He abruptly turns towards them and waves his hat in their direction. 'Hello there,' he says with forced cheer. 'Welcome. Nice to see you.'

'We wanted to observe. I hope you don't mind,' Mrs B says sweetly. 'Please, carry on. Act like we're not even here. We're excited to see Toby Swan in action.'

*

Pops is awake. I can hear his laugh from the corridor. I sprint into the room and ignore the wires and machines and hug him anyway. Nan wants to know what took me so long. But I'm not going to tell them. Not yet.

THIRTY-FOUR

We meet after rehearsal and quietly develop the plan. We don't tell Mrs B or Mr Healy what's going on. We don't mention it to anybody outside the group. This is our secret. The cast and the crew. Every single one of us. Except Noah. Noah says I'm being too sensitive. Taking it too personally. That I need to chill out.

And that Toby is his friend.

He says he feels bad for him.

I think about that a lot. I don't sleep. I stare at the ceiling, at the dead stars, and I wish Mum would call me. I wish Mum would respond to one of my texts. I check my phone constantly. Waiting for her. Worried I have done something wrong, messed it all up again. That she's gone for good this time. And it's then I realise. That feeling I get when I'm desperately wishing for Mum is the same feeling I get when I think about losing Noah, when I think about how I'm losing

Aubrey, when I freak about losing the scholarship. So, I hold on tighter and tighter. Because I don't want to be left behind again. I don't want to be abandoned. Even when, perhaps, I should be the one doing the leaving.

I ask Noah to meet me in the rose garden. It's dark now. Quiet. Most of the cast have gone. I can hear some of the crew packing up.

Noah wants to know if I'm still pissed off about the Juliet thing. *The Juliet thing.* That's what he's reduced it down to – bribing someone to give me a part, humiliating me, demeaning me and my acting ability, not to mention Imogen's – like it's no big deal. I tell him yes, I am still pretty pissed off about 'the Juliet thing'. He tells me to let it go. I tell him he is a manipulative piece of shit.

He says, 'Calm down.'

I say, 'I think we should break up.'

He goes very, very quiet. Bites his lower lip. I have never seen Noah do that before. I thought I knew all his faces. All his moves.

Here's the thing about Noah Winters. He is charming and handsome and can be surprisingly kind and generous, and he is totally not used to being told *no*. Noah always gets what he wants. It's not his fault. It's the luck of his draw. The fact he was born into the right family at the right time. But even though he doesn't often hear the word no, that's what he's getting today.

'You're not thinking right,' he says. 'You're upset because of your grandfather.'

I am upset. And Pops is part of the reason, I suppose. Pops

would never lie like that to Nan. And I'd never mismatch my earrings over Noah.

'Thing is, I was actually going to break up with you,' he says moments later, and I almost believe him. He really, really wants me to know that it's not because of anything I have done. And is definitely, one hundred per cent, not because I'm poor.

'Poor?' I say. 'Wow.'

'I didn't mean ... well, you're not – but compared to us, I mean – but it's not a – that isn't what I'm – sorry,' he stumbles and splutters, and I think he's actually a little embarrassed. Which is probably a big deal for Noah Winters.

'Compared to your family, I think most of the population would be considered poor,' I say. He laughs like he isn't sure if he should. I tell him to relax. *Calm down*. That it's OK. It's not really. But I get why someone like Noah would think we're poor. I used to think I was too, but that was only because I kept comparing myself to the kids at Arcadia. I'm trying not to do that anymore.

'I'm sorry, Edie,' he says. And I can tell he means it.

'Me too,' I say. Because I am.

'I assume it's Will.'

'Excuse me?'

'The reason you want to break up with me? You like Will.'

'No,' I say. 'I'm breaking up with you because you lied to me. And manipulated the whole situation and –'

'OK, OK, I get it. I'm a dick. Like you always thought. But you're not perfect yourself.'

'I know that.'

I didn't think this was going to hurt. I thought I was going to break up with him and feel bad about it, but not hurt. Not rejected. But maybe that's what all break-ups are meant to feel like. Maybe I was being naïve to think I was going to get away without feeling like shit.

'I still like you,' he says.

'And one day,' I say, 'you'll find someone who likes you back.'

As I walk away, I wonder if he is feeling rejected. If he feels like shit. I don't think he does. I don't know if he'd ever feel that way. He is Noah Winters, after all.

THIRTY-FOUR

I love this moment. The butterflies that tornado around my stomach and flutter down my legs and up my body and through my skin. Fluttering. Glittering. In the darkness of the wings I bounce up and down on my toes and try to get into the right mode.

I'm not going to be Juliet tonight. Tonight I'm going to be me. And suddenly, I'm freaking out again. I can't do this.

But I can.

And I will.

Imogen squeezes my hand.

It's a full house. And it's not just all family and friends. Toby Swan's name on the poster has drawn a different crowd. Agents, including Imogen's Condola; Toby Swan's contacts and colleagues from the industry; heads of acting from the big drama schools; reviewers and critics. People who could give me an opportunity. Open a door. Except, I've realised, I have to open the door myself.

The cast and the crew take to the stage. Every single one of us.

This is not Toby Swan's vision for the opening scene of *Romeo and Juliet*. This is not what we have rehearsed. This isn't even what Mrs B and Mr Healy expect to see right now. But this is what we're doing.

We stand. We wait. I wear the red wedding dress, because why the hell not? Imogen, beside me, is in the pant suit Riz reworked for her. Makayla's in her long white gown. Mei's in her white, beaded jumpsuit. Darcy's in a black T-shirt and jeans, headset on, clipboard pressed against their chest. Noah, sulking, is in his white linen trousers and shirt; Dom and Cody are standing a little further back, looking serious and sincere. Every single one of us is on that stage.

A hush falls over the audience.

They think this is Toby's avant-garde take on the show. They think he is some sort of genius. Breaking the form. Shattering their expectations.

I step forward.

I've spent so long speaking the lines and singing the songs of characters that I forgot I have a voice, too. I think I lost it somewhere along the way. Lost it and had it taken from me. I always thought the dialogue in my musical would be all *umms* and *ahhs* because I never knew what to say or how to say it. But I think I'm learning. I think I'm finding my voice. Or at least I'm starting to. I steady myself.

'We will not be presenting *Romeo and Juliet*,' I say. There are some whispers. A gasp. They love this. They still think this is part of Toby's vision. It's experimental. Risky. Different. Exactly what they expect from the incredible Toby Swan. 'Toby Swan has harassed, bullied and abused the students in this production. He has used his position of power and privilege to hurt us, intimidate us and make us feel small.'

Something has shifted in the audience now. No-one is smiling anymore.

'Toby Swan is a known offender. His behaviour is the worst-kept secret in the industry but still, he gets hired. And still, you are here. Still, you see his shows and marvel at his genius. Toby Swan is not a genius. He is a bully and an abuser. He has bullied and abused me. He has bullied and abused others in this cast. And because of that, we will not be performing tonight. Thank you.'

There is absolute silence.

And then someone in the crowd starts to clap. And someone else joins them, and then another. But among the clapping is the sound of anger: people getting up and leaving. Someone shouting, but I can't make out the words.

I look out at the theatre, at the audience slowly emptying out. Some grumbling, some excited. Toby is nowhere to be seen. And, just because it's a habit, I find the best seat in the theatre. Row E. Seat 15. And tonight, she's there. Mum. Sitting in that seat. Watching me.

Mum is here.

I blink away the hotness in my eyes.

I'd imagined she would sit in the audience – middle seat in the middle row to get the full effect, the *mise en scene*, like she always said – and watch me play Juliet. I'd imagined that she would see me, up on stage, and fall in love with me the way mothers are supposed to love their daughters. I thought she'd be overcome with this sense of pride. That she'd say, *That's my daughter up there!* to everyone who asked, and even those who didn't. That she'd see something special in me again, something worth sticking around for. And that she'd finally become the mother I'd always longed for. I wanted to follow in her footsteps and be a triple threat too, because I thought that would bring her back to me. The way my performance as Merry the Christmas Elf did all those years ago.

I have been building my hopes and dreams on the idea of her.

Maybe she built her hopes and dreams on the idea of me.

And tonight, I destroyed it all. I could have just performed the role the way we'd rehearsed it. We were ready. I could have done it. And Mum would have finally seen it. Would have finally seen me as the actor she always wanted me to be.

But would she have seen me as *me* – the real me, the person I've become without her?

*

'What the *fuck* was that?'

She's screaming at me. In front of everyone. This is not the post-show foyer scene I've always dreamed of. This is not how it's supposed to happen. She's been drinking. Her eyes are bloodshot. She's thinner than I've ever seen her. The veins pulsate on the side of her head.

I try to pull her away, out of the foyer, but she shoves me away. I want to die. I want the ground to open up, right here, and swallow me whole. Everyone is staring. I can't blame them. It must look frightening and strange to them.

I turn to look at the crowd. Imogen is with her agent. I want to throw up. Darcy looks like they're about to jump in and try to save me, but I shake my head and they back away. *It's not worth it*, I want to tell them. *Don't get involved.*

This was meant to be a moment of triumph. A moment to celebrate what we'd managed to do. Together. But now … Now Mum is here. The Mum they all think is some Hollywood actor. Swearing and hitting me and out of control.

She looks nothing like the version of her I've spent all these years creating for my friends. I don't know why I ever believed I could keep the lie going. That she would come through for me. When has she ever, ever come through for me?

'You selfish, *selfish* girl.'

Maybe I never really thought she would turn up, that I'd never have to prove she was something she's not. Maybe I thought, for all those years, that my lie would remain intact.

But it's not now.

'I'm so sorry, Mum,' I whisper, trying to get her to bring her voice down. To stop making a scene.

'Sorry?' she laughs. 'You're sorry? Too late for sorry. Too late!'

She isn't even making sense. People are starting to leave, taking a wide berth around her. I'd leave too if I could.

'Everything all right, Edie?' Mrs B steps in.

'Fuck off!' Mum hisses at her.

I'm scared she is going to hit Mrs B so I tell her it's fine, I have it under control. She quietly mentions the police, and I say *Please, don't, I can handle it.*

I wanted Mum to meet Mrs B. I wanted Mrs B to meet my mum. Not this version of her. I wanted the version who talks about the *mise en scene* and Meryl Streep and famous directors, who can recite Portia's monologue from *The Merchant of Venice* beautifully and sings Fantine's song from *Les Misérables* with such feeling you can't help but cry. The version who can crack you up with her silly jokes and stories from the cruise ship days. The version who loves me.

'I said, fuck off.' Mum moves in closer towards Mrs B. Now I don't care if she hits me. I grab her, hard, and drag her outside. The cool air seems to calm her down a bit.

'I'm getting you an Uber. Where are you going?'

'I don't want anything from you,' she spits at me. 'Come all this way to see that. That? What a fucking disgrace.'

'You have no idea what's been going on.'

'Oh, boohoo, poor little rich girl with all her stuck-up friends couldn't deal with the real world. I'm so embarrassed.' She starts on her rant again. I just wait. Wait for it to stop. I know it will, eventually. She'll wear herself out. This is what she does.

I watch her face contorting. Hear the mean words she is spitting at me. I have to remember this isn't about me. That's what our psych said. *This is about her, not you. You can't take it personally.* But it's hard. It's so hard.

She starts to get quiet. This is when the tears will start. I know the routine. I ask her, again, if she needs an Uber.

'No,' she sniffs, 'I have a lift coming.'

I stand there in silence, waiting for her lift to show up. Waiting for her to leave. Again. I wonder if anyone is still in the foyer. I don't dare turn around to check. I can't deal with the thought of them still watching me. Seeing all of this. All this stuff I've worked so hard to hide.

'Thought I might meet Toby Swan,' she says finally. 'You messed that up for me though, didn't you?'

'Yeah,' I say. 'I did.'

And it hits me. What am I waiting for? Why am I waiting? I look at her, this woman who is supposed to be my mum, and I can't find her. Can't find Mum in the spit and vile words, the bloodshot eyes and curled lip, the vicious slaps and acid breath. She isn't there. Not anymore.

And I'm not waiting for her to come back.

I'm not waiting anymore.

And so I stop. I stop waiting. I leave her. Right there. Walk away. Ignore the shouts and sobs that follow me.

I leave her. This time, at least, she can't leave me. I'm the one doing the leaving.

And I won't look back.

*

'You're early!' Nan says as I come in the front door. My eyes are puffy. My face is red. I cried all the way home.

'Cup of tea?' she calls from the kitchen.

'No.' I try to make my voice sound steady. 'I think I'll just go to bed.'

'But I want to hear how it went ...' She sees me then. Her face falls. 'Edie? What's the matter?'

*

That night, after a long talk and lots of tea, Nan tucks me into bed like I'm a kid again, because sometimes we all need that, and says, *Good night, love you*. And I realise that all this time I've been longing for a mother, I've had one. My nan.

THIRTY-FIVE

Old Man Healy is in crisis mode. According to Shelley at reception, the phone hasn't stopped and the emails are never-ending. A message went out to every Arcadia Grammar family telling us to say 'no comment' when approached by the media. There was a small pack of journalists out the front of the school this morning. Just by the front gates. As close as they are legally allowed to get. The video of my speech is doing the rounds on social media. I'm trying to ignore it. Imogen has already sent me a message warning me that I should absolutely, positively NOT read the comments. I'm trying very hard not to.

Shelley tells me she is very proud of me before waving me through to Mr Healy's office. Mrs B is there, too.

They don't look very proud of me at all. I wonder if they even left last night or just came straight here, to the office, to fix the mess I seem to have made.

'That wasn't the deal, Edie,' Mrs B says. 'You have really put the school in a difficult situation.'

'Are you expelling me? Taking away my scholarship?' It had been my worst fear, but right now I don't think I'd care. I think I'd actually be all right.

Old Man Healy laughs. 'No! Not at all. It was very impressive. We just have some fires to put out.'

'A lot of fires,' Mrs B echoes.

'But all publicity is good publicity, so they say, and we can work this to our advantage. You'll be our spokesperson. I'm sure you won't mind doing us that little favour, will you?' he says.

They want me to be the face of the movement. To talk to the media. To give a speech at a press conference.

'You spoke so eloquently last night, and we think you should keep doing it. Using your voice like that, Edie. You can make a difference,' Mrs B says.

'What's the catch, though?' I look at Old Man Healy.

'No catch,' he says. 'But if you could mention how Arcadia gave you the confidence to stand up for yourself, that sort of thing, I would be grateful.'

'Roman!' Mrs B snaps at him. 'Edie can say what she likes. We want you to be honest. That's all. Just be yourself, Edie.'

'Of course, yes, be yourself, Edie,' Mr Healy echoes.

I don't know if I've ever had the chance to be honest during my time at Arcadia. Not really. I feel like I've always been playing this version of me. Hiding my mum, my home, my insecurities, my true self. But now it's all out there. There's nothing left to hide. And if I don't talk about the stuff that happened with Toby, the only person who wins is him. And that man does not deserve to win.

But I'm not going to agree so easily.

'There's an empty theatre sitting there now. And I want to use it. For Will's musical. Give us three weeks and we'll be ready,' I say. I haven't planned this. Haven't mentioned it to Will or Aubrey. But it feels right.

'*Romeo and Juliet* is the scheduled performance –'

'Mrs B is going to need time to fix it. Toby did a horrible job. You should have let her do it in the first place.'

Mrs B sits a little higher in her seat.

'And she'll need to find a new Juliet. We can do the musical while they get the play ready. I think that's a good deal. I think a spokesperson for the school would be really happy with that decision.'

*

Last night, I added a long message to the group chat with Will and Aubrey about Mum and all the things I'd been hiding, and when Aubrey asked me why I did it, I said, *I don't know*. Because I don't know why I lied about it, especially to my best friends. But I was lying to myself, too. Creating a version of Mum I could carry with me more easily than the truth. Aubrey removed herself from the group chat before I could even try to explain.

I sent Will a text to see if he hated me, too. He called me instantly.

'I could never hate you,' he said.

'But I lied.'

'You can tell me the truth now. Or whenever you're ready. I'm here for you, Eds.'

So I told him all the parts I could manage for now and promised to tell him the rest when I felt I could. Because it's a lot. We talked long into the night. It felt like I'd been sort of holding my breath since our fight but now, hearing his voice, I could finally exhale. I could breathe easily. It was a relief, having Will back. But Aubrey never called. Never texted.

She's standing by my locker now. My stomach flips at the sight of her. I know what's about to happen. No-one talks about that. How breaking up with a best friend can feel even worse than breaking up with a boyfriend.

'You lied to me,' she says.

'I'm sorry.'

'You know I hate liars. After everything with my dad. You saw all of that. You were there.'

She wants to know the details. Exactly what parts are true (none of it) and what's a complete lie (all of it). She wants to know why I lied, so I tell her all the stuff about Mum that I've never told anybody. All the stuff only Nan and Pops know. More than what I told Will last night. Everything.

'You could have told me this. I don't know why you lied to me.'

'I don't know either.'

'I can't trust you, Edie. And if I can't trust you, I can't be your friend. Not right now.'

'What? So, that's it. Our friendship is just done. Over this?'

'Not just this.' She sighs. 'You don't even remember. You promised me we'd go to Singapore together. I was so excited, thinking of everything we could do there together. And then you just said no. And you didn't even care. Didn't give a shit what that meant to me. How that affected me. Cos it's always about you.'

I am so confused. I have no idea what she's talking about because it wasn't like that. It isn't like that. 'You know why I can't go.'

'It's an excuse, Edie. You could if you wanted to. You let me down and you hurt me.'

'I'm sorry,' I say, but it sounds like too small a word, too fragile and insignificant, against the pain in Aubrey's voice. I had no idea she felt like that. No idea I'd let her down, hurt her, so badly.

'And now this, with your mum. Hiding that from me? I feel like I don't know you at all.'

I want to tell her I love her. I want to tell her I'll make it up to her. That our friendship will be what it used to be, but even better because there will be no stupid secrets. Just honesty. And trust. And that if she'd just hear me out, give me a chance, I could prove to her that I'm worth it. I want to say that I was embarrassed about Singapore, about not being able to pay my way, about the fact I don't even have a passport, that I have never been anywhere. That I need her to keep encouraging me to take those little steps, even though I've taken the biggest steps of all – standing up to Toby Swan, dumping Noah, leaving Mum – without her. That I want her by my side, always.

But do I?

I think back to the way she's treated me since she met Lexie. The way she's called me naïve, ignored me, told me to sort my own shit out. She never made room for me. She hasn't been on my side for some time now. And I realise it's not just my fault that our friendship is over. It's hers, too.

But I don't say any of that. I just say, *Sorry*. Again. Because I truly am. And one day, maybe, she'll know that I mean it.

THIRTY-SIX

It's Pops's first night home. He says they've sent him home because he is fighting fit and they have really sick people who need the bed. I know that's not true. And I know he knows I know it's not true. But he needs to tell me that story, and I need to hear it. So that's how it is.

I have attached some *Get Well Soon* helium balloons to the back of his armchair, and bought him some new crossword books, which I've piled on his side table along with a jar full of chocolate-covered liquorice (the fancy kind he only ever gets for Christmas) and a small vase of roses from his garden.

'This is too much, Little Ed,' he says, wiping his eyes. He has been very emotional lately. It seems like just about anything can make him tear up. In the hospital he would get all choked up over ads on TV, and the moth that fluttered around his bedside lamp, and how orange the orange juice looked. It makes my heart hurt to see him like that, and I have to turn away for fear it will crack my chest my open.

'I was thinking a lot in there, and I … I need to tell you something,' he says. I nod. I can't speak. I'm too scared to hear whatever it is he wants to tell me.

'I was a carpenter because my father was a carpenter,' he says.

'I know, Pops, you've told me.'

'But I wanted you to know I wouldn't change it for the world. Don't regret it. Any of it. Because that led me to the best dream of all.' He takes my hands in his. 'Dreams can be sneaky like that. All right, Little Ed?'

'All right, Big Ed.'

*

I busy myself with tea-making duties while Nan helps Pops get into the shower and changed into his pyjamas, and try not to think about the fact he needs help with that stuff now.

The doorbell rings and I shout, *I'll get it.* It's late, and I'm already in PJs because I was hoping to curl up at the foot of Pops's chair and watch some bad TV with him. Or, at least, I'd watch while he slept.

I didn't expect Will to be at our door, but he is. Standing there with his hands shoved into his coat pockets like he's trying to keep warm.

'Hey,' he says. 'How's Pops doing?'

He doesn't want to come in, even though I ask him to and even though I know my grandparents would love to see him. I step outside and close the door behind me. He tells me he has a bit of a monologue and that I need to listen, to just stand right there and not say anything until he's done. I tell him I don't know if that's possible and could you be more demanding and OK, OK, OK, I got it.

'I should have brought a speaker and some giant cue card things,' he says.

'What are you talking about?'

'That bit in *Love Actually*.'

'Never seen it.'

'What? Of course you have. It's like the all-time greatest Christmas movie. According to Wanda. And you know she's always right.'

'We're a *Die Hard* family.'

'Ah.' He smiles then. 'Are you cold?'

'Do I look cold? I mean, check me out,' I say. I'm wearing some very unsexy flannelette pyjamas and fluffy slippers.

'You look cute,' he says.

We stand there saying nothing for a while until I ask him to please, continue, and promise I won't interrupt.

He takes cards from his pocket, the type we would use in debating or for an oral presentation. He has written this whole thing out. I try to hide my smile. His hands shake, ever so slightly, as he shuffles them into place. Standing there, under the dull light of our front porch, I get a glimpse of the doctor William will become one day. He'll take his job very seriously and be very committed and kind and compassionate to his patients – and a little silly now and then, which will make them feel better, even if it's just for the tiniest moment. I can see it.

'I've been given a chance to do the musical at Arcadia. I don't know what made Old Man Healy change his mind. I don't know why he is suddenly so eager for it to happen, in the big theatre, with all the support we need. But he is. I have a second chance to make it happen. But what I'm asking for, tonight, under the stars' – and we both check but there are no stars – 'just imagine they're there, OK? What I'm asking for, tonight, under the stars, is for a second chance with you.'

'Will,' I start, but he won't let me finish. He shakes his head, motions to the cards in his hands.

'I said you were selfish, among other things, but I was being selfish, too. Maybe even more so. I put all my hopes and dreams for this musical on you. And that's not fair. Hopes and dreams shouldn't be tied to anybody except yourself. So, I am telling you, without any expectation and without any need for a reply, that I love you, Edie. Probably have since that day at the ice-skating rink. And I wrote this musical for you because I love you. And I want you to be a part of it. Not because I love you, but because you're fucking amazing. But if you can't or you don't want to, that's OK, too. I just wanted you to know. All I am really asking for is a second chance to be your best friend. Again. If you'll take me.' He lowers the cards. 'The *Love Actually* thing would have been better. Sorry. But, yeah, that's it. That's my bit. No need to say anything –'

In the musical version of this moment, we would be lifted up into the heavens like Zac and Zendaya as they sing about rewriting the stars – floating and soaring, bodies close, arms wrapped around each other. That's what it feels like. Right now, in real life, under the starless night sky, kissing William Yoon. Properly. Because I want to. I've always wanted to. Probably since that day at the ice-skating rink.

AFTERWARD

The audience is so loud. Clapping and cheering and stamping their feet. Will and I wait together in the wings, stage left, where everyone is gathered awaiting the curtain call. One by one, they head out. Yazi first, followed by CJ, followed by Martha and Samrah, and Kellen, then Tara and Caleb. And then it will be our turn. Will holds my hand tight and I can feel him shaking, ever so slightly. I look at him. He is focused on the stage. Concentrating on the music. The music he wrote, which is being played by the orchestra. A smaller-scale orchestra than other productions would have, but an orchestra all the same. He did this. We did this.

Jack & Lily, he called the musical. Like *Romeo and Juliet* but better, he'd joked. I said it should be called *Lily & Jack* because why can't the woman's name be first for a change? And so he changed it. And he added something else: Music and Lyrics by Willian Yoon; Book by Edie Emerson and William Yoon.

'I think you showed Arcadia what you can do,' I whisper.

'I think you did, too,' he says.

Aubrey stands on the other side of Will. Puts her arm around his shoulders. I put my arm around him, too. Will's arm slips around my waist. The three of us. Arm in arm. We made this. We did this. Together.

I love this, and I will do it for the rest of my life – even if it is hard, even if it's a struggle, even if I never make it, whatever that means. I will never stop doing this. I was born to do this. And no-one can make me feel otherwise.

But I also know, no matter what the future holds, nothing will ever beat this moment, this feeling, right here. Right now.

It's my cue to bow. I step out of the wings and walk downstage. My eyes are blurry with tears, but I can see them. Nan and Pops. Row E. Seats 15 and 16. The best seats in the house.

THE END

If you need help, please reach out — to a trusted friend, relative, health professional or teacher, or the following services.

IN AUSTRALIA
Kids Helpline
Free, confidential support for people aged five to twenty-five, available 24 hours a day. Phone 1800 55 1800 or visit kidshelpline.com.au

Lifeline
Free crisis support and suicide prevention, available 24 hours a day. Phone 13 11 14 or visit lifeline.org.au

ReachOut
An online mental health service. Visit au.reachout.com

IN NEW ZEALAND
The Lowdown
Free mental health helpline for young people, available 24 hours a day. Phone 0800 111 757, text 5626, or visit thelowdown.co.nz

Youthline
Provides support to people aged twelve to twenty-four, with a free 24/7 helpline service as well as other services. Free call 0800 376 633, text 234 or visit youthline.co.nz

Aunty Dee
Free online tool to help people work through problems. Visit auntydee.co.nz

ACKNOWLEDGEMENTS

I would like to acknowledge the Traditional Owners of the Country on which I wrote much of this book; the Bunurong Boon Wurrung and Wurundjeri Woi Wurrung peoples of the Eastern Kulin Nation. I would like to pay my respects to Elders, past and present. And acknowledge First Nations peoples' continuing connection to culture, land, sea and story. Always was, always will be.

Huge thank you to Marisa Pintado for her support of Edie and her story from the initial pages and conversations, for the phone calls and advice, and her all-round amazingness. Thank you, Marisa, for your support of authors and championing of books for young people.

And I honestly don't know what I would have done without the editing geniuses/dream team of Luna Soo and Johanna Gogos. Their thoughtful, insightful feedback and ideas have helped shaped this book so much. Absolute superstars. I am indebted to you both, you creative, clever, talented women. Thank you.

Thank you to the immensely talented Holly Ovenden for the beautiful cover. And to the entire team at Hardie Grant – thank you for working with me, again!

A shout out to my fabulous, wonderful agent Grace Heifetz (Left Bank Literary), who I adore.

The origins of this book started at the Jacky Winter Gardens artist-in-residency, on the traditional lands of the Wurundjeri and Bunurong people. Thank you to Lorelei, Jeremy and the team. It was such a privilege to have that beautiful space and time in which to write.

To my parents. Thank you. I love and appreciate you both so much. Thank you Ma for instilling in me a love of theatre and reading and writing. Thank you Dad for believing in me and always checking in. Thank you both for creating a home in which we always felt loved and safe, and able to sing and dance and act and play.

Thank you to my wonderful siblings who also happen to be my best of friends: Claire and Clint, Jess and Chris, Ash and Luke, Ethan and Caitlyn. Thank you for your love, support and patience! Thank you for being the actors in my first plays, and the readers of my first drafts.

To my lovely in-laws, Sue and Paul, Kristyn and Adam, Matt and Nat, who have been incredibly supportive especially over these past few challenging years. Thank you for always being there.

This one is for my beautiful nieces and nephews who I promised myself I'd include in an acknowledgement by name if I ever got another chance to write a book! Thank you for being such an inspiration – Jake, Lewis, Abby, Max, Billie, Tessa, Violet, Amelia, Leo, Alfie, Grace, Arielle, Blake and Xander ... and of course the little one who is on her way very soon.

Much of this book was written in Melbourne during lockdown, which was tough and challenging but also made me realise how important my friends are. They have been a lifeline and I am so grateful to all my mates, in particular Lyall (who gets the credit for Okey Dokey Karaoke – gold!), Adam, Sharon, Zoe, Hannah, Maddy, Jesse, Lucy, Jayne, Syrie, Hayden and Kate. Thank you for the text messages and Zoom calls and socially distanced walks and coffees.

During the darkest days of lockdown the cast recordings of so many musicals got me writing and inspired me to keep going. So, thank you *Hamilton* and *Six* and *Dear Evan Hansen* and *Anything Goes!* and *Rent* and so many, many more.

And finally, as always, thank you Steve. For your encouragement, support, nagging and celebratory pizza. I love you. Even if you're not a fan of musical theatre.

ABOUT THE AUTHOR

Katy Warner always thought she wanted to be an actor and for a big part of her life that's what she did – until she realised she actually preferred writing the words herself. Now, she's an award-winning playwright and author. Even though she misses the costumes, Katy is much happier as a writer. Her plays have been performed across Australia and in New Zealand, London and Edinburgh. Katy lives in Tasmania with her husband, their cat and a lot of books. Her debut novel, *Everywhere Everything Everyone*, was shortlisted for the Readings Young Adult Book Prize.